THE
SECRET RITES
of
SOCIAL
BUTTERFLIES

LIZABETH ZINDEL

THE
SECRET RITES
of
SOCIAL
BUTTERFLIES

viking

Published by Penguin Group

Penguin Group (USA) Inc., 345 Hudson Street, New York, New York 10014, U.S.A.

Penguin Group (Canada), 90 Eglinton Avenue East, Suite 700, Toronto, Ontario,

Penguin Books Ltd, Registered Offices: 80 Strand, London WC2R 0RL, England

First published in 2008 by Viking, a member of Penguin Group (USA) Inc.

1 3 5 7 9 10 8 6 4 2

LIBRARY OF CONGRESS CATALOGING-IN-PUBLICATION DATA
Zindel, Lizabeth.
The secret rites of social butterflies / by Lizabeth Zindel.
p. cm.
Summary: Sixteen-year-old Maggie's fears about making friends as an incoming senior at
an exclusive New York City girls school are allayed when she is invited to join an elite secret
society devoted to eavesdropping and recording the "truth" about students and faculty.
ISBN 978-0-670-06217-1 (hardcover)
[1. Secret societies—Fiction. 2. Gossip—Fiction. 3. High schools—Fiction.
4. Schools—Fiction. 5. New York (N.Y.)—Fiction.] I. Title.
PZ7.Z646Sec 2008
[Fic]—dc22
2007042540

Printed in U.S.A.   Set in Centaur   Book design by Nancy Brennan

Butterfly information from chapters 1, 2, 7, 8, 9, 10, and 20: Scott Shalaway, *Butterflies in the Backyard*, Stackpole
Books, 2004; from chapters 1, 2, 3, 4, 6, 13, 14, 15, and 17: Phil Schappert, *The Last Monarch Butterfly: Conserving
the Monarch Butterfly in a Brave New World*, Firefly Books, 2004; from chapters 2, 4, and 6: Judy Burris and Wayne
Richards, *The Life Cycles of Butterflies*, Storey Publishing, 2006; from Chapter 16: Maraleen Manos-Jones,
The Spirit of Butterflies: Myth, Magic, and Art, Harry N. Abrams, 2000.
Other butterfly information is from the following Web sites: http://www.earthsbirthday.org/butterflies/bflys/
faqs.asp, http://www.riverdeep.net/current/2000/09/092900_migrations.jhtml, http://www.earthsbirthday.
org/butterflies/bflys/faqs.asp, http://archives.cnn.com/2001/NATURE/01/18/butterfly.mimicry.enn/,
http://www.sciencedaily.com/releases/2006/09/060926072401.htm, http://www.hmnh.harvard.edu/travel/
pdf/broch_monarhs08.pdf, http://answers.yahoo.com/question/index?qid=20070922081104AAjGj4u,
http://www.riverdeep.net/current/2000/09/092900_migrations.jhtml

To Regina Hayes and Joy Peskin,
for capturing stories and setting them free

THE
SECRET RITES
of
SOCIAL
BUTTERFLIES

Perhaps I should have run away the moment I was invited to become a member, but I was curious and lonely—a dangerous combination. If I had jetted in the other direction, maybe the shocking things that happened this past December 10th, the day of Berkeley Prep's Winter Formal, would never have occurred.

When I first heard of the Revelers, I thought they were just a fun group of girls who cared about having a good time, and about each other. But now I think Victoria, the group's leader, cared more about the rules she created than she did about her own best friends. And their covert circle of truth mattered to her most of all.

I can't expect you to understand everything completely yet. If I told you the details right now, I'll bet you would feel as surprised as I did the day Victoria told me that the Revelers existed. But don't worry: like me, you, too, will come to see the light, or shall I say, the writing on the Wall.

SEPTEMBER: INTIATION

CHAPTER one

A butterfly begins its life as an egg. Mothers generally lay their eggs on the tender shoots of milkweed plants. Pale yellow or ivory when laid, the eggs darken as the caterpillars develop inside of them.

Today is the first day at my new school, so it's game time, a chance to start senior year of high school with a clean slate. Not every kid is lucky enough to have this sweet opportunity for rebirth.

Of course, I'll miss parts of my life in Jersey—my dad; our miniature poodle, Moose; my cool-ass best friend, Kelsey; and the cute skater guy behind the Clove Deli counter who made my egg-and-cheese sandwiches every Sunday—but I'm jazzed by this chance to reinvent myself.

None of the students at Berkeley Prep know anything about me yet. That means they're clueless that I: a) went through a temporary chunky stage when I started puberty in fourth grade and my face looked like a giant penny on the body of an Oompa-Loompa, b) got a rose petal stuck up my nose in sixth grade during science class, and c) had a "One Night Boob Stand" the night of Lucy Clark's Bat Mitzvah when football player Felix Mack felt me up and threw me to the curb all in the amount of time it took for the song "Moondance" to play one time through. This list, plus many other embarrassing mishaps, are now miraculously erased from my social transcript. Zap. Delete. See ya.

To get ready, I go through my underwear drawer, pick out some cute panties—not that anyone but me will see them—and get ready to face the day. My room is clean and organized, but only because we just moved and my mom forced me to unpack everything before school started. In a few days, the place will be covered with dirty laundry, clean tank tops, flip-flops, loose change, magazines, sparkly bracelets, and empty glasses. I don't like throwing stuff away because you just never know when you might lose five pounds so you can fit into the red skirt that is oh-so-very cute and just a teensy-weensy bit too tight.

I don't like to spend much time getting dressed, so I climb into my Angel jeans and a pale pink T-shirt. Then I throw on blush and gloss and shoot my strawberry-blonde hair up into a ponytail. I say, "So long" to my mom and feed my blue Siamese fighting fish, Tahiti, before heading out the door. He only eats the most expensive pellets, Bio-Gold, but that's okay 'cause it makes his scales stay extra vibrant blue.

I walk over to Central Park West from our apartment on Broadway and 64th Street and ride the M10 uptown. Then I switch to the 86th Street crosstown bus and head over to the Upper East Side. Last week, I practiced the route, so I know exactly where to go. The difference is, now that the school year has started, there are tons of other kids in transit, too. At Berkeley Prep, we don't need to wear uniforms, but a lot of other private-school kids do. I notice a group of debutante-types in identical navy-blue jumpers sitting in the front section by the "Reserved for Elderly" seats, and toward the back of the bus, I see a posse in green checkered skirts with white blouses. I'm standing in the middle section, where there just so happens to be a crew of good-looking guys dressed in button-down shirts and khaki pants. What a nice way to start the morning. Straight-up hotness, if you ask me.

I get off the bus and walk along Manhattan's ritzy Park Avenue, passing upscale apartment buildings, with uniformed doormen standing outside. This neighborhood drips with luxury. Lincoln Town Cars with tinted windows swoop by to pick up silver-haired businessmen in crisp, pin-striped suits. Mom-types clank down the sidewalk in their loafer high heels, toting oversized designer bags while clutching fistfuls of coffee cups.

As I make a right on 89th Street, my heart beats fast. There in the middle of the block stands my new school. It's a six-story redbrick building, which is set back from the sidewalk by an iron gate. Over the entrance hang an American flag and a navy-blue one that says in white writing, THE BERKELEY PREP SCHOOL FOR GIRLS. Other than last week, I've only been here once before—last spring, when I came for my interview.

I pass clay pots filled with red azaleas and walk through the school's wood-paneled French doors. I was instructed to meet Mrs. Hanover, the head of student affairs, twenty minutes before the official school day starts. As I enter the lobby, I worry that I won't be able to find her office, but a security guard points me in the right direction.

"You must be Maggie Wishnick," Mrs. Hanover says as

I step into her doorway. Her hair is flipped up at her shoulders and she is wearing huge pearl earrings and a matching pearl necklace. "Welcome to our community." She hands me my class schedule, the school phone directory, and the huge student handbook, which looks like it must be filled with a zillion rules and regulations.

"It's your responsibility to go over the handbook, cover to cover," Mrs. Hanover says. She makes me sign a form promising to read the packet and adhere to its principles. Then she explains that the high school takes up the entire six-floor brownstone, with the auditorium on the main floor, the library on the top, and the other levels devoted to specific departments like math, English, and history.

"Ready to dive in?" she asks.

I nod and she leads me out of her office. I already saw the school after my interview last spring, but the hallways feel different now.

These girls look very smart and sophisticated—much more so than the kids at my school in Montague, New Jersey. Here, as I walk the halls, I worry that I stand out like a stained, drooled-on pillow in a shop of fine, down-feather ones. Maybe my outfit of jeans and pale pink T-shirt is too lame-o. I could have at least spiced it up with some accessories. Everyone else did, as I can see from the montage of oversized sunglasses, beaded bracelets, unusual book bags, designer jeans, crystal rings, laced-up booties, worn-in leather jackets, chandelier earrings, and bright patterned scarves tossed sloppily yet glamorously around slender necks.

My mom's voice echoes in my head: *It may be hard for you to start so late in the game. These girls have been good friends already for a long time. After all, Berkeley Prep begins in seventh grade."* I remember how ecstatic she was when the headmistress, Principal Hudgins, called and said she'd allow me to enroll as a senior. The news came after two other private schools in Manhattan wouldn't accept me because it was against their policy to "welcome" new students after junior year.

My mom told me about Berkeley's reputation for educating the offspring of wealthy business moguls and media tycoons. I'll bet they live in the kinds of places I passed on my walk to school—nothing like the simple two-bedroom I live in with my mom. I look around the hallway trying to imagine where these girls came from and who gave birth to them. Are their parents as messed up as mine?

Mrs. Hanover shows me the auditorium, where, for a fifteen-thousand-dollar donation, you can have a chair named after you. Afterwards, she walks me down the hallway of the prestigious Golden Wreath Girls.

"Every year, we pick one senior girl and present her with the school's greatest honor, the Golden Wreath. It's Berkeley Prep's equivalent to valedictorian, except not only must the student have top grades, she has to present an eloquent paper to a committee of administrators that argues why she should receive this award. "We announce the winner on the night of the Winter Formal, and the lucky recipient gets to give the graduation speech," Mrs. Hanover says with obvious school pride.

She points to framed photographs of smiling girls. "We've found in the past that winning a Golden Wreath usually cements acceptance into an Ivy League school."

We move down the corridor and into the main lobby.

Mrs. Hanover lifts her pearl necklace and lets it drop against her collarbone. "We've assigned you a student buddy named Anne Marie Schneck. She's in your homeroom, which is typically first period, but today we have an extra long back-to-school assembly. I'm sure you'll find Anne Marie a great resource."

We take the elevator together to the fifth floor. Mrs. Hanover shows me my locker, where she says Anne Marie will meet me in a few minutes, and then she takes off, leaving me to the pretty wolves.

A pack of three skinny girls rushes past me, laughing and sharing sips from a Starbucks iced coffee. The tallest of them knocks into me. "Excuse you," she says, and then keeps going.

I notice a fashionable blonde bragging to her friends about her summer internship working for the senior photo editor of *Italian Vogue*. "My boss bought me lunch every day and gave me a ton of free Rebecca Taylor and Cynthia Rowley clothes."

None of them seems to give a damn that I am standing right here. Hello, world. It's Maggie Wishnick. I've arrived on the scene and I'd like to be your friend!

I am solo, single, alone, party of one—the hole in a bagel. If my grandpa hadn't offered to pay for this tuition, I wouldn't be here. He values education more than anything else. When I think about how sending me to a private school for this one year is costing him forty-five thousand dollars of the life savings he earned as a tax accountant, I feel overcome with gratitude. And pressure.

"Do the best you can. I know it'll be better than most people, because you're my gal," Grandpa Jack told me the first day my mom and I moved here. We were all eating Chinese food at Sammy's Noodle Shop by his apartment in Green-wich Village, and he was wearing one of his jogging outfits. Then he broke into a line from one of those old-fashioned songs he likes to sing. *"If you knew Susie, like I know Susie—Oh! Oh! Oh! What a gal."*

Yeah, sure. No problem. I'm gonna get straight As, I say to my-self. But my mom told me about Berkeley Prep's competitive reputation. She's also warned me that my course load will be much harder than at my last school. Still, I know there's plenty in being here for me. Not only am I bound to become a more highly evolved and enlightened chick, I will increase my chances of getting into a better college.

A girl waves at me while walking down the hallway.

"Hi, you must be Maggie," she says. "I'm Anne Marie."

"Hey, what's up?" I say. I notice she's carrying a purple-and-white striped bowling-ball bag with a black strap. *What a cool vintage idea,* I think to myself. *Using an old-school bowling bag for books.*

She has curly brown hair just past her shoulders, glasses, pale skin with some acne scars, and no makeup. Something about her reminds me of those girls from that ancient televi-sion show *Little House on the Prairie.* Like she could be Laura Ingalls Wilder's cousin or something. She's wearing a vintage-looking baby-doll dress with an orange-and-brown pattern. On her feet are worn-in black Chinese slippers.

"Hope I didn't keep you waiting. Today's the first meeting of the bowling club, and I couldn't find my new shoes for the life of me," she says.

Oh, she's actually keeping a ball inside the purple case. It's the forest-green JanSport over one shoulder that's for the schoolwork. "No prob," I tell her. "Did you track them down?"

"Yeppers. They're in my Stevie."

"What?" I ask.

"That's the nickname for my backpack. As in Stevie Wonder. I'm a huge fan of old-school R&B. My brother goes to Columbia and deejays at some clubs in the East Village on the weekend."

"That's awesome," I say.

"Yeah. I started my own vinyl collection last year, too. You'd like my brother. A lot of girls think he's hot. My boyfriend, Robby, and I just saw him spin at Soulgasm last weekend. He ripped it up."

Anne Marie's locker is two down from mine, and I wait for her while she stuffs her bowling bag and shoes in there. "The summer went by way too fast," she says. "Except for the end of it when my mom left me behind while she went on a seven-day cruise to Paradise Island in the Bahamas with my brother."

"Why couldn't you go?"

"I didn't get the straight As I promised her in the college-level psychology classes I took this summer, so my brother got to take his best friend in my place."

"Ouch," I say. "That really sucks."

"Yeah, well. My mom can be a witch sometimes. But some days, she's really nice, too."

Anne Marie leads me into the section of the auditorium where our homeroom is assigned to sit. Before the assembly begins, I tell her a bit about my summer—my parents' separation, splitting time between my mom at her hotel room at the Montague Days Inn and my dad at our family's town-house ten minutes away. It's inside a residential community called Highpoint Country Club where for July and August, I worked at the clubhouse restaurant.

"Don't be fooled by the name. Even though it's called a country club, it's totally not a swanky setup with guys in white shorts and pink polo shirts swinging croquet mallets. Yeah, there's a golf course, but the people who live at High-point mostly fall into two categories—low-income families and senior citizens who spend their winters in Florida."

"But why did your dad get the house and your mom move? Usually it's the other way around," Anne Marie asks as the auditorium fills up with people.

"My mom never liked living there. Plus, she couldn't stand our neighbors. This one woman who lived in the townhouse below us used to hit the ceiling with a broom whenever we didn't walk quietly enough. And this other guy who lived next door had Tourette's and was always cursing near our driveway."

The president of student government, Jacqueline Moore, a big-boned girl with pretty features, walks onto the stage and welcomes us back for the new school year. The audience of students and teachers erupts in applause.

Then she encourages us to get involved in the diverse as-sortment of extracurriculars. As Jacqueline announces the groups, the head of each committee walks onto the stage and says a few words. Anne Marie whispers about each club to fill me in. There's the James Bond group, which watches mov-ies like *Casino Royale* while drinking ginger ale out of martini glasses; the high-school newspaper called *The Scarlette*, which reports on all the latest news; Potty Rings, a club dedicated to *Harry Potter* and *The Lord of the Rings*; a Cheese Club committed to sampling fine cheeses; the Walk-and-Talk Club, which sounds like an excuse for exercising minimally while gossiping; an a cappella group called the Fresh Melodies; and a performing-arts committee that organizes Phase, the school talent show.

Anne Marie goes up onstage to announce the Bowling Club, and a screen lowers down from the ceiling. As a recruitment video plays, I watch footage of Anne Marie and other members of the team knocking down pins at a bowling alley and yelling at the camera, "Come on over and help us strike!" Anne Marie and her teammates have a lot of spirit, and they don't seem embarrassed by the potential dorkiness of being in a bowling club.

I'm amazed by the wide range of unique organizations. Jacqueline continues by introducing the Anime Club, which promotes Japanese animation. There's also the LSEN committee (Anne Marie explains that it's a gay-rights group, commonly known as GLSEN at other schools, but since there are no guys here, they dropped the *G* and kept the *L* for lesbians); the Ballet Folkloric, a dance troupe; and *Salon #33*, the school's literary publication.

Jacqueline wraps things up by saying, "And last but not least, I'd like to welcome Victoria Hudson, the president of the Social Committee, to the podium."

I watch as the girl who must be Victoria struts up the stairs and confidently stands before the entire student body. "This year I have the privilege of planning the Big Three—

Winter Formal, Spring Fling, and Junior/Senior Prom," she says, flipping her chestnut-colored hair over one shoulder as she speaks. Her long layers fall alongside her heart-shaped face and no hair looks out of place or fried.

The girls in the audience clap in excitement as she describes the details of the Winter Formal, which she says she planned over the summer: a yacht cruise, cuisine made by a protégé of Wolfgang Puck, and a world-renowned DJ spinning till midnight.

"Trust me, it's going to be the best year yet. So save the date, December tenth—you have almost three months to find your date, your dress, and your best dance moves. Plus, the proceeds will be going to the ASPCA to fight animal cruelty. Ta-ta."

Anne Marie leans over toward me and whispers in my ear, "If you're gonna go to this school, you might as well know now: Victoria Hudson's the most powerful girl in our grade."

"I was starting to sense that," I say. "What's her story?"

"Dad's, like, the next Donald Trump," Anne Marie says. "Her mom's on the Berkeley parent council, which reports to the Board of Trustees. She's also a big-time doctor at the OBGYN unit of Roosevelt Hospital, does award-winning research into fertility, and delivers famous people's babies. I heard Victoria's linage can be traced back to descendants of the *Mayflower*. We're both ranked academically at the top of our grade and compete in lots of classes."

I watch as Victoria walks off the stage and joins two pretty girls in the audience—a girl with long, blonde, wavy hair who was introduced earlier in the assembly as the head of the a cappella group, the Fresh Melodies; and a tan girl with dark brown hair pulled back in a high ponytail who was introduced as the captain of the girls' varsity tennis team.

Anne Marie and I continue to whisper as Principal Hudgins takes over the podium and welcomes the students and teachers back for what she calls "a vibrant and exciting new school year."

"Are those her best friends?" I ask.

"Yeppers," Anne Marie says. "The blonde's name is Sydney Orandello and the tan one's Lexi Cutter. If you're lucky, you'll get invited to the exclusive back-to-school party they organize every year."

I turn my head quickly from Mrs. Hudgins to look at Anne Marie. "How do I get invited?" I ask, then turn my focus back to the stage, where the principal sounds like she's wrapping up her speech.

"You're asking the wrong chick. I never even know about it till afterwards when I hear kids whispering about it in the hallways. Last year, I think five girls from our class met their boyfriends that night. Victoria seems to know every cute guy in the city."

Note to self: *Must keep a lookout for this party.* It sounds like the best way for me to crack into the scene.

During the rest of my first day, I get introduced to all my classes. For English this semester, I have Modern Drama, where we will be reading plays like Henrik Ibsen's *The Wild Duck* and Edward Albee's *Who's Afraid of Virginia Woolf?*. My foreign language is French, math is pre-calculus, science is astronomy, and my history elective is Western Philosophy, which sounds like a load of B.S. I don't get the importance of learning what a bunch of toga-wearing dudes came up with while getting high on 400 B.C. cannabis. My philosophy teacher, Mr. Z, is like no other instructor I've ever had. He dresses extra cool for a sixty-year-old guy, in a leather jacket and jeans. Plus, he's got a salt-and-pepper ponytail, a perfectly shaven face, and sparkling blue Santa Claus eyes. He tells the class that he likes to drive his motorcycle up to his weekend house in the Berkshires every Saturday, where he enjoys writing poetry and drinking ginger tea while staring off at the lake in his backyard and contemplating the universe. He reminds me of a mixture between Anthony Hopkins and a member of the Hell's Angels.

When he asks who put philosophy down as their first choice for a history elective, I'm one of the few kids in the class that doesn't raise their hand. I think he hates me already.

At the end of the day, I spot Victoria, Sydney, and Lexi leaving the school. As they charge out the front doors, they wave to a group of good-looking boys waiting for them on the stoop across the street. The guys are wearing different combinations of leather jackets, flannel shirts, and beat-up blue jeans. The crowd of them hangs out laughing for a few minutes before heading down the street to Lexington Avenue. I can't help but stare.

What I would give to be part of their good times, I think to myself. Victoria and her friends seem like the kind of group I always hoped to be part of. Growing up back in Montague, I had my wonderful best friend, Kelsey. But I never belonged to a pack of girls, even though that's what I wanted more than anything.

CHAPTER TWO

Caterpillars eat voraciously and grow quickly. In only ten to fourteen days, depending on temperature, the caterpillar will grow to more than 3,000 times its hatching weight. During this time, a caterpillar can shed its skin up to five times. Caterpillars should never be disturbed during this process, as they are extremely vulnerable to stress and injury.

The first week and a half at Berkeley, I am on the outside looking in. I can't decide which sucks more—being at home or being in school. My mom is a mess. She closes herself in her room early at night, and I can hear her crying behind the door. I want to knock and see if she's okay, but I also know she doesn't want me to see her like this, so I respect her privacy. Knowing she's so sad makes me feel sick inside. And the stuff I found out about my dad before we left New Jersey makes me feel even worse. I can't decide if I should tell her what I know about him.

I wish I could turn to my brother, Jason. I call him in his dorm room at Tufts and he doesn't even call me back. He's probably busy with his film classes and hanging out with Chloe, his girlfriend. Still, I can't help but wonder if he's avoiding me. Things between us seemed ice-cold the last few days before he left for school. Jason probably thinks I'm selfish and manipulative just like my father does. But then again, Dad seemed to think women in general were selfish and manipulative, starting with his own mother and continuing on to Mom and me. It was like he thought all females were controlling him, even when they weren't.

Now my dad and I mostly keep in touch over e-mail. Right after my mom and I moved out, he sent a note yelling at me for leaving my room at our house a mess. *Sometimes you don't think enough about other people,* he wrote. *Sometimes, I just hate family,* I think to myself.

At Berkeley Prep, the cliques seemed sealed tight with crazy glue. Despite the fact that there are forty-three girls in my grade, I often sit alone at a table in the cafeteria.

On a few occasions, I grab lunch with Anne Marie and her two best friends, Grace Mills and Robin Waldron. But that's only when they poke their buried heads out of their textbooks like prairie dogs. Most of the seniors aren't around, because you're allowed to leave school and eat anywhere in Manhattan as long as you're back in forty minutes. Meanwhile, I am stuck in the cafeteria eating French-bread pizzas, sloppy joes, baked ziti, and meat-loaf casseroles, and drinking syrupy-sweet lemonade. I sit all by myself in the corner and probably look like a hardcore dorkilingus.

Since Berkeley is located on some of Manhattan's prime real estate, there's no room for baseball diamonds or football and soccer fields. So for phys ed, the school herds us off in orange buses to Randall's Island, a big city park, which is a fifteen-minute ride away over the Triborough Bridge. Anne Marie tells me that lots of the New York City prep schools use this place for sports and gym classes.

Anne Marie always sits on the gym bus with her best friend, Grace, and I often get stuck alone, or sitting with Anne Marie's second-best friend, Robin, who seems to have zero personality and no sense of humor. Victoria and her two best friends, Lexi and Sydney, squeeze into one seat in the back of the bus and I can faintly hear them whispering and giggling.

I have so much homework to do and I do it on the bus. I also finish reading the student handbook, which ends with the school's Credo:

All members of the Berkeley community are expected to live honestly, with appreciation and respect for the feelings, needs, and activities of others. In keeping with the tone of community life that we wish to establish, we should be conscious to exclude abusive language in our interactions with one another. These expectations are based on the values identified by the community as essential to ethical and responsible behavior: courage, respect, fairness, responsibility, caring, and honesty.

Who the hell actually sits down and writes the student handbook? I wonder if the person who wrote it thinks she's like a female George Washington making a constitution for all Berkeley Prep girls to follow.

It's during the second Thursday of school on the bus for gym class that I finally get wind of Victoria Hudson's back-to-school party. I'm sitting alone in my seat, leaning my head against the window, watching the city skyline over the Tri-borough Bridge. I overhear two girls sitting diagonally behind me whispering. The girls' names are Olivia and Fredrika, and I recognize them as two members of a clique that's on the fringe of Victoria's A-group. These girls wear mostly worn flannels, jeans, and just a little makeup. They spend a lot of time on the stoop around the corner from school smoking cigarettes.

Olivia has thick, long blonde hair, a perfect body, and nice features, except for her strange nostrils that are big and curved up like a horse's. She acts like she's older and more mature than the rest of us. I've seen her skateboard to school a few times. Fredrika is pretty homely and tries to pretend she's a hippie sometimes. I remember trying to say hi to her on the first day of school, but she just looked away.

"I got the details for Vic's party this Friday," Olivia says.

"Nice work," Fredrika says. "Where is it this year?"

Olivia pulls a red piece of paper from her grungy blue gym bag. "The garden at her dad's new building on Thirty-Ninth at the East River. Eight o'clock sharp. BYOB and your own flashlights."

Olivia notices I'm watching her. She flips her hair and quickly turns into the seat, hiding behind Fredrika's big-boned, flannel-coated body.

I blush, embarrassed that she caught me eavesdropping, but at least now I know this Friday's the date and it's on East 39th Street. The only problem is I'm not invited. Shit. Plop. Suck. Poop. Blow.

As the bus pulls up to Randall's Island, the girls from my grade pile off the orange bus that smells of salt, sweat, and vanilla body spray. The gym teacher, Mrs. Foster, makes everyone line up and picks two team captains for a game of softball. As usual, she chooses Victoria's jock best friend, Lexi, as one of them.

Lexi stands confidently before our grade picking members of her team. She picks Victoria and Sydney first—as always—even though they are definitely not the top athletes. Lexi grins at them as she calls them over to her team.

Anne Marie was right—Victoria definitely is the most powerful girl in our grade. I've been watching her closely to try to learn the secret to her success. She always seems in control and never seems mean, but rather, exclusive. If you aren't in her tight group of girlfriends, she won't give you the time of day, unless she has to. There's a rumor she dated a baseball player on the Yankees, and I never see her wearing the same outfit twice. Whenever I spot her in the hallway, she is looking straight ahead with her chin slightly lifted. It doesn't seem like she's ignoring me, but rather like she has something more important on her mind that's distracting her from seeing me.

I end up on Lexi's team. I make sure to stand next to Victoria while Lexi assigns positions. I wish I could ask her for a red party invite, but I feel too intimidated. The words just won't come out of my mouth.

"Go play left field," Lexi says, pointing to me.

I grab my mitt and run out into the field. I spend the next ten minutes poised and ready to catch a ball that never comes.

~~~~~~~~~

When Friday night rolls around, I throw on a casual floral sundress and flip-flops. The only problem is I'm not heading to Vic's big, hot back-to-school soirée. I'm going out with my mom for dinner at her old friend Karen's house. All week, I never got my hands on a red flyer, and I don't have the guts to crash without being invited.

Karen's my mom's best friend from high school and she still lives in Manhattan, but now with her sexy husband, who is an attaché for the Turkish embassy. My mom stands at the door holding her purse. I notice she has white roots growing in on the side of her hairline by her ears. She's usually so on top of getting her hair colored every three weeks.

"I'm not really in the mood to go out," my mom confesses to me in the elevator down to the lobby. "But when I tried to cancel, Karen wouldn't let me get out of it. She said she had a million stories she wanted to tell me about their trip to Istanbul."

"Why'd you want to skip out?" I ask my mom, surprised. "You haven't seen her since we moved here."

"I guess I'm rundown from unpacking all those moving boxes and learning the ropes at the new office. Frankly, I'd prefer to stay in bed and watch the Jane Austen miniseries on PBS."

When I started school, my mom began her new job working at a district public health office that handles East and Central Harlem. She's a health-promotion coordinator, which, from what I understand, means she helps oversee a wide range of programs for nearby schools on stuff like asthma, vision, fitness, and mental health.

My mom certainly seems lower on energy lately and not herself. She's usually what she would call "a live wire."

In the cab on the way to Karen's, my mom points to the identification card posted on the glass partition behind the driver's seat. "See that? If you ever take a cab alone, I want you to call me with the driver's name and his medallion number. I don't care what time it is, you can wake me up. I like having it for safety."

"Sure, Mom," I tell her. Now if a deranged cabbie tries to kidnap me or take me hostage, she can track him down and rescue me. Since moving to New York, she has been a walking almanac of caution. Don't go into Central Park after sundown or you might get mugged. Stay away from dark and empty streets. If the elevator door opens and there's a weird-looking stranger standing inside it, pretend you pressed the wrong button and don't under any circumstances step inside. My mom wasn't as safety-conscious back in Montague. I guess she had less to worry about back there.

Karen lives in a brownstone on 43rd Street between First and Second Avenues. In the distance, I see a hundred world flags blowing in the breeze outside the United Nations. As we walk up the front steps of the townhouse, I notice how much bigger Karen and Omer's home is than the squishy apartment where Mom and I live. Their place is three stories tall with flower boxes filled with magenta azaleas outside the windows.

"Wow, do they own this place?" I ask my mom as she rings the doorbell.

"No, the Turkish government does," my mom says. "Since

Omer is a member of the consulate's staff, they provide them with a place to live."

"Nice gig," I say.

"And technically, once we step inside, we're on Turkish soil. It's pretty wild, but Omer has diplomatic immunity. Even U.S. law enforcement agencies aren't allowed in."

"That's crazy," I say.

A moment later, Karen answers the door. She has light brown hair to her shoulders, big blue eyes, and an open smile. I like the lemon dress she is wearing.

"How good to see you!" she says, greeting my mom and me with big hugs. It's been about two years since I last saw her, and she looks like she hasn't aged one bit. I wish my mom looked like that, too. Not for superficial reasons, but because it worries me that she's getting older.

"We just got back from Istanbul last night! I had to see you right away. Welcome to New York!"

"It still hasn't hit me yet that we're really here," my mom says.

"I can't tell you how happy I am that you and I are in the same city again." Karen puts her arm around my mom's shoulders as we walk into her living room. "We haven't been in the same place for more than a few days since Hofstra. Your mom and I in college were something else," Karen says, looking at me.

I smirk. "Really?" I ask. "What did you guys do?"

"Oh, your mother was a real beauty. All the boys loved her."

"I didn't know that," I say, smiling.

"Please, stop." My mom shakes her head. "Little did they know what a chubby frump I'd grow into."

"No, you look fantastic," Karen says. I wonder if she's just saying that to be nice. Since my parents separated three months ago, my mom's gained at least twelve pounds, and the skin under her eyes looks droopier.

"Anyway, Omer wanted me to order in Thai from this place we love up on Forty-Seventh, but I insisted on making some traditional Turkish food. I've learned to cook a few dishes, and I thought, no better time to show off." Karen turns to me. "Your mom knows. I used to be a horrendous cook. Almost poisoned us with a batch of lemon chicken when we were roomies in college."

"It's not your fault the supermarket mislabeled cow brains," my mom jokes.

Omer waves to us from where he stands, opening a bottle of red wine. I notice he has black cuff links that look like delicate knots on his crisp, white shirt. He kisses my mom on the cheek and puts his hand on my shoulder.

"Nice to see the both of you," he says.

I look up at his face. He is very handsome, at least for a member of the Older Man Crew, with short brown hair, olive skin, and almond eyes that seem to wink at you as he talks. He has a refined and charming quality about him, like he could moonlight as a maître d' at a ritzy restaurant. If I were from Turkey, I would certainly be very proud to have him representing my country.

Omer pours three glasses of cabernet and hands them out to my mom and Karen while keeping one for himself.

As Karen and Omer tell my mom all about their recent vacation in Istanbul, I notice a side table filled with a collection of kaleidoscopes. I glance out the window, spot the sign for 43rd Street, and remember how close I am to Victoria's back-to-school party. It's only four blocks downtown and one avenue to the east. I wish so bad that I was there. I lift up one of the kaleidoscopes and turn the tube. The street sign outside spins and turns into patterns of green and white light.

Karen announces it's time to sit down to dinner. She and her hubbie take the far ends of the table, while Mom and I sit across from each other. My mom picks up her wineglass and takes a sip. I try to figure out what she's feeling as she swirls the red liquid. It must be strange hanging out with these married types, while she's separated. I imagine it's one of the few times in the last eighteen years she has gone to a dinner party without my father. It must feel weird being dateless. Even though I'll be the first to admit that my dad can act like a dickwad, I kinda wish he was here. He always tells such great jokes and stories at dinner parties. Besides, I got kinda used to having him around.

As Omer helps serve the food, Karen looks at me. "So the million-dollar question," she says. "What on earth are you doing hanging out with old fogies on a Friday night? You should be out having a blast with your friends."

I laugh, surprised by her directness. "I, uh, wanted to see you," I said.

"There must be something more fun going on, no?" Karen looks at me and raises her eyebrows.

I shrug my shoulders. "Well, I guess, tonight, there is a party that one of the girls from my school is throwing." I take a bite of the lamb shank that Omer put on my plate. "In fact, it's just a few blocks away, I think. On Thirty-Ninth Street."

"And why aren't you there . . . ?" Karen says, wiping her mouth with a red cloth napkin.

"She's not invited. Mags has been having trouble making friends at Berkeley Prep," my mom announces. "It was hard moving her to a new school for senior year and asking her to adjust. I feel bad for putting her through it. Maybe it's all my fault."

I throw my mom a shut-up look. "I'm doing just fine," I say. "I have tons of friends. In fact, I can hardly make time for all of them."

Karen leans her elbows on the table and holds her head in her hands. I feel like she's looking right through me.

"You know, sometimes you just have to go for it and put yourself out there." She smiles at Omer across the table. "Eight years ago, I was out to dinner with a girlfriend of mine at Cipriani. We heard there was a private party in the back room, and after dinner, we decided to sneak in. Minutes later, I met the love of my life beside the dessert buffet of miniature éclairs. Now look where we are today."

Omer nods and his eyes wink. "Except they weren't mini éclairs, they were vanilla cream puffs."

Karen rolls her eyes as if they've already been through this many times before. "Maggie, you have plenty of time in this life to stay in on a Friday night eating lamb shank," she says.

I look at my mom, hoping she'll give me advice. "Honey, it's up to you," she says. "I just want you to be happy."

"I guess . . . I would really like to go," I admit.

My mom nods at me slowly while she chews. "All right," she says. "Then I'll walk you over there right after dinner."

"No, I can go myself," I say, looking at my watch. It's eight thirty. "And I should probably leave now. The party started half an hour ago."

My mom smiles at Karen. Then fiddles with the napkin on her lap. "It's dark out, and I don't want you walking alone."

"I'll be fine," I say. Then I stand up from the table. "If I'm old enough to have my driver's permit, I really think I can walk six blocks."

"Magpie," my mom says. "Please don't cause a scene. I'll walk you over when we're done with the meal and then come right back."

"It's not fair," I say. "I want to go alone. If anyone sees I'm being chaperoned, I'll look stupid."

Karen clears her throat. "Sarah, I think you should let her go by herself," she says.

I stare at my mom and raise my eyebrows, waiting for her response.

She looks down at her plate and then lets out a loud breath of air. "Okay," she says. "But be careful."

I smile big. "Always am," I say. Then I turn to Karen and Omer. "Thanks for dinner!" I say. But deep down, I want to thank them for much more. Like helping to get my neurotic mother off my back a little bit.

"Our pleasure," Omer says.

"Come back anytime," Karen says.

"And thank you, too, Mom," I say, giving her a quick kiss on the cheek good-bye.

"Be home by midnight," my mom says. "And take a cab."

"I will," I call, as I grab my pocketbook and head out the door.

I feel the three of them watching me. Maybe this was just the right kind of nudging I needed.

CHAPTER THREE

Upon completion of the caterpillar's growth, which is mediated by hormone balances, the caterpillar leaves its host plant and crawls around to locate a place where it can begin to build its cocoon, which is also known as a chrysalis.

Nerves fill my stomach as I walk toward 39th Street and the East River. I look around for where the party might be. I finally spot what seems to be a newly constructed building. Through the windows, it appears as if there's no one living there yet. Parts of the lobby are full of paint cans and are covered in tarps.

I notice two girls from my grade dressed in short black skirts, tight tops, and high, stiletto heels, clanking along the pavement. I've noticed these girls at school hanging out in Olivia and Fredrika's clique and I've overheard their names in the hallway. One girl is called Sadie, and the other, Dakota. They look like clones of each other, with dark hair and smoky eyes.

The two girls stop at one of the side doors of the vacant building. They look left and then right before quickly opening the door and running inside. *Bingo.* I hurry over to the side entrance and put my hand on the doorknob. To my relief, it opens. As I step inside, the girls are now out of sight, but I still smell the lingering scent of their mango perfume.

The room I'm standing in now looks like it's a side foyer of the building's main lobby. There are marble floors, crystal chandeliers, and black leather couches. I notice a huge mirror hanging against one of the walls and straighten my sundress in the reflection. Back in Jersey, we dressed super casual for a night out on the town—not in lycra miniskirts and high-heeled shoes. I'm wondering whether I should've worn something more sophisticated when out of nowhere, I hear a guy's voice.

"Like what you see?" he says.

I jump, startled. To my right stands a boy about my age in jeans, a black Izod shirt, and trendy-looking tan sneakers with blue and white stripes. He's finger-licking cute, so I can only glance at him for a few seconds. Keeping prolonged eye contact with hot guys makes me nervous. He has brown, slightly messy-styled hair, bright green eyes, and a confident smile. Plus, he seems so comfortable here, with one of his hands tucked inside a front jean pocket.

Play it cool, Maggie. You can swing this. "I'm just checking this place out, that's all," I say.

He raises one eyebrow, inquisitively. "Didn't you read on the invite to make a sharp left as soon as you get inside the door?"

"Oh, yeah, I, uh, must've overlooked that part," I say.

"Take out your flyer," he says. "It's right there."

"I, um, didn't bring mine," I stammer. "Left it at home." It's hard to look at him without blushing.

He takes his own crumpled flyer from his back pocket. "See, it says it right here." He gestures with his head toward the center of the building. "There's a security guard in the main lobby. If he hears us, he'll call the cops and that girl Victoria will get in huge trouble with her dad. Even though he's the real-estate developer, no one's moved in yet, and he wouldn't want her here. Or us."

Anne Marie mentioned to me during the first-day-of-school assembly that Victoria's father was a big real-estate mogul in New York, and now I'm starting to put things together. Victoria's throwing a party in one of her daddy's skyscrapers before any of the tenants have moved in yet. Dangerous, but also kind of genius.

"Good thing I snuck back here to take a leak and saw you," the cute boy says.

"Yeah," I said. "Seriously."

"Are you and the hostess with the mostess good friends?" he asks.

"Oh, no," I say. "Just acquaintances from school. And you?"

"Don't really know her. One of the guys from my soccer team had a few extra invites and he gave me one. Come on. Follow me," he says. "The party's in what's going to be the vegetable garden. This building's green, and I heard the plan is to have a small organic farm for the tenants."

"That is so cool," I say. There are a bunch of farms out in Montague, but none that sound as sophisticated.

The cute guy leads me down a long corridor. As I walk behind him, I can't help but notice how tall he is, almost six feet.

"So what do you think of Berkeley Prep?" he asks, glancing back at me.

"Still getting used to it," I say. "I'm new. Just started this year as a senior."

"That's kinda weird," he says. "Why so late?"

"Long story," I say. I don't want to get into all the gory details. "My mom wanted to move. She grew up here and missed it tons. Plus, my grandpa lives here still, and now that he's older, she wants to be closer to him." I speed up so I'm walking right beside him now.

"Gotcha," he says. "I moved here two years ago, but from Lancaster, Pennsylvania. You know, Amish country?"

We make a left turn and head down another hallway. I notice a silver door at the end of it.

"Wow, are you Amish?"

"You should've seen me when I moved here. I wore suspenders, rode a horse, and had one of those cool black felt hats," he says seriously. Then he laughs. "No, I'm not Amish."

I suddenly feel stupid. *Why on earth did I ask that? Of course he's not Amish. He looks like he just stepped out of an Abercrombie & Fitch catalog.* "Well, what I meant is maybe your grandmother is or something," I say, trying to recover quickly.

"Far from it," he says, staring straight ahead. "When I was born, my dad's mom was my only grandmother still alive, and she was a country-club socialite." His voice grows quieter.

We arrive at the silver door. He turns the knob and we take a few steps outside. "By the way, my name's Connor. What's yours, redhead?" he asks.

I stop in my tracks. "Maggie. And my hair's not red," I

correct him. "It's strawberry blonde." God, I hate being described as a redhead. There were those annoying jokes I endured in middle school about being a mutant. Kids called me "Bozo the Clown," "carrottop," and "Cheeto crotch." And there are all those stupid stereotypes about redheads having huge tempers, major mood swings, and small boobs. Plus, my dad has balding red hair and although I like being smart like him, I don't want to look like him.

Connor stops in front of me and jabs me lightly on the shoulder. "Oh, easy there, tiger. I see I pushed a sore spot."

"I don't like thinking of myself as a readhead, that's all."

"Well, just so you know, I've had a thing for redheads since the girl I dated in kindergarten."

Hmm. All right, fine. I guess that makes things a little better. We continue along the outdoor redbrick path. As we head into the main garden area, I realize it's a stroke of luck to enter the party by his side. At least this way, it may seem more like I belong. The garden area is a large rectangle, with paths of trees and wooden benches swirling around a central gazebo. The lights of flashlights moving back and forth illuminate the gray of night a little, but it's pretty dark out here. Once my eyes adjust, I can make out groups of prep-school boys and girls hanging out in clusters, posturing, flirting, laughing. I notice that Sadie, one of the girls I saw enter the party from the street, is now perched on a guy's lap, nibbling on his neck.

Victoria, Lexi, and Sydney are lounging inside the prime gazebo area. Victoria's in a black-and-blue-striped dress and motorcycle boots with several black and gold chainlink necklaces. Lexi wears a pair of dark jeans with a black sequined

tank top and headband, and Sydney's in a floral dress with
snakeskin boots. They're chatting with a bunch of good-
looking guys who look like grungy, intellectual rock stars
that could've stepped out of *Rolling Stone* magazine.

"Come meet my buddy Teddy," Connor says to me. "We
play on the soccer team together at Chesterfield."

"Where is he?" I ask, making sure he's not one of the boys
on the gazebo. The last thing I want to do right now is walk
right up to Victoria.

"Over there by the cooler," he says, nodding at a boy with
round glasses who's standing by a white plastic trunk filled
with ice.

The cooler isn't on the gazebo, thank God, but it is pretty
close by. I decide it's probably best to stay near the door where
Victoria won't see me. "I'll just hang out over here," I say.

"Don't be silly. Come hang out with us." Connor grabs
my hand to pull me along. I feel the warmth of his palm next
to mine, and part of me doesn't want to let go. It's like my
body is turning into Laffy Taffy.

Connor introduces me to Teddy, who's kinda cute, but
pretty short, with a big nose, brown eyes, and curly brown
hair. He's wearing a burgundy polo and a pair of khakis. As
he talks he likes to play with the bottom of his shirt and lift
it up slightly to expose his abs.

"Hey, whaaat's up?" Teddy says, slapping me a high five.
Then he turns back to the girl he's been talking to and puts
his arm around her shoulder. I recognize her from my school.
She's a member of my grade's jock clique. She's short, with
big boobs, and eyebrows tweezed too thin. I can hear her

laughing really loudly at whatever Teddy is whispering into her ear.

"That's his girlfriend, Nikki. They started dating when they were counselors at this sports camp in New Hampshire," Connor says. He dips his hand into the white cooler and takes out two cans. "Want one?" he asks.

I haven't drunk much before, but I am curious. There was just that one night back in Montague when Kelsey and I shared a six-pack with her older sister, got a teeny bit buzzed, and mooned her sister's cute friends Pete and Trevor. I wish Kelsey was here right now. Although we still e-mail and text, it's not the same as having her around as my day-to-day, living-and-breathing partner in crime.

"Sure," I say.

I glance over at Victoria and her friends. They look too busy flirting with their group of guys to notice me. Connor flicks back the beer top and hands it to me. "Here ya go, me lady," he says.

"Thanks." I look down at the huge pile of cans in the ice chest. "How did they get so much?" I ask.

"There's a bodega on East Eighty-Third Street, and this guy who works there, Tomiko, sells beer to underage kids. You just slip him your backpack and the money, and he takes your bag behind the cash register and sticks the six-pack or whatever you're getting inside."

Connor and I sit down on a bench. As I take a sip, I can't help but feel a little guilty. I know my parents wouldn't be too happy if they knew I was drinking. My grandfather on my father's side who died before I was born was an alcoholic, so they're always extra strict about letting me try any booze.

Teddy walks by us holding Nikki's hand. He shines his flashlight into our faces. "Hey, sexy people. Nikki and I are gonna take a walk and find some privacy."

"All right there, man," Connor laughs, then turns back to me. "I swear, he's one of my best friends, but he's always causing trouble."

I laugh, then glance over at Victoria again. This time, she's looking in my direction. I flip around and focus back on Connor's yummy-looking profile. He's got the cutest little sideburns, small ears, and kissable lips.

He turns and catches me staring at him. Who knows what kind of silly, orgasmic look was plastered on my grill as I studied his features? I feel so nervous that I lose my balance and rock backwards. Connor sticks out his arm and grabs on to me so I don't fall off and land on my head in the grass.

"I'm so clumsy," I say, shaking my head.

"Near miss," he says. "But I got you."

"I don't why, but I always do stupid stuff like that. Knock my elbows into doorways, stub my toe on couches, and fall down on the street. Once I even hit myself in the eye with my hair dryer." My mouth is jabberwacky.

"Ouch," he says. "Were you okay?"

"Nope, I got a black eye." Then I laugh at myself. "I don't know why I just told you all that. Like, I mean, do you really want to hang out with klutz central?" I stop talking and listen to myself. Being within one foot of this guy's adorableness is making me act like a colossal weirdo.

Just then, I feel a tap on my arm. I turn and the world freezes. There's Victoria beside me and standing next to her are Lexi and Sydney. "Can we talk to you privately?" Victoria asks.

My heart is beating fast and loud like quarters dropping out of a slot machine. "Oh, yeah, sure," I say, casually standing up from the bench. "I'll be right back," I tell Connor as cheerfully as possible.

My hands start to sweat as Victoria takes me over to a spot under a tree away from the rest of the partygoers. Lexi and Sydney stand around me, looking at Victoria, waiting for her to begin.

"I didn't want to embarrass you in front of everyone," Victoria says. "But what are you doing here?"

It's like a searchlight is now pointed right at my face. "Um . . ." I say. It's the only sound I can get out.

The girls stand there with their hands on their hips waiting for an answer.

"We're just really confused," Lexi says. "How'd you get here? We didn't invite you."

"Yeah, it's supposed to be a small soirée," Sydney says, curling one of her long, blonde ringlets around her index finger.

"Look," Victoria says, "I don't want to sound mean, but we need to know if word of this got out. If it gets crashed by three hundred people, I could get in huge trouble with my dad. If he finds out, he'll royally flip the crap out on me."

"Uh, I, yeah, um," I say, stammering. I look over at Connor. He's sitting where I left him, but now he's watching me. He raises both hands up in the air as if to gesture, *Is everything okay?* I flash him a small wave and a mini smile, trying to look as casual as possible.

"Come on. Out with it," Victoria says.

"Well, I have to admit that, uh, because I never lie, that I did get wind of the flyer." Somewhere in this response, I hope I'm giving them part of the answer they want to hear.

"Do other people know?" Victoria asks.

"What are their names?" Lexi asks.

"Tell us everything," Sydney says.

The trio fires off questions at me with a swift *bang, bang, bang.* I try to come up with the right words. "I was on the gym bus, and I overheard something. No one else knows. I swear. I'm sorry if I crashed, it's just that—"

Just then, I see Nikki run out into the courtyard. Her overplucked eyebrows look arched in panic. Teddy quickly emerges by her side. "Victoria! Victoria! Where are you?" Nikki screams.

Victoria turns to Nikki. "What is it? Keep your voice down," she says.

Nikki runs over to us. "Teddy and I were making out on the couches in the side lobby and—"

"Why were you in there? I told everyone explicitly not to hang out in that area and to come immediately back here."

I look over and see Teddy talking with Connor by the cooler. He's moving his arms frantically in the air.

"I know, I know. I'm sorry, we just got carried away." Nikki throws her hands down by her side. "Teddy stuck his tongue in my belly button as a joke and it made me laugh and the security guard must have heard 'cause he called to us so we ran back out here."

"Nikki, I swear. Your laugh is way too loud for this planet," Victoria says. "Now look what you did."

"I'm sorry, Vic. I am. And the guard said he was gonna call the cops."

Victoria covers her face with both hands and lets out a loud sigh.

"This party was just getting started," she says. Then she turns to the center of the courtyard and calls out loudly, "Everyone! Get out of here! Pigs are coming! Someone grab the beer chest! Turn your flashlights off! And run for it!"

Just then, we hear the side door open. "Is that the guard?" Lexi says, squinting in the sudden darkness as everyone turns off their flashlights.

"I'm not sticking around to find out," Victoria says.

I watch as kids start running down the courtyard toward the other end. I spot Connor and Teddy carrying the cooler between them. Connor looks back at me as they take off.

I find myself running away from the party with Victoria, Lexi, and Sydney.

"This is the fastest way out," Victoria says, pointing toward a side wall. "We gotta jump over this."

"But I'm in cobra-snakeskin boots with three-inch heels," Sydney complains.

Victoria, Lexi, and I jump down the four-foot drop. I stumble when I land, almost twisting my ankle. "Just throw yourself over and I'll spot you," I yell up at Sydney, who's looking down at me, panicking.

"Oh my God," she's saying over and over. "He's coming! I hear him! The guard is coming!"

"Just start climbing over and we'll help you the rest of the way," I encourage her.

Sydney holds on to the top and throws herself over. "Oh,

please God," she says, dangling a few feet off the ground. Lexi and I help her down. Then the four of us start sprinting down the block.

As we run, I look over at Victoria. She's shaking her head, breathing heavily, and moving her lips without saying anything. It's the first time I've ever seen her lose composure.

We are two blocks away when I look back and see a cop car pull up to the building. We turn around to see two officers get out of the patrol car and go inside.

"I'm fucked! I'm fucked!" Victoria says. "I can't get caught. I just can't. My dad's gonna ground me forever."

"Me, too," Sydney says. "I told my mom I went to the movies with you at the AMC in Murray Hill. She'll know I lied."

"If I get arrested, I'll never get to become a lawyer," Lexi said. "Tonight could ruin my entire career."

"I know where we'll be safe," I blurt out.

The girls look at me with curiosity. "It's only a few blocks away. Follow me."

"You'd better know what you're doing," Victoria says. "If not—"

"Trust me," I say.

The four of us keep running. We pass a Chinese restaurant, a Bank of America, then a drugstore. "I'm getting blisters the size of gerbils on my big toes," Sydney screams out.

"Almost there," I say. As we run up First Avenue, I spot the flags from the United Nations getting closer. We turn down 43rd Street, and I lead the girls up the steps to Karen's brownstone. Then I ring the doorbell.

"Where the hell are we?" Victoria asks.

"It's this guy's apartment. He works for the Turkish consulate," I explain, in between gasping for breaths.

"Yeah, so what?" Lexi says.

"NYPD aren't allowed to set foot inside. Diplomatic immunity," I say.

Karen swings the door open, smiling. "So I see you've found some friends, after all," she says.

"Can we come inside?" I ask urgently.

"Please do," Karen says.

The four of us run through the front door like we're reaching home base. Karen gives us a funny look and then shuts the door. "Just in time for my favorite Turkish dessert," she says, leading us into a salon area.

My mom and Omer are already enjoying spoonfuls in front of a window facing out onto the street. She's telling him about her new job as we walk in.

"This week, it's planning a vision screen follow-up at the public schools in my district," my mom says. Then she turns and looks over at me. "You're back. That wasn't very long. I thought I'd lost you forever." As she looks behind me and notices Victoria, Sydney, and Lexi, she smiles.

"What happened to the party?" she asks.

"Oh, it ended early," I say. "I told my friends from school about Karen and Omer's amazing brownstone and they were dying to see it."

"Well, if you think this is more exciting, you're welcome to stay," Karen says, and motions us to sit down in the living room.

As I walk past Karen, she raises her eyebrows at me. I sense that although she might not buy my excuse entirely, she's willing to play along.

I introduce Victoria, Lexi, and Sydney to the rest of the group.

"I hope we're not imposing, though," Victoria says.

"Shush, shush. So who wants baklava with scoops of pistachio ice cream?" Karen announces.

"Count me in," I say, smiling at Victoria. She grins back at me.

"I just love baklava," Victoria says.

"Me, too," Lexi says.

"So do I," Sydney agrees.

In the salon, the four of us squeeze together on a dijon-colored divan. Karen hands us dessert plates and we balance them on our laps.

It's while Karen pours us tea that we noticed a police cruiser drive down the street. Lexi sees it first and nudges Victoria in the arm. We watch as it slows down for a moment, and then it drives off. Out of nerves, we burst out laughing.

"What's so funny?" my mom asks me.

"Yeah, what is it?" Karen says.

"Nothing," I say, shaking my head, smiling.

"Girls will be girls," Omer says. "You remember when you were that age."

"I guess I do," my mom says.

After we finish our plates, Victoria, Lexi, and Sydney excuse themselves and say they have to get home. It's only ten o'clock, and I doubt that's where they're really going, but I imagine they must have something more fun to do than stick around the consulate.

I walk them to the door and after we say our good-byes, Victoria lags behind for a moment. "Thanks," she says. "I really appreciate what you did tonight. You're a lifesaver."

"Don't mention it," I say. "I'm happy it worked out."

She nods and walk down the steps. "Cool," she says. "Your number's in the school directory, right?"

"Yeah," I say.

"I'll give you a call soon. We should all hang out again, Maggie."

"That'd be great," I say. And then it hits me. Although I never told it to her that night, she already knew my name.

I watch Victoria, Lexi, and Sydney take off down the street and hail a cab. *Tonight was big-time,* I think to myself. *I did exactly what Karen told me to do, and now, look how it's paying off.*

CHAPTER FOUR

Once the cocoon hardens into a brilliant green chrysalis with metallic gold spots, the caterpillar undergoes what is called complete metamorphosis. During this stage of development, the caterpillar changes into a completely different creature before it emerges from the chrysalis.

The next morning, I wake up to the house phone ringing at ten o'clock. Then I hear the sound of my mom's feet walking toward my bedroom. She knocks with her familiar style, three short taps, then opens the door.

"Sweetie, are you still asleep? Phone call for you," she says.

I roll over on my side and look at her through half-open eyes. "Who is it?" I ask.

"One of the girls from last night," my mom says. "She said to call her Vic."

I sit up quickly.

"I'll take it," I say, jumping out of bed. I hurry into the living room and grab the phone by the couch. I clear my throat before talking into the receiver. "Hello, Vic?" I say.

I hear Victoria's voice on the other end. "Did I wake you?" she says.

"I've been up for hours." I try and make my voice sound as peppy as possible.

"Okay, good," she says, sounding like she believes me. "Then you can meet us at Sheep's Meadow in Central Park in half an hour, right? We really need to talk to you."

"Is everything all right?" I say. "Did your dad find out about last night? Are we in trouble?"

"Miles, my dad, got a call from the building about the party, but there was no evidence it was me so I denied it and he believed me."

I exhale. "Then what do you need to talk about?"

"We want to tell you in person," she says. "We'll be by the tree cluster in the middle of the north end at eleven o'clock. You know how to get there, right? It's in the center of the park near Sixty-Seventh Street. We'll be lying out, so wear a bathing suit. Look for me in a red Dior bikini."

"But it's almost the end of September."

"It's seventy-five degrees. Gotta make the most of every Indian summer day there is. Now hurry up and get over there. Ta-ta," she says.

I look through my closet and pull out my one-piece gray suit from last summer. I left all my bikinis back at my house in Jersey because I didn't think I would be swimming much in New York. Great, now I'm stuck wearing a Marshall's special.

I tell my mom I'm going to meet the girls from last night in Central Park. She looks happy to hear that I'm finally making some friends. I take the West 67th Street entrance and walk straight toward the center of the park. Since it's Saturday, the inside roads are closed to traffic and have been taken over by bicyclists, Rollerbladers, and joggers. A cute boy my age runs past me with his shirt off and I can't help but look at his perfect pecs.

When I reach the Meadow, I stop in front of the gate that surrounds it and peer inside. I've walked by here before but have never actually ventured in. It reminds me of a crowded beach filled with sunbathers, except instead of sand there is rich, green grass, and the expansiveness of the ocean has been exchanged for the sweeping city skyline.

I spot the girls lounging on their towels, wearing bathing suits and oversized sunglasses. Victoria notices me heading over to them. I see her say something to the other girls. Then she stands up and waves.

"Great, you're here!" Victoria says. "Come on, grab a seat." She pats the patch of grass beside her. "Oh, I brought this for you." Victoria reaches into a white canvas tote bag with her initials monogrammed in red and pulls out an oversized, lush beach towel.

"Thanks," I say. As I spread the towel out on the ground, I notice it has the Dolce & Gabbana logo sprawled across it. I lean back on my hands and the softness of the material rubs against my palms. I notice they have bottles of Diet Coke and stacks of magazines, including *Vanity Fair*, *Hamptons*, *Wallpaper*, *W*, *Interview*, *The New Yorker*, *Elle*, *Teen Vogue*, and *Cosmo Girl*.

These girls seem very different from the popular girls back in Montague Township, who spend the weekend at the Middletown Mall and don't seem to have any interests other than getting trashed on spiked grape Kool-Aid in the gazebo behind Highpoint's clubhouse.

As I lie there in my gray one-piece, I feel pretty homely

compared to the glamour peacocks to my left. Lexi's wearing a pair of tinted Ray Ban aviator glasses and a white bikini with the Lacoste insignia, showcasing her tanned, perfect body. Sydney's blonde curls flow out from beneath her straw fedora hat, and her crocheted yellow two-piece displays her smoothly shaven long legs. And Victoria's in that red Dior bikini she mentioned on the phone with her Chanel sunglasses resting on top of her long, layered hair. Around her neck is a stack of delicate gold chains with charms of stars and hearts hanging from them. Despite their individual styles, I notice that each of the girls is wearing copies of the same bracelet. It's a stretchy silver band with an ID plaque that's inscribed with a cursive, uppercase *R*.

Victoria turns and smiles at me. "First of all, I want to thank you again so much for last night," she says.

"Totally loved your escape route," Lexi says, taking a headband out of her bright modern paisley LeSportsac and putting it over her dark brown hair.

"And your mom and her friends were so cool. I've never been to Turkey, but now I'm dying to go," Sydney says, playing with her wooden elephant pendant necklace.

"But can you pretty please come clean about how you got to my party?" Victoria says. "You were starting to tell us when all that stuff happened with Nikki and Teddy."

I sit up and tell them about how I overheard Olivia and Fredrika's conversation on the gym bus. "I feel silly, but I guess I just really wanted to go," I say.

"I get you," Victoria says. "It's hard being new. We just didn't know you yet or we definitely would have invited you."

"Really?" I say.

"Absolutely," Victoria says. The other girls nod in agreement, saying, "Of course," and, "For sure."

"Thanks," I say. "That's nice to hear." I settle back onto the towel.

I notice that Victoria's staring off into the distance about a hundred feet outside the Meadow, where a group of guys our age is playing a pickup game of soccer.

"Wow, look at them go," Victoria says. "He just scored another goal!"

"The way my guy dribbles that ball sends chills down my thighs," Sydney says.

"Who are those boys?" I ask.

"The one kicking the ball right now and I started hanging out about a week ago. He was at the party last night," Victoria says.

It's hard to make out the guy's features from this far away, but he looks like Jim Morrison.

"And I've got a mother-huge thing for his friend in the green T-shirt," Sydney says. Green-Shirt Guy is a tan stud with a short ponytail of light brown hair that looks like it naturally gets blonder in the summer.

"They told us last night that they were playing here today," Victoria says.

"So are you going to go over and say hi?" I ask.

"No way," Sydney says. "They didn't invite us to watch them, and it would be obvious we followed them."

Victoria flips her hair. "It's much more fun spying."

"Mmm," Victoria and Sydney say, staring off at their

crushes running down the dirt field. They sound like they're tasting melted chocolate.

After watching the boys for another moment, Victoria snaps back to reality. "Anyway, I know I acted a bit mysterious on the phone, but we've got some extremely fantastic news for you."

My ears perk up. "Really?"

"This is gonna rock your world," Lexi says, twisting her ponytail.

"*¡Bueno!*" Sydney says.

"What?" I ask, not understanding.

"Sydney's traveled to a zillion countries and sometimes pops out with foreign words. It's just her thing." Lexi takes a Barney's shopping bag that's next to her and moves it behind her neck so she can relax onto it like a pillow.

"It means, 'Good,' in Spanish," Sydney says.

"Gotcha," I say. "I like that. *¡Bueno!*"

"Speaking of wonderful," Victoria says, "I can't take it anymore. I really want to begin!" She plays with her stacked gold necklaces.

"Yes, let's!" Lexi says.

"Please do," Sydney says.

I look around and notice that all three of them are looking at me, biting their lips and smiling, like they're trying to hold in great news.

"On this auspicious date of the twenty-fourth of September," Victoria says, "we officially tap you to join the Revelers."

The girls look at me, their faces serious.

"The Revelers?" I ask. "What is that?"

"Wikipedia says it's those who live large, whoop it up, and paint the town red," Lexi says, tightening her ponytail.

"It's also defined as people who rise up in rebellion," Sydney says.

"But most important, it's the name of our group," Victoria says.

"Our secret society," Lexi adds.

"You guys have a secret society?" I say, surprised. "Are you serious?" I start laughing out of excitement.

"*Assolutamente*," Sydney says. "Since freshman year."

"That is the coolest thing I've ever heard!" I say.

A group of meatheads wearing worn-in baseball caps start throwing a football near us. I notice the three girls look over at them. From that moment on, they lower their voices. I match their volume so the boys don't hear what we're talking about.

"Our fourth member, Tracey, moved to Japan this year for her mom's job," Lexi says.

"And we decided you're the girl to replace her," Victoria says.

"Wow, I can't believe this," I say, trying to process what they're telling me. "I don't know what to say. I mean, this is the coolest thing ever. I'm so excited."

"You should be," Lexi says. "Your life is about to change for the better."

It's extremely flattering that they're singling me out for this honor, but it seems kind of sudden. I mean, only two days ago, they acted like I didn't even exist on this planet. "I'm really touched," I admit. "But why me?" I ask slowly. "Why are you picking me?"

The girls nod to each other in silent agreement.

"We like you," Victoria says.

I let the words echo in my ears.

"But don't forget—everything we tell you is top secret," Victoria says.

"The Revelers have a lot of fun and party," Lexi says.

"But we also devote ourselves to a unique social cause," Sydney adds.

"What's the social cause?" I ask.

That's when all of the girls lean in toward each other. I lean in, too, and our four heads meet over the center of Victoria's crisp white towel.

"The Wall," Victoria says, squinting her eyes and looking at me with the utmost seriousness.

"The Wall?" I say. "Which one?"

I've read about the Berlin Wall, but that was already torn down in the eighties. Growing up, I heard of the Western Wall in Jerusalem and the Great Wall of China, and listened to the music from Pink Floyd's *The Wall*, but I have no idea which one they're talking about. Maybe it's a new wall I've never even heard of.

Victoria leans back and picks up the tube of SPF four Bain de Soleil from beside her. "I'm really sorry, Maggie, but that's all we can tell you right now." She rubs the orange lotion into her legs. "First, you have to complete Pledge Week."

I'm dying to know more about their hush-hush under-world. "What do I have to do?" I say.

"For this coming week of school, you can't wear makeup, talk to boys our age, or use your cell phone," Victoria says.

"Also, you must have our favorite candy on hand every second—all things gummy—and Trident, the whitening kind. Plus, wear only clothes out of this bag to school," Lexi says. She passes me the black Barney's shopping bag that she's been lying on. "Don't be fooled by appearances. Nothing inside actually came from Barney's. It's all weird stuff we picked out from the thrift store. Plus, we subdivided the stuff into plastic bags and labeled them Monday through Friday."

I look inside and pull the outfit out of the oversized Ziploc bag labeled MONDAY. There's a sweatshirt with a huge wolf painted on it, a bright, rainbow-colored skull cap, and a pair of acid-washed jeans. "Wow," I say, rolling my eyes. "Stylin'. Are you serious? I really have to put these on?"

Victoria nods her head. "And if anyone asks you why you're dressed so strange, you have to play it off, and just say, 'Because I feel like it.'"

"And last but not least," Sydney says, "you have to bring each of us a vanilla cupcake with chocolate icing from Baked on Friday, the last day of Pledge Week."

"Okay," I say. "But what's so hard about that?"

"It's over the bridge. In Brooklyn," Lexi says.

I scrunch my face at them, confused. "Yeah, so?"

"When you're born and bred in Manhattan, you never go to the outer boroughs," Lexi says.

"We barely go beyond the range of Soho up to Ninety-Sixth Street," Victoria adds.

"The society convenes every Friday night, seven o'clock at my house," Victoria says.

"Here, I'll write down the address for you." Sydney takes out a purple sparkly pen from her suede bag and writes on a high-end, pink Post-it that's been designed in the shape of a small leaf. "It's on Fifth Avenue and Ninety-Fourth Street, overlooking Central Park."

"If you play your cards right and do what we've told you, everything will become clear on Friday night and we'll introduce you to the Wall. Does that make sense?" Victoria says.

I nod in agreement, although part of me feels a little scared. What if I mess up and fail? They may take back their offer to have me join their group. Or maybe they'll give me even worse tasks to do to make up for it. Plus, it's gonna be so embarrassing dressing like a total dork all next week. Thank God we go to an all-girls' school and no boys will be there to see me. Although I'm bound to pass some on the street.

Victoria must notice my inner panic. "I hope we're not overwhelming you," she says.

"Not at all," I fib. "I can handle it."

"Well, I just want you to know that I'm super excited you're coming on board. Oh, and if it all works out, which I'm sure it will, I want the four of us to go to my parents' place in the Hamptons next Saturday—the morning after our meeting. It'll be a celebration of you as the newest member of our group. We have Monday off from school because there's a professional development day for the teachers, so we can stay Saturday and Sunday nights."

"I've never been out there before," I say. "Isn't that where, like, P. Diddy throws his White Party? And I read in some magazine that Leonardo DiCaprio and Orlando Bloom have had summer houses there."

"Yeah," Victoria says. "It's off season because it's after Labor Day, but we always have a great time. Doesn't matter the time of year."

"Wait till you see her place," Sydney says. "Right on Georgica Pond and a two-minute walk to the beach."

"And the guys out there are really cute," Lexi says. "There's this dreamboat I've seen a bunch of times running on the beach, and I just want to tackle him into the sand and make out with him in the waves. Looks like a young Keanu Reeves."

"Lexi's a kissing bandit," Sydney says, giggling.

Victoria turns to me. "Which means she makes out with tons of guys, but doesn't go much further."

"What can I say?" Lexi said. "I love Frenching boys and they love smooching me."

"She just never sticks around very long," Victoria says.

"I get it. I'm as boy crazy as the rest of them," I admit, and an image of Connor's face flashes through my mind. I could've handled making out with him last night at the back-to-school soirée. He was so cute and seemed really nice, too. I wonder if these girls know anything about him. At the party, he mentioned that he didn't really know Victoria but was given a flyer from one of his soccer buddies. I can imagine Victoria handing some dude from his school extra invites and instructing him to bring a few extra cool guys to add some red hots to the eye candy.

"Then you're in the right company," Lexi says.

I laugh, and for the first time, I feel like I'm part of their conversation. Not on the outside looking in.

"Anyways, my mom will be out there, too, so you can tell your mom not to worry," Victoria says. "I know Lexi's mom, for one, is super overprotective. She's a reporter and acts like one, too, when it comes to Lexi's life."

"Every night I get home late, she gives me a hug and I can hear her sniffing my hair for cigarette smoke and my breath for beer," Lexi says.

"Yeah, my mom can be pretty intense, too," I say.

"How 'bout your dad?" Victoria asks.

"Not so much. When I was living with him and my mom in New Jersey, he was never as strict as she was," I admit.

"He's not living with you right now?" Victoria asks. The girls look at me.

"Yeah, well, they're separated," I say. "He lives at our house in Montague with our poodle, Moose, and my mom and I are here in the city. I have a brother, too, but he's a sophomore at Tufts."

"Why did you and your mom move to New York?" Lexi asks.

I look down at my chipped pale pink nail polish.

"We don't mean to pry. . . ." Victoria says. "Just trying to get to know you."

"That's all right," I say. "My mom grew up here, and her dad still lives downtown in the Village. My grandpa's, like, seventy-eight. I guess he's the main reason we came. He thought my mom would have a bigger support system here and more things to do. Plus there's this small incident that happened at the end of last year."

"What happened?" Victoria asks.

"I don't know . . . my grandpa had a small aneurism or something. It's like a mini stroke."

"I'm so sorry," Victoria says.

"That's terrible," Sydney says.

"Like, the cleaning lady found him on the floor of the bathroom in his apartment, and he looked up at her and thought the porcelain sink was a hat she was wearing. He was that disoriented. But when they took him to St. Luke's Hospital and did some tests, he snapped out of it."

"*Mon dieu,*" Sydney says.

"That sounds really tough. Is he okay now?" Victoria says.

"Everything's fine now, it's just I think he's part of the reason we moved. Like my mom wanted to be closer to him. I don't know, it's complicated." I look away, off at the city's skyline.

Victoria says, "If you ever want to talk about anything, you can come to me. My grandma died a few years ago from cancer and it was devastating. She was the most beautiful woman in the world. A member of the Daughters of the American Revolution. She spent a lot of time volunteering. It royally messed up my family for a while, especially my mom."

"I can imagine," I say. "Or I can't imagine, really. I mean, I can, but I can't."

"I think I know what you're trying to say," Victoria says.

I bite my lip, ashamed by my lack of eloquence.

Then Sydney changes the topic. "I better get home," she says. "I need to finish reading for English before I burn. Plus, I have to memorize my part in 'Somebody to Love' and 'Kiss from a Rose' for the Fresh Melodies 'cause we have rehearsal tomorrow afternoon."

"Oh, that's right. You're head of the a cappella club. I saw you get up at assembly on the first day of school."

"It's not actually a club," Sydney says. "It's a real group and it's pretty big at Berkeley Prep. We do a variety of songs, old rock and newer stuff like 'Say My Name' by Destiny's Child. We had a benefit last spring and performed 'Dock of the Bay' at last year's graduation. My dream is to record a CD of the group this year."

"Yeah, you guys are awesome," Victoria says.

"Freshman year, I thought I wanted to be in chorus, but Mrs. Mack, the conductor, has a substance-abuse problem. She showed up to rehearsals last spring with six-packs, which she drank right there—in front of everyone. And apparently she almost got fired because she groped some soprano."

"You don't know if that's true," Victoria says. "About the beer and the groping. Sounds like stupid gossip to me."

"I heard it from a reliable source."

"We've been through this already. There's an important difference between truth and gossip," Victoria says.

"I know, I know," Sydney says.

"It's just sometimes you forget," Victoria says.

"I'm not in the mood to argue. I have to get ready for tomorrow's Fresh Melodies rehearsal. We have a bunch of songs we need to learn for Phase." Sydney throws some of the magazines into her patchwork suede hobo bag.

Victoria turns and explains to me. "Phase is like our high-school version of a talent show. Student rock bands jam. Girls do dance routines that look like they came right out of MTV music videos. And all the guys from the boys' schools come to watch us."

"Lexi, do you want to walk together?" Sydney asks.

"Yeah, sure," Lexi says. "I should get to work on my three pages of proofs due Tuesday in geometry. I messed up and got a C on our first quiz. I have this new teacher, Mr. Dumont, who just moved here from Grand Rapids, Michigan, and he's mean as hell," Lexi says. "Plus, I have a tennis match away on Monday against Riverdale and I heard they're good this year." She unzips her LeSportsac and throws in her suntan lotion.

"You'll have to see Lexi in action one day," Victoria says. "She's like the next Sharapova."

"I've been playing since I was three years old," Lexi says.

Lexi and Sydney say good-bye and we all exchange quick pecks on both cheeks like Europeans do.

After they leave, it's not long before Victoria says, "I should take off, too. I've got a killer test in AP Calc this week, and Mr. Hackman is like a transvestite witch." Victoria puts her tortoiseshell sunglasses into a Chanel case and throws them into her black leather Marc Jacobs bag.

"There are, like, twenty new verbs I have to learn to conjugate for French and I've got reading by Socrates for philosophy class with Mr. Z," I say, standing up and folding up the beach towel.

Victoria laughs when I say my teacher's name.

"What?" I ask.

"He's just such an eccentric," she says.

I'm certainly on the outside of her joke. Victoria and I finish gathering our things and then walk toward the north edge of the Meadow.

"Here," I say, handing Victoria her Dolce & Gabbana towel back. "Thanks for letting me borrow it."

"Oh, you can keep it," Victoria says. "I have a bunch more just like it back at home."

"I wouldn't want to take it from you," I say.

"Don't be silly," Victoria says.

"No. I just couldn't," I say.

"It suits you. I insist." Victoria forces the towel into my arms and leaves it there.

I look down at it. "Well, thanks," I say. "That's really nice of you."

We say good-bye and then I walk out of the Meadow, holding the towel in one arm and the Barney's shopping bag in the other.

CHAPTER FIVE

*During the metamorphosis stage, the caterpillar liquefies inside the cocoon.
Some tiny clusters called imaginal buds remain intact. These growth centers
contain the chromosomes that carry the butterfly's genes. They have been
inactive throughout the caterpillar's life, protected deep inside its body.*

The no-makeup thing isn't so hard on me, other than my freaking addiction to lip gloss. I just love the way it feels—so soft and slippery. Throughout Pledge Week, my mouth feels like a dry cake craving frosting.

The no-cell-phone policy makes me realize what a communication junkie I've become. My fingers want to poke the numbers and send fantastic text messages to Kelsey in Montague, but I can't. Instead, I spend more time online e-mailing and instant-messaging. You can't shut me up that easy. So there!

I go to Dylan's Candy Bar near Bloomingdale's and stock up on all sorts of gummy candy—Swedish Fish, gummy cherries, sour bright crawlers, chocolate-covered gummy bears, Sour Patch Kids, and gummy Coke bottles and cherries. I carry them in a lunch box–shaped tin in my backpack and stick plenty of Trident teeth-whitening gum in the front pocket.

I wear a bunch of unfashionable clothing items and notice girls in my school looking at me funny. These pieces include a hot-pink dyed fake-rabbit-fur jacket, two pairs of contrasting-colored socks, purple overalls, red stirrup pants, a navy blazer from the 1980s with shoulder pads, and clown pajama pants. I leave my apartment in my normal clothes then change in the lobby bathroom so my mom won't notice and ask me what on earth I'm up to. I don't have to worry what I wear home from school because she doesn't get back from her public-health gig until six at night.

On Tuesday, Anne Marie stops by my locker. She takes out her earphones and asks me why I'm wearing a ratty old IMPEACH NIXON T-shirt with orange sweatpants. I tell her, "Oh, ya know. Because I feel like it." She just shrugs her shoulders and says, "Whatever floats your boat." I kinda like how she doesn't seem to judge me. Then she puts her white earpieces back in. "Now back to the Commodores," she says, and bops her head a little as she walks down the hall.

Wednesday morning I take the bus wearing an abomination of an outfit that I pick out of the bag. It's a dress with a million polka dots of bright pink, red, green, and blue, with a red handkerchief over my hair. I climb onto the bus, flash the driver my bus pass, and take a few steps back. Then to my shock I see Connor's face stuffed among the crowd of commuters. He's standing up holding on to a silver bar on the back of a seat and looking right at me, smiling. My heart beats fast, and I grin back at him. Then I look down and remember how I am dressed. In a second I spot a second familiar face. It's Lexi wedged in the way back of the bus. It's too hard for us to get to each other, so we just wave.

Connor's walking toward me now, making his way through all the bodies. I guess his school has a dress code 'cause he's in a white button-down shirt and light blue tie with small white polka dots on it.

If Lexi wasn't here, too, maybe I could cheat and break the Pledge Week rule: *Thou Shalt Not Speak to a Boy Our Age*. Perhaps I could've chatted quietly with him, and no one would ever have known. From one to ten, this will be a 9.5 on the embarrassment scale.

"Hey," Connor says. "Do you always take this bus?"

I smile and nod.

"Me, too," he says. "Today I left ten minutes early 'cause I promised my buddy Teddy—you remember him, right?"

I nod my head up and down.

"Well, he needs help on this physics assignment, which he left to the last minute 'cause he's been spending every free second with Nikki."

I giggle but wish I could say something. There's an awkward silence. He looks down at my silly outfit and I blush.

"I see we both brought out the polka dots today." He holds out his tie. It's funny how tasteful his polka dots look like compared to mine. Who knew one pattern can go from J.Crew stylish to a psychedelic optical illusion.

I feel Lexi's eyes on me and look over. It's clear she wants me to know that she's monitoring my behavior.

"The other night was crazy," he says. "I really wanted to say bye to you, and maybe get your number so we could hang out sometime. But the next thing you know, I'm lugging a hundred-pound cooler."

I nod my head up and down. Connor looks away and I stare at his profile. It's the same view I had at the soirée. The short brown hair, side burns, big green eyes, and cute ears.

"Well, I guess, um . . ." he says, scratching the back of his neck. "Is everything okay?"

I nod my head quickly up and down.

"It's just . . . you haven't said anything."

I bite my lip and look back at Lexi. She waves at me and smiles, then takes a sip from her Starbucks coffee.

Connor looks out the window and is no longer smiling. "This is my stop coming up." His eyes search my face. Then he tightens his grip on the strap of the messenger bag thrown across his chest. "Alrighty then. See you around."

I feel terrible. I squint my eyes and look down at his black shoes, then watch them take off down the steps of the bus. I realize too late that I should've taken out a piece of loose-leaf paper and written to him. Why didn't I think of that sooner? Crap. Shoot. Plop. Damn.

As soon as I get off at my stop, Lexi runs over to me. "I'm so freaking impressed," Lexi says. "That guy was a total cutie and you didn't make a peep."

"Do you have any idea how hard that was? He probably thinks I hate him now. Or I'm a complete mean nutcase. I bet he'll never talk to me again."

"Don't worry. I'm sure he will," Lexi says. "Guys love it when girls play hard-to-get." She holds out her coffee to me. "Here, have a sip. Latte with skim milk and sugar-free caramel syrup," she says.

"Thanks," I say, taking a small taste. I'm not a big coffee drinker, but right now I would possibly drink anything stuck in front of me. "Do you know anything about him?"

"Negative," Lexi says. "I've seen him around. But I think he's relatively new on the scene or I'd have more dish to dirt. I mean, the other way around."

Lexi turns down 89th Street toward our school. "Anyway, wait till I tell the other girls. They're gonna be blown away by your commitment."

"I hope so," I say. "That was certainly a challenge."

As we walk through Berkeley Prep's doors, Lexi asks me for a handful of gummy cherries. Then she heads off to her first class, Spanish, and I go to mine, philosophy.

"See ya later," I say.

"Take it sleazy," she jokes as she walks away.

In philosophy, I sit there cringing as I replay the incident with Connor in my mind. It's hard for me to pay full attention to Mr. Z as he paces around the classroom in his leather jacket and jeans. His salt-and-pepper hair, like usual, is pulled back in a low ponytail. I can imagine him racing back to us on his motorcycle from his weekend house in the Berkshires. I zone in and out of his lecture on Aristotle.

"He was a brilliant Greek philosopher who believed that each object has its own essence. An essence is the property or properties that make an object what it is. Let me illustrate this point further with an experiment." Mr. Z takes an old baseball cap out of his desk drawer and starts cutting it with a pair of scissors. First, he snips a hole in the top and asks, "What am I holding in my hand?"

"A baseball cap, of course," Mia Bernstein, the class kiss-ass, yells out.

"Precisely," Mr. Z says.

Mia smiles to herself, satisfied. *Big whoop, you know what a baseball cap is,* I think. *Congratulations.*

Next, he cuts off the plastic band on the back that fits the cap to your head. And then, to my surprise, he rips off the actual brim.

"Now what is it?" he asks.

Mia's best friend, Jenna, says, "It's still a hat, obviously."

Mr. Z doesn't say anything. Instead he takes the scissors and really cuts the hat to shreds, totally mutilating it.

"Oh, no!" Mia squeals out in pain as he cuts the hat. "What are you doing? That was a cool hat. I would have bought that at Bloomingdale's. The worn-out look is totally in."

"Shh," Mr. Z says. "Relax and watch." He holds up the remains. "Now what is it? Is it still a hat?" he asks.

The class stares at him speechless and confused. Mia and Jenna look at each other, trying to figure out the right thing to say.

"Yeah, of course," Jenna says, speaking up.

"No, it's not," Mia says. "That's definitely not a hat anymore. It's just a rag now."

"There seems to be some confusion," Mr. Z says. "According to Aristotle, a hat, just like every other object, has its own, unique essence and set of qualities that make it what it is. Was there a moment when I deconstructed this hat when it lost enough of its properties that it was no longer a hat? Did this cease to be a hat when I cut off the plastic strap or the brim? Or is it still a hat at this moment—but no longer a perfect or absolute hat? Think about it, class. And we'll talk more next time."

I'm not sure what Mr. Z does in the Berkshires, but I'm starting to worry he's hanging out with the wrong crowd and has lost some serious brain cells. That was a fairly trippy experiment.

As I stick my notebook in my bag, Mr. Z calls me over to speak to him in private. "Maggie, it doesn't seem like you've been paying close attention," he says, resting the elbows of his leather jacket on the desk.

"Oh, but I've been completely focused the whole time," I say, tucking my overgrown bangs behind my right ear.

He cocks his head to the side and opens his eyes wide with disbelief. "Can I see your notes from today's class?" he asks, and puts his hand out, gesturing for me to hand over my notebook.

I freeze. I didn't take detailed notes today. Just in-depth doodles of Connor's face, his short, disheveled haircut, and that polka-dot tie. "Do you have to?" I ask.

Mr. Z looks up at the ceiling. I can see him debating in his mind what to do. "Okay, Maggie," he says. "Consider this a warning. I've got a reputation for giving pop quizzes, so make sure you're up to date on the reading assignments. Focus on the substance and essence section of *Metaphysics.*"

"I definitely will," I say. "For sure."

Mr. Z organizes the papers on his desk into a stack. "Now get going to your next class," he says.

"Okay," I say. "Thanks." Then I take off out the door. As I run down the stairs to English, I worry about getting on Mr. Z's wrong side. If he dislikes me early on, it will only make the rest of the year in his class even harder. And I promised Grandpa Jack I would deliver excellent grades.

That evening, I try to read Aristotle's *Metaphysics* but can only get through three pages of it. The text is so dense and it doesn't make any sense. I end up throwing the book across the room.

On Friday, it's time for my final Pledge Week assignment. The directions to Baked are posted online. The Web site tells me to take the F train to Smith–9th Street and then the B77 bus to Van Brunt Street. After school, I change out of my crazy outfit in the bathroom and put on regular jeans and a T-shirt. Then I ride the subway over to Brooklyn. It's silly, I know, but somehow leaving Manhattan makes me feel like I'm traveling far from home and into another country. I didn't tell my mom where I was going because I promised the Revelers to keep all Pledge Week assignments secret. She thinks I'm going directly from school to Victoria's.

After I get off at the Smith–9th Street station, it takes me a while to find the B77 stop. When I do, it's already five o'clock. As I sit on the bus, a strange woman plops down across from me. She appears to be in her thirties, wearing dirty jeans, flip-flops, and an Iron Maiden concert T-shirt. Her eyes look red. I wonder if she's on drugs as she sits there talking to herself. Then she takes out nail clippers from a brown supermarket bag and starts to cut her toenails. She notices me watching her.

"Be careful, or you're gonna die soon," she says.

This freaks me out, so I walk to the front of the bus and stand by the driver. I don't look back at her once. Thank God my stop is next. I want to get back to Manhattan quick.

Finally, I reach Baked and get my hands on the buttercream goods. I run back to the bus, hop on the train, and make it to Victoria's apartment on the Upper East Side just in time for the meeting.

The apartment is completely posh, a penthouse in one of those white-glove doorman buildings. After the doorman calls up to announce me, a uniformed elevator operator takes me to the top floor.

The elevator doors open right into the apartment. Victoria stands waiting for me in the foyer. She's wearing a black-and-white-striped top with jeans and black boots. I peek behind her at the rest of the apartment. There's an impressive floral arrangement in the foyer with stargazer lilies and pale pink roses, a French-blue dining room with a long oak table that looks like it could seat twenty people, a reading room filled with bookcases, and a series of marble statues that look like they came from ancient Rome. I'd love a proper tour, but Victoria's already guiding me toward an elaborately carved wood door.

"My parents are at a fund-raiser tonight, so we have the place to ourselves. They live up here, but I spend most of my time on the bottom level 'cause I have it all to myself." She runs her fingers over her gold-stacked necklaces, untangling two of the chains.

We pass an antique-looking chest covered in framed photographs. "Are those you as a little girl?" I ask.

"Yes," Victoria said. "But don't look at that one," she says, covering a photo with her hand. "It's me one day old, and I swear I look like an alien."

I laugh. Then I notice a picture of a man in a tux and woman in a wedding dress. "Are those your parents?" I ask.

Victoria nods.

"She's really pretty," I say. Victoria's mom has what my mom would call all-American good looks.

"I told my mom about you and she can't wait to meet you."

"That's so sweet," I say, touched.

"She likes staying involved with all my friends. Rosalind's known Lexi and Sydney since we met in seventh grade. She totally adores them."

"Rosalind's your mom?" I ask.

"I call both my parents by their first names. Rosalind and Miles. Anyway, she always buys them presents for their birthdays and holidays."

"That's very generous," I say.

"She's super giving. You'll see when you meet her."

"Can't wait," I say, taking my last step toward the door.

Now, Victoria opens it to reveal a winding staircase that leads to an entire lower level of the apartment. Upstairs seems more like an English manor, but downstairs looks like a trendy modern boutique hotel. There are large beveled mirrors, white shaggy carpets, and a huge silver lamp with a marble base. Oversized cherry-and-ivory-beaded pillows are thrown across the black leather couches.

"Welcome to our headquarters," Victoria says.

Lexi and Sydney come over and say hi.

"You have so much space for yourself?" I ask.

"Rosalind and Miles never come down here. The only person who bothers to set foot on this floor is Yelena, our

Russian cleaning lady. But she doesn't speak English well and she's about a hundred years old, so a lot of things just go right past her. I mean, like, words and stuff. Not dust. She's very good with a wet Swiffer."

I walk around the room, admiring the artwork. The walls are covered in five-foot-tall framed and signed photographs of different female icons like Debbie Harry, the lead singer of Blondie, giving a sassy look to the camera while wearing pink sunglasses; a young Katharine Hepburn bike-riding through a studio lot; and a young Marilyn Monroe posing in a red bathing suit.

"These decorations are unbelievable."

"Sydney designed almost everything," Victoria says. "She's got that creative flair."

"I bought most things at ABC Carpets and Barney's home department," Sydney says, tightening the drawstring of her long turquoise skirt. "Oh, but I got the ghost chandelier from the Museum of Modern Art and the photos from a gallery in Chelsea. I want to be an interior designer when I grow up."

"Look at this," Lexi says, waving me over to the lava lamp positioned next to one of the leather couches. "This is my favorite piece," she says. "A lava lamp in the shape of Venus di Milo's body! Isn't that hot, hot, hot?"

"*¡Que bueno!* I adore the shaggy rugs from Ireland," Sydney says. "Sometimes I like to lie down and do stretches on them. They're so soft and cuddly."

"And this is my special collection," Victoria says, waving me over to the fireplace area. There's a lineup of small objects on the mantelpiece. A framed painting of an Egyptian woman in a large headdress. A thick candle with a red Chinese letter on the side of it. A vase filled with white flowers. A decorative pin made of diamonds surrounding a large blue sapphire. And a white marble sculpture about six inches tall that looks like a Greek goddess.

"What are all these things?" I ask.

"Symbols of truth," Victoria says. "My favorite pieces are the miniature copy of a statue of Athena holding a parrot out on her arm—she was the Greek goddess of wisdom—and the framed painting of Ma'at, the Egyptian deity of truth, order, and balance."

"I like them," I say.

Then Victoria switches the topic. "So are you ready to begin? We need you to sit down in that chair," she says, pointing to a black leather swivel chair. "That's an Eames original," she brags. "It's considered a piece of contemporary art, and there's even one on display at the MoMA."

"What's Eames?" I ask.

Victoria smiles. "Charles Eames is like the pimp-daddy designer of all present-day furniture. But don't worry. Once you start hanging with us, you'll know all that and more. We're gonna teach you everything you need to know about life."

"Okay." I spin the chair to the left and to the right slightly. Then I place the cupcake box on the table as an offering.

Lexi opens the box and digs in. She swirls off a chunk of icing with her finger. "Did you know chocolate is an aphrodisiac?" she says. "I heard if you sat and just kept eating tons of it, you'd eventually have an orgasm."

"That is not true!" Sydney says.

"It is so!" Lexi says. "I read all about it in *Glamour!*"

"I've read something about that before, too," I offer.

"Chocolate contains stimulants, but there's no proof it's actually some sort of love potion."

Lexi looks at me. She seems a bit surprised that I corrected her. "Well, whatever. I think it would still be fun to try anyway."

"Ladies!" Victoria shushes us up.

"Sydney, you can be so annoying sometimes," Lexi mumbles.

"It's not my fault that you get facts wrong," Sydney says back.

"Focus! Focus!" Victoria dims the lights and flicks a switch that turns on a disco ball hanging from the ceiling. Then she sits down on the couch across from me. Sydney and Lexi flop down on either side of her.

"You've reached the end of Pledge Week and completed all the tasks we've asked you to do," Victoria says. "Are there any transgressions you want to confess?"

I shake my head no. It's true. This week, I followed their orders to the T—even when I was alone. At home in the evening, I imagined the girls watching me through my bedroom walls and perched outside my window. And when I walked down the streets, I envisioned them hiding behind fashion magazines in cafés or ducking into alleyways, monitoring my every move. "I did everything you asked me to do," I say.

"Then congratulations, Maggie," Victoria says, grinning wide. "I officially welcome you to the Revelers. We can now tell you everything."

CHAPTER SIX

*A few hours before the butterfly is ready to emerge, the cocoon changes
color, darkening before turning translucent. An intake of air is used
to expand and split open the chrysalis. Using its new long legs,
the butterfly pulls itself out of the chrysalis and clings to the empty
shell so that its crumpled wings can hang down freely.*

Victoria walks over to the far end of the room, where there is
a bookcase that takes up a small portion of the wall.

"I don't want to get all Scooby Doo on your ass," Victoria says, "but this is the coolest part of downstairs. The man
we bought this apartment from installed a concealed room.
He was a billionaire and incredibly paranoid about robbers
breaking in. Come here and look very carefully."

I walk over and Victoria points out the small telltale
signs. Hidden hinges, rollers, and a handle. "How badass," I
say. "I've never seen anything like this before in real life."

"According to an article in *The New York Times*, concealed
rooms are actually growing in popularity," Victoria says.
"Not to defend against intruders, but 'cause people like creating a sense of wonder and mystery."

"Architects are getting many more requests," Sydney says. "I hope to interior-design a bunch of hidden rooms one day."

"So what's behind there?" I ask.

"You'll have to go in and see," Victoria says. She pulls a huge art book on Picasso off the shelf, revealing a gold doorknob. When she sticks a key in the doorknob and turns it, the bookcase swings backwards like an actual door.

"No way. That's awesome," I say.

"After you," Victoria says, ushering me into the private room.

I step inside and look straight ahead at a plain white wall. "I don't get it," I say. "There's nothing in here."

"Turn around," Victoria says.

I do, and that's the first time I see it. One complete wall of the secret room is covered in countless writings scribbled over a massive mural.

"Oh my God. What is all that?" I ask.

"Everything you ever wanted to know about the girls in our class, and the teachers, too," Victoria says proudly.

I examine the Wall more closely. There are three long panels of thick white paper, placed next to each other, but instead of being glued down, they're held in place by silver tacks. I notice tons of handwritten notes sketched in various types of pens. There are many different colors, too—red, black, green, blue, orange, sparkly purple, silver, and gold. And written in so many different styles—cursive, caps, all lowercase, calligraphy, neat, messy, large, and small. I recognize names of girls in our class and teachers from Berkeley. I read some parts quickly:

Fredrika binges on food when she is alone in her room.

Sadie's parents made her break up with her boyfriend because he
  wasn't Jewish.

Mia gets verbally abused by her father, who tells her she's not
  good enough.

Mrs. Hilback, the physics teacher, is trying to have a baby, but
  her gyno said she's infertile.

Mr. Vogel was just left by his wife for a woman and is going
  through a dirty divorce.

There are also photographs posted up there. One picture is of a girl from our class, Gwendolyn Marks, at a tattoo parlor, getting an image of lucky dice inked onto her lower abdomen. And another photo is of Laticia Smith drinking from a bottle filled with green liquid marked ABSINTHE.

"Isn't it beautiful?" Victoria says.

"I've never seen anything like it," I admit. "But why do you have this?"

"Tradition, power, and legacy. You know how parents and teachers want to see us in a certain way? Like we can't show them everything inside or they'll disapprove?" Victoria says.

"Yeah," I say. There are things I don't feel like I can tell my parents. Like how I tried beer the other week with Connor 'cause I was curious. And took the train to Brooklyn when I said I was going to hang out at Victoria's house right after school. And how pissed I am at my dad for being such a jerk and screaming so loudly sometimes. And although I am so grateful my grandpa sent me to Berkeley Prep for a top-notch education, I hate the pressure to get perfect grades. Oh, and I detested the time my pseudo-boyfriend from sophomore year, Chad, took me for a walk around the country-club lake, and my dad followed twenty feet behind us pretending he needed to walk Moose when all he really wanted to do was make sure Chad didn't put the moves on me.

"On this wall here," Victoria continues, "we can say it as we see it. No holding back—and not just about ourselves, about everyone at school, too."

"So this is all gossip?" I ask.

"No, no, no," Victoria says, shaking her head as if I offended her. "Gossip is for Gawker, TMZ, and Billy Bush. We only care about the truth 'cause that's what really matters. The Wall needs to reflect our lives as accurately as possible or it's of no use."

"And we're not the generation to start it," Lexi says.

"My mom began the Revelers with her friends when she was in high school over twenty years ago. Now the tradition continues with me. Picture this. The summer before my freshman year, Rosalind takes me out to a lunch while we are on our mother/daughter European vacation. We're sitting at one of the beach dining tables across the street from the Carlton in Cannes and she tells me all about it," Victoria says.

"So your mom *knows* you have this?" I ask.

Victoria nods. "She encourages it. The three scrolls of paper are held up with pushpins 'cause on graduation day of high school, we're going to take them down, roll them up, and put them in a box. And after we store the box away in the highest shelf of my walk-in closet, my mom and I are going to have a celebration, open up the Wall she made while she was in high school, and read it together. Then when I have a daughter one day, I'm gonna pass the tradition down to her, and when she graduates high school, she's gonna get to read *our* wall."

"I still think it's totally unfair you get to keep it," Sydney says. "We've all written on it, too."

"Sydney, I'm not going over this again. It's my family's tradition, and I want it to stay in my apartment."

"I'm just saying . . ." Sydney says.

"End of conversation," Victoria says. Then she turns back to me. "This is all ours. We're preserving what it's really like to be a girl today. Our voices will not be squashed."

"Like, look here," Lexi says. "Under my name, I list all the guys I've made out with. See, I suffer from the the False Loosey-Goosey Theory. Guys can kiss as many girls as they want and don't get judged, but if a girl hooks up with a lot of guys, even Kissing-Bandit style, some people call her 'easy' or 'slutty.' Maybe she just can't find a nice guy to date seriously and in the meantime doesn't want to be alone? Huh? Do they ever think about that?"

"Or, like, look here," Sydney says, pointing toward a few lines written in thick black marker. "A classic example of the Three-Prong Theory. Nanette Beauchamp from the Snobby Indies. Most people in our grade stereotype her as a bitchy, smart, pretty girl, but she's actually very nice if you take the time to get to know her. People in our world have a hard time believing a girl can be pretty, nice, *and* smart. They tend to think they can only be two of those things at once. If a girl is smart and pretty, then she must be a bitch. Or if she's pretty and nice, she must be stupid. Like in my case. I know some girls at school think I'm stupid when I'm not one bit."

"What are the Snobby Indies?" I ask.

"One of the cliques at school. They all have names," Lexi says.

"We have a lot to teach you," says Sydney as she eats a gummy Coke bottle.

"Definitely," agrees Victoria. "But back to the Wall. I have to deal with the Strutting in My Mother's Shadow Principle. Rosalind's the first female head of the OBGYN unit at Roosevelt Hospital. She's won countless awards for her research on fertility. And I'm her only child. If I don't live up to what she's accomplished, then I'll feel like a failure. Like I haven't lived up to the lucky moment my dad's sperm hitched with my mom's egg. I mean, do you have any idea the odds? I read online all about it. If you go back twenty-five generations, the chance of you being born is at most one divided by six times ten to the hundredth, which is . . ." Victoria looks up and to the side and it appears as if she is doing a calculation. "One in 600000000000000000000000 00000000000000000000000000000000000000000000000 00000000000000000000000000000000000000."

We stare at Vic in awe as she actually says all the zeros.

"Did you *really* just do that math?" Lexi says when Victoria finally stops.

"I was trying to emphasize a point," Victoria says.

"Which is what?" Sydney asks.

"What a nothing I will feel like if I don't succeed. See, so that is the Strutting in My Mother's Shadow Principle. And Maggie, I'm sure you suffer from your own angst."

"If you only knew," I say.

"We want you to know you're not alone. No matter how hard things get. Now that you're part of the Revelers, we've got your back. If you ever need to talk—and I mean any time of night—you can always call me."

"Any of us," Sydney chimes in.

"We mean it," Lexi says.

"So everything written on the Wall is true?" I ask.

"Yep. Or at least, to the best of our abilities," Lexi says. "We're not, like, robots or anything. We try to be as accurate as possible. If something is found to be wrong, we cross it out immediately."

"But how?" I ask. "How do you collect all this info?"

"There are tricks you can learn," Victoria says. "Like being a good listener. Eavesdrop on people's conversations. Really look at them. Pay attention to the small things like the details of what they're wearing. Their facial expressions. We've read articles on how to tell if people are lying by under-standing body language, and the mannerisms they use while they speak."

"Also you'd be surprised by how much you can overhear in the bathroom," Lexi says. "If you hide in a stall for a free period, girls come into the bathroom and pour out their hearts to their friends."

"Another tip is if you see a piece of paper on the floor or if someone leaves a notebook around, take it and read it. Usually kids write private thoughts inside them, and poems," Sydney says.

"Our class is pretty small. There are forty-three girls, so

there are some things that are just common knowledge. If something crazy or spectacular happens, the news usually spreads like wildfire. You have to keep in mind we have been in school with most of these kids for years already, so we've accumulated some good stuff," Victoria says.

"Nowadays, some girls post their most intimate details online. You know, like on blogs or those million 'Be My Friend' sites. Brianna Russo in our grade posted pictures of herself topless online. They were up for a week before her parents found out and made her take them down," Lexi says.

"I would never do that in a million years," Sydney says. "Why on earth would anyone do that?"

"She thinks she can become famous online since a million people can see her," Victoria says.

"Or it's like a power trip," Lexi says. "Like no one has control over what she can or can't do."

"Total exhibitionist, if you ask me," Victoria says. "Anyway, we have our classmates organized alphabetically by first name. A's starting on the left. They're also color-coded by clique starting from the most powerful and working all the way down the ladder. Gold ink is reserved for us, followed by black for the Snobby Indies. Red is for the Cheers and Beers. Those are the jock girls who party hard."

"Orange is fitting for the Orange Shoppers," Lexi says. "They dress in all top-designer labels and wear pearls, and their faces always look oddly orange from using too much self-tanner. Sparkly purple is for Les Artistes, the artsy crew who sometimes wear costumes as their everyday clothes."

"Blue stands for the I-Have-No-Lifers," Sydney says. "The girls like Anne Marie Schneck and Grace Mills who work all the time with barely any social life. Silver's for the Gay Asians. They're not all gay or Asian, but every member of their clique is super into Asian studies and gay rights. And last but not least, we use green for the Warriors—the sweat-pants-wearing clique obsessed with playing that online video game Rabbit Wars and having imaginary sword fights in the hallways."

"Let me see if I've got it straight—gold for us, black for the Snobby Indies, red for Cheers and Beers—"

"There's a color code on the bottom right-hand corner. But while that soaks in, come on," Victoria says. "I want to show you the best part of the Wall."

"What's that?" I say.

"How to use it. Is there anything that you really want a lot? Something you want to achieve in school? A girl you want to get back at? Or some boy you like?"

Connor pops into my head and my face gets flushed. "I suppose there is a guy I have my eye on . . ."

"Ooh, yeah?" Sydney says, giggling. "Do tell!"

I smile a little.

"Dish it," Victoria says. "I'm dying to know."

"I bet I have an idea. That tall, hunky, yum-yum machine from the bus?" Lexi guesses right on the dot.

I smile wide, my face giving it away.

"What's his name?" Victoria asks.

"Connor," I say.

She bites her lip as she thinks. "Hmm. There's a few Connors in the prep-school circuit. Tell me everything you already know about him."

"Plays soccer. Goes to The Chesterfield School. He

moved here two years ago from Pennsylvania," I say.

"Not ringing a bell," Victoria says. "Which is odd for us. Are you sure that's his name?"

"I saw him," Lexi says. "He was one of the new cute faces at your party."

"A newbie. That's why," Victoria says. Then she goes up to the Wall. "Let's see . . . my ex-boyfriend Jake goes to Chesterfield, but we're on terrible terms. I dumped him when he became too clingy." She studies the Wall, then places her finger on the name "Olivia" from the Snobby Indies written in black pen. "Olivia's younger brother goes there. He's a junior, but I'm sure she can ask him if he knows anything about Connor. We'll find out how to get you and Connor in the same room together. If you want Connor, Connor we shall deliver," Victoria says.

"Really?" I say. "That would be awesome. I mean, I bumped into him on the bus this week, but I couldn't talk to him. What if he hates me?"

"We're on it now," Victoria says. "The only thing you should be worrying about is going home and packing your weekend getaway bag for our trip to the Hamptons tomorrow."

"*Fantástico*," Sydney says. "I'm taking a Bikram yoga class at eight A.M. so we need to leave after that."

"Trust me, I'm sleeping in," Victoria says, rolling her eyes. "Besides, I already made the arrangements. A Town Car's gonna come pick us up in the morning."

We finish making plans and decide to meet at Victoria's house so the car can get us all together.

"You're *in* now," Victoria says. "Just like one of us."

～～～～～～

When I get home, I tell my mom about the Hamptons invite. "The place is right in East Hampton near where celebrities spend their summers. I've always wanted to go!"

"It's kind of last-minute."

"But I just found out for sure tonight, Mom."

"Well, I should probably call Victoria's parents and introduce myself."

"Please don't," I say. "You have nothing to worry about. A car's picking us up, and it's gonna be a straight mom-to-mom drop-off."

She has a hard time arguing with me. "That does sound reasonable. Karen was probably right when she said I need to relax a little and let you loose into the world. And New York is much safer than it used to be. . . . Just remember all the street smarts I taught you, and leave me the phone number for Victoria's Hamptons house in case of emergencies."

"I'll leave it on the fridge," I say, rolling my eyes. I'll have to text Victoria later to ask for it. How embarrassing. "But no matter what, always try my cell first."

"I always do," she says.

My mom stays up and helps me pack for a while, but then she says she's ready for bed.

"But it's only nine o'clock," I said. "You usually stay up till at least ten thirty."

"I guess I'm feeling tired. I don't know why."

"You're just not yourself lately. What's happened to all that energy?"

She shakes her head. "There've been a lot of changes, and I'm just run-down."

Alone in my bedroom, I take a few minutes to finish throwing my stuff into my Puma duffel. Then I go and check on my mom. She's under the covers in her room watching television. It looks like another English romance on PBS.

"Do you have any plans for the weekend?" I sit down on the edge of her bed and run my fingers along the big purple flowers in her duvet spread.

"Karen and Omer are going to visit her parents in South Carolina. I might meet your grandpa for Chinese, but I'm not sure." She pulls the blanket closer to her chin and glances up at me. The look in her eyes reminds me of a little girl's.

Just then, I feel guilty leaving her alone for the weekend. "I think you should grab egg fu yung with Grandpa," I say.

"I'll see how I feel," she says.

I look over at the empty space on the far side of the bed. I'm still not used to seeing my mom alone in bed at night. The mattress looks so huge and empty. At this hour, Dad used to always be lying beside her, eating from a huge bowl of chocolate Häagen-Dazs ice cream that was resting on his belly.

"All right. Sleep well," I say. Then I give her a kiss on the cheek.

"Sweet dreams," she says.

I head off to my room, change into my Victoria's Secret pink pajama bottoms and white tank top, then crawl into bed. As I lie there, my mind still wants to worry about my mom and dad, but I quickly divert my thoughts in another direction. *I am the newest member of the Revelers,* I think to myself, and smile. *And there are so many wonderful new things ahead of me.*

OCTOBER: Transformation

CHAPTER seven

Butterflies are single-minded and can fly for thirty miles per hour all day long. They use the position of the sun as it crosses the sky, landmarks, the moon, and the stars to keep going in the right direction.

The Town Car picks us up at the lobby of Victoria's apartment building at eleven o'clock, as planned. She has Starbucks Frappuccinos and hot, buttered bagels from H&H waiting for us. Victoria's mom—I just can't think of her as "Rosalind"—already went out to the house bright and early that morning, and her dad is staying behind in the city for work, so it's just four high-school girls in transit.

We squeeze into the black leather seats and I watch the New York blocks whiz by outside my tinted window. The car drives south on the East Side Highway, but then it makes a weird turn, and we end up at a heliport.

"Oh my God," I say, laughing nervously. "What on earth is that?"

Victoria points to a white-and-red chopper sitting on the tarmac. "That, my friend, is a Sikorsky S-76 ready to rock out," Victoria says.

"We're flying in a *helicopter* to the Hamptons?" I ask, my jaw wide open.

"Yeah, girl!" Lexi says. The chauffeur opens the car door and she pops out.

"This one's even nicer than last time," Sydney says, sticking her long legs out onto the ground, one after the next.

"But you didn't mention that," I say, following Victoria out into the open air. "I told you I took care of the plans, right?" Victoria says, smiling.

I bite my lip and look at her. "Yeah, it's just that . . ."

"Uh-oh. What's wrong?" she asks.

I look over at Lexi and Sydney. They're fifteen feet away from us, flirting with the young pilot. "I'm not allowed to take helicopters," I say quietly. "They're really dangerous and might crash."

"That's ridiculous. Actually, they're even safer than cars," Victoria says. "Come on. Have you ever done it before?"

I shake my head no.

"Don't you wanna try?"

The truth is I do want to try, even though I'm scared out of my mind. I take a deep breath. "Kinda," I say.

"Then come on, sister!" Victoria says.

As I walk beside her, I reach inside my Puma bag for my phone. I take it out and consider calling my mom, but then decide against it. She might stick a fork in my party and leave me stranded in the city. I put the cell back in my duffel.

The rotors are spinning, but not at full speed, as we step on the platform and climb into the helicopter's open side door. Inside the streamlined interior are blue leather seats that look like they've been plucked from the back of a high-end SUV, except they're facing each other.

I dig my fingernails into my leg when the helicopter takes off. My adrenaline is pumping and I feel like I'm about to go on a roller coaster. It's just sometimes I don't do so well on those types of rides. Like when Kelsey and I went to Six Flags in New Jersey freshman year, she dragged me on the Great American Scream Machine with her and I came off with an asthma attack. I don't even have asthma.

As we get settled in the seats, Victoria taps the aircraft's wooden paneling with her raspberry-painted nails. "This one's super high-end with lots of sound-proofing material so we can actually hear each other."

"Perfect. I hate wearing those headphone thingies," Lexi says. "They make my ears sweat."

The helicopter flies up about a thousand feet in the air, according to the pilot. Because we're lower than an airplane, we can feel a lot more of the bumpy air. As we head over the Atlantic, the pilot hits some turbulence, and the chopper drops about ten feet. I let out a yelp.

"Oh God, oh God, oh God," I say. "We're gonna die."

Victoria pats me on the arm. "Don't worry. We're on the safest kind. The British royal family only flies Sikorskys, too."

At this moment, it doesn't matter what Prince Harry and Prince William do, I'm still having a hard time breathing. Once the flight becomes smooth again for a good five minutes, I'm able to calm down and actually enjoy being airborne.

"My sister has a guy friend who's an investment banker in

New York," Lexi says. "And he take helicopters back to work every Monday morning from the Hamptons so he can stay out there and party an extra night."

"Wow," I say. "Hardcore."

The flight takes forty-five minutes. When we arrive at the East Hampton Airport, we sit on benches outside waiting for Victoria's mom to pick us up. Victoria tells us that her dad decided to stay in the city for the weekend to supervise the finishing touches on his East 39th Street luxury high-rise, where the party was. As we sit there waiting, Lexi says she wants to play the Penis Game while we wait for Victoria's mom to pick us up. I admit to Lexi that I don't know how to play, so she explains the rules to me.

"We take turns, and each girl has to say the word *penis* louder than the next, until no one will go next, and there's a crowned winner. I'll go first," Lexi says. Then she whispers the word *penis* very softly so we can barely hear it over the sound of a Mercedes driving by.

Victoria says it next, a little louder. "Penis."

Sydney shakes her head. "This game is so silly," she says. "Besides, I always lose."

"Lighten up, Sydney," Lexi says. "Just play along."

"Ugh. Penis," Sydney says, and we can hear her now as if having a normal conversation.

Now I'm up to bat. I decide to go for it. "Penis!" I say, raising the volume. Then I laugh. It's actually kinda fun to say the word out loud. It's such a silly-sounding word, really, and so taboo to say. In fact, I can probably count on one hand how many times I've said it in my entire life.

"Penis!" Lexi says, clapping her hands loudly. "Now top that," she dares us.

"Peeeeenis!" Victoria yells out louder.

An old lady crossing the street stops and looks back at us. We look away and pretend to be innocent. Then we burst out laughing.

"See, that's the best part—shocking people," Lexi says.

"I'm out," Sydney says. "No more for me. It's down to you three."

I wanted to stay in and impress them with my fearless-ness. *"PENIS!"* I yell.

"PENIS!!!" Lexi shouts.

A dad-type in an open-air Jeep drives past. He gives us a disapproving look.

"Okay, do you guys forfeit?" she says.

"That was pretty loud," Victoria said. "I'm out."

"PENIS!!!!!" I said, screaming even louder.

Lexi glares at me. "Are you serious?" she says. "Do you actually think you can take away my crown? I don't think so." Then she squints her eyes and grows ultra competitive, hollering like a wild woman, *"PENIS! PENIS! PENIS! PENIS! PENIS!"*

I stare at her with my mouth open. She certainly got su-per into this game. If she gets that into her tennis matches, I would be scared for my life to score a point on her.

"I'm out. You win!" I say. I can sense it wouldn't be a good move to keep challenging her.

Lexi smiles big. "That's what I thought," she says.

Victoria's mom pulls up in a dark blue BMW convertible

with the top down. She's a Denise Richards type, pretty in a cute way, wearing khaki capri pants and a pink sweater with white sneakers.

"Hi, girls!" Rosalind says, coming out of the car.

"Hi, Mrs. Hudson!" Lexi and Sydney say.

"So great to see the bunch of you out here." She gives Victoria, Lexi, and Sydney hugs and then turns to me and smiles. "And this must be Maggie. You get a hug, too!" she says, throwing her arms around me. "So nice to meet you! Your mom called already, and I spoke to her. She is just so nice."

"She called?" I say, humiliated.

"Yeah. She mentioned you didn't tell her anything about the helicopter. I told her not to worry a wink about you. That you'll be fine and I'll keep my eye out. You're in the Hamptons, after all. It's not like Nicaragua."

I smile shyly. I can't believe she called after I asked her to try my cell first if she needed to talk to me. She must be mega pissed about the 'copter. The five of us get into the car. Rosalind hits the gas and we take off. It's a warm fall day, and the sunlight feels good on my face.

"I'm taking the scenic route back to the house so we can show Maggie the beach. Victoria, I was thinking of getting all of us two-pound lobsters for tonight and eating them in the backyard. It can be like our own little seafood fiesta. What do you say? Lexi, I know *you* love shellfish!"

"You remember the time I came to stay with you at the house you rented in Martha's Vineyard," Lexi says, leaning toward the front seat, "and ate, like, twenty pounds of lobster in one day?"

"I was surprised you didn't grow a hard red shell," Rosalind says. "Anyway, Marcos brought the bikes out on the front lawn if you want to ride to the beach. Or else I can drive you."

"We'll just bike," Victoria says.

"Who's Marcos?" I ask.

"The helper/gardener," Victoria says. "He's super nice."

"Yeah, let's definitely bike down to the beach. I'm totally on edge today from not working out," Lexi says.

"I want to do yoga on the sand! Can I teach you guys a class when we get down by the ocean?" Sydney says.

"I hate yoga!" Lexi says. "It's too still and peaceful. I need to be running around a court whacking balls."

Victoria laughs. Sydney snorts. I giggle with them at Lexi's innuendo.

"Did you hear what you just said?" Victoria says sheepishly.

"Yeah, and I meant to say it," Lexi says. "So chew on that!"

"Ooh, in front of my mom? Really?" Victoria squeals.

Rosalind just laughs and turns up the dial on the air-conditioning with one hand while driving with the other. "Oh, girls. There are so many hormones in this car. I think the windows might fog up. To be sixteen again. Who are you ladies gonna take to that big dance Vic's planning?"

"I bet I know who Maggie's gonna go with," Victoria says. Then she turns to me. "I've been texting with Olivia, and she said there's only one Connor in high school at Chesterfield. His last name is Pederson and he's a senior. She's gonna get the 411 from her brother this weekend. The Wall is in effect.

As soon as I hear anything, you'll be the first to know."

"I hope it works out," I say.

"Vic and I want to go to the formal with those guys Jayden and Diego," Sydney says. "They go to All Saints Academy."

"Ooh, those names should go in the Archive of Cute Boy Names," Rosalind says.

"Are those the guys who were in the gazebo with you at the party and the ones we watched at the Meadow that day?" I ask. But as soon as I soon as I say it, I realize that I shouldn't have.

"What party?" Rosalind says. Her voice sounds suspicious.

Victoria looks back at me and shuts me up with her eyes. Lexi jabs me in the arm.

"Yeah, what party?" Victoria says, sounding completely convincing. "I don't think I've been to any parties this year yet. Not one." She and her mother exchange a look.

"I, uh, don't know what I was talking about," I say. "Must've imagined a party . . . ?"

"Victoria, did you throw a party in your dad's new building?" Rosalind says, pounding the steering wheel. "How dare you! We told you not to."

There's a tense silence. Then everyone except me in the car bursts out laughing. "Only kidding! I knew all about it!" Rosalind says, cracking up.

Victoria smiles. "My mom helped me plan it. We just kept it a secret from my dad. He's the hard-ass in the family."

I let out a loud sigh of relief. "I thought I was getting you into trouble."

"You're too cute," Rosalind says, smiling at me in the rearview mirror. "I like this one."

I force a smile, but part of me is hurt to be the butt of their joke.

We turn off Route 27 and onto a side road that takes us past several large estates.

"See it just down the street from us now?" Rosalind points out. "The blue of the water over there out the right-side windows?"

I look out and see a strip of the dark aquamarine. But then I notice something else. Closer to us, up ahead, just outside the car windows, there's orange specks everywhere.

"Look, what are those?" I say, pointing. And then I realize for myself as we drive closer. "It's tons of monarch butterflies," I say, pointing.

The girls sit up in their seats, stretching their necks. There are tons of orange wings flying now on the sides of the car and in the air just around us. We look all over the place, craning this way and that, trying to take in the three-hundred-and-sixty-degree winged spectacle.

"Vic, I meant to tell you. It was in the local paper." Rosalind taps her red manicured nails on the steering wheel. "The butterflies are in town!"

"Mom, what are you talking about?" Victoria says. "Are you on crack?"

"No, silly," Rosalind says. She turns her head so she can talk to Lexi, Sydney, and me in the backseat. "Monarchs are like geese—they migrate south in the winter. We've been coming out here for years, but this is the first year they've been spotted right down the road from us on Georgica Beach. I'll show you the article when we get back to the house."

"Pull over. I want to get out of the car," Victoria says. Her mom listens and stops the car over on the side of the road. Victoria flings her door open. Lexi, Sydney, and I follow her lead, climbing out of the backseat.

"Be careful of traffic!" Rosalind yells after us. Then she gets out and leans against the car, watching us. There are barely any other cars on this road, so I feel safe standing right in the middle of it. There are more butterflies than I can count—more than I've ever seen in one place at the same time. They spread their wings and sail like kites, fluttering and darting all over the place, before landing on our car and closing their wings together like thin pieces of origami paper.

"There's one on the side mirror!" Victoria says.

"And a ton on that patch of grass," Lexi says.

"If you look up, there's a bunch flying over our heads," Sydney says.

"That one looks like it's gonna land on my arm," I say, pointing to a single monarch in the air just beside me. It flies so close, almost teasingly, before darting away. I want to catch it in my hand, but I know I shouldn't, because they need to be free and go where they want to go. After watching them for a few minutes, we get back inside the car and drive off.

"*Molto bello!*" Sydney says.

"Yeah, that was really cool," Lexi says.

I look back at the butterflies as we drive down the road. They seem to land, but only for a moment, before taking off again, flying independently and then all together in circles.

We turn down a private road and approach Victoria's family's estate. It's located in what appears to be an exclusive area filled with mansions that all border a pond.

Rosalind pulls into the long driveway and parks in front of a huge white mansion with black shutters. As soon as we carry our bags into the house—with its cathedral ceilings, blue-and-white-striped couches, and vases filled with sunflowers—Victoria asks for the newspaper.

Rosalind grabs it off a banquette in the kitchen. Then she searches for a page and opens to it. "Here you go."

Victoria scans the article. "I don't get it. So, like, a zillion monarch butterflies migrating down from Canada to Mexico are passing by here right now?"

"Yes, love, it's some scientific phenomenon that happens every year in the fall, just not always right over the Hamptons. They actually migrate all the way south for the winter to stay warm. It's wild. The entire journey's, like, three thousand miles long. The paper says they may use the sun as their compass. It's still somewhat of a mystery how they know to fly every year from Canada down to the same seven mountaintops in Mexico. They have to make it down there before winter comes, or they'll freeze to death."

"Wow," Victoria says. "That's trippy."

"I'm so happy we saw them," I say.

Victoria offers to take me for a tour of the house while Lexi and Sydney settle into their rooms and unpack. I'm blown away by the setup. There's a grand entrance foyer, formal dining and living rooms, reading room, professional kitchen, eight bedrooms, and eleven and a half baths (I count). The

place also has a steam room and sauna, beauty salon, screen-
ing room, an all-weather tennis court, and my personal favorite, an indoor wave pool. I can't get over that.

The grounds include an outdoor pool with what Victoria
calls a "gracious loggia," which looks like one of those long
first-floor walkways out of ancient Greece that have one side
open to the air with ornate columns.

If I had a place like this, I would feel like I'd arrived in
heaven. I would never want to leave. I'd even be willing to be
home-schooled. (I never thought I would *ever* say that.)

When we get back to the living room, Victoria announces
she wants to head down to the beach. Her mom is sitting on
the couch with her legs curled under her. She's wearing glasses
now and appears engrossed in a book on her lap called *Impo-
tency and the Modern Age*.

"Do you want to come with us?" Victoria asks her mom.

"I'm going to stay back. I have a lot to do. Have fun,
though. There are wraps for you girls from Loaves and Fishes
in the fridge."

"Right. I should have seen you were already in work
mode."

It's strange, but now that Rosalind has her glasses on, it's
like she's switched roles from fun mom to serious doctor.

Victoria, Lexi, Sydney, and I go upstairs, where we each
have our own room on the second floor overlooking Georgica Pond, and change into our swimsuits. Victoria lets me
pick out a new bikini from her hall closet, where there's a
box marked GUEST SWIMSUITS next to a stack of extra tooth-

brushes. I find a cute bright blue one in my size with a green hibiscus flower print. No more nasty gray one-piece. Hurray!

"It's about sixty-five degrees. Probably too cold to lie out," Victoria says. "But just in case."

Then we help her throw some napkins, the wraps, and cans of Diet Coke into a white plastic shopping bag. When we're all set, we walk out to the front lawn. Thanks to Marcos, the bikes are outside waiting for us to climb on. Victoria takes the only bike that has a basket attached to the handlebars and stuffs our food into it. I walk over and take a blue mountain bike that's positioned next to hers.

"Oh, are you taking that one?" Lexi asks.

"Is that all right?" I ask.

"I guess. It's just I usually ride the blue one. . . ." Lexi says, swishing her ponytail around.

"I'm sorry," I say. "I didn't know."

"You can take the one Tracey used to ride," Lexi says, nodding to a black bike. "That one's actually a better bike, I'm just used to this one 'cause the seat's high off the ground."

"No prob," I say, walking over to the black bike. It's weird, but when I climb on, I suddenly feel like I'm Tracey's replacement, and that I'm trespassing on a piece of space she left behind.

We ride our bikes along the winding road next to Georgica Pond, passing other multimillion-dollar houses that border the waterfront. Then we pass through a small gateway out onto the main street, and bike past a small farmstand selling apples and corn. To our left is a field with pumpkins that look almost ready to be picked.

It's about a five-minute ride down to the beach, and along the way, Victoria's pointing out houses.

"The son of some big oil magnate lives here. Oh, and they filmed a Scarlett Johansson movie there. And this house has a son our age and sometimes he rides a tractor around the cornfield with his shirt off. And this house over here once had a huge party with a big white tent and dancers performing on the grass that looked like they were right out of Cirque du Soleil."

When we get down to the water, we leave our bikes by a rack in the parking lot. The shoreline is beautiful. It's covered in dunes and seems very private. We only see a couple—a white-haired man and woman—reading in beach chairs under a hunter-green umbrella. I assume the one car in the parking lot, a silver Lexus, must be theirs.

As soon as we start walking down the beach, Lexi's already taking off her T-shirt to show off her bikini physique. Note to self: *Keep trying to lose those ten pounds.* Next summer is gonna be the year I have a concave stomach and perfect, runway thighs. Will also have a boyfriend by that time, hopefully, and when we go on spring break, I want to look ripping hot for him. Won't ever gain the freshman fifteen.

As we walk along the sand, Lexi asks, "You know what? I talked to my sister last night, and she said that a few of her sisters in Kappa Kappa Gamma at UC Santa Cruz wear thin panty liners every day—even when it's not that time of month—just because it makes them feel fresher. Don't you think that's weird?"

"Ouch! That sounds so uncomfortable!" Victoria says. "I would never do that. Not in a million years."

"She also said that sometimes because of our culture, it's hard for guys to say they want to hug or hold you, so instead they just say they want to hook up."

"You're right," Sydney says. "When I dated Geoffrey last year, he never once said, 'Please can we cuddle or spoon?' I wish our world wasn't so messed-up and boys could say that more."

"We could add that to the Wall," Victoria says. "It's important to put these keen observations about life today alongside the Truths we collect. It gives the Wall more texture."

"Totally. And maybe next time a guy says he wants to get with me, I should just try holding him?" Lexi says. "It's weird, but lately, I'm getting a little sick of so many empty kisses. They just never seem to go anywhere."

"Maybe you should get to know the boy first just as friends?" I suggest. "The one boyfriend I ever had, we started out as friends first."

"How long were you two together?" Victoria asks.

"Five months."

"Wow," Lexi says sincerely. "That's a long time."

"Hey guys, is it cool if we do some stretches over here by the dunes?" Sydney asks. "It's such a gorgeous day out, and I want to feel alive!"

"No way," Lexi says. "I want to keep walking down to the breakers. Besides, yoga is gay."

"No, it's not!" Sydney says. "I hate when you say that."

"I'll go with you," Victoria says to Lexi. "Wanna come with us, Maggie?"

I look over at Sydney and feel bad leaving her behind alone. "I'll stay back," I say.

"'Kay, see you in ten," Lexi says. I watch as the two of them take off toward a jetty of black rocks.

"Have you ever done yoga before?" Sydney says, reaching down to her toes.

"Never," I said. "But I'm willing to try."

"*Perfecto.* We'll just do some basic moves." I can tell she's happy to play teacher.

Sydney puts her hands in front of her as if she's praying. "Copy what I'm doing," she says.

I put my hands like hers and smile, amused. Then she sits down on the sand, and reaches for her toes. I copy her movements. It feels a little New Agey standing out here in broad daylight on the beach doing yoga stretches. I remember how silly a man looked in Central Park one day when I walked by and saw him standing alone on the Great Lawn moving air with his hands and doing tai chi.

"Tracey was terrible when she started, too," Sydney says. "But by the end of last year, she could do even complicated moves like the Mountain and the Monkey Pose."

"Do you and Tracey still talk a lot?" I ask.

"Not that much. It's been hard," she says. "I mean, she's so far away, living in Japan and everything."

"There's some really affordable ways now to talk long distance," I say. "My brother's girlfriend, Chloe, was in England a few weeks this summer, and he found this Web site that sold calling cards he could use to talk to her for five cents a minute. Do you want me to find out the name of it for you?"

"No, that's okay," Sydney says.

"Or he also talked free sometimes using some programs on his laptop computer."

"I wouldn't know how to do that," Sydney says.

"I'd be happy to teach you how. Maybe we can use the computer at Victoria's and connect the two of you this afternoon." This would be a great way for me and Sydney to bond. I know a lot on the subject of long-distance communications from my brother, and now I can use it to help her out.

"Let's just skip it, okay?" Sydney says quickly.

I bite my bottom lip and nod. Clearly, I just hit a nerve. "Just trying to help," I say.

"I appreciate it," Sydney says. Her voice softens. "It's just a sore subject, okay? So can we drop it?"

"Yeah," I say. "Of course."

Sydney quickly switches the topic. "What would be fun to try? How about the Warrior Two? Put your legs in a lunge and then reach out like this with both hands."

After Lexi and Victoria come back from their walk, the four of us lounge on towels in the sand and eat our gourmet wraps. We sit in a line looking out at the ocean. It's the first moment I really get to take in how beautiful it is here. The golden light. The dunes with the long weeds growing beyond the wooden fences. All the small white-and-black rocks washed up on the sand. And the few strips of clouds against the blue sky in the horizon.

When we finish eating, we lie out in the sun for about an hour before heading back. It's while strolling to the parking lot that I notice a small speck out of the corner of my eye flying around the dunes. I turn and look. There, darting back and forth, is a single monarch.

"Hey, look," I say, pointing with my Diet Coke can.

The girls look over where I'm pointing.

"It's just one," Victoria says. We walk closer.

"But where are the rest of them?" Sydney says.

The four of us look around. The only other winged creatures in sight are a flock of seagulls.

"It's lost its crew," Lexi says.

"This one must've not kept up with the rest," Sydney says. "Or it got lost or left behind."

"What do you think will happen to it?" I ask. Then I remember what Victoria's mom said, about how they try to get down to Mexico before winter comes.

"Might not make it . . ." Victoria says.

I can't help but look over at the solo monarch, flying close to the ground along the dunes, and feel sorry for it.

"Hey, lookie lookie," Lexi says, nodding up ahead. "It's my Keanu Reeves look-alike."

I follow the length of her stare. There's a cute guy hopping off his skateboard. He's average height, with short brown hair, wearing khaki cargo shorts and a white polo.

"You *have* to talk to him this time," Victoria says. "When we saw him here in the beginning of the summer, you chickened out."

"I didn't," Lexi said. "Sydney just got her period so we had to go back early."

"Don't blame it on me!" Sydney says.

"Go up to him," Victoria says.

"No," Lexi says. "My sister taught me that guys like a challenge. I have a better idea."

We watch as the guy walks down to the beach away from his skateboard. He glances our way, nods his head, and then jogs off in the opposite direction.

"Too shy to talk to us, huh?" Victoria says.

"Watch this," Lexi says. She hurries up to the parking lot as if on a mission. We watch as she goes up and picks up the boy's skateboard.

"What on earth are you doing?" Sydney asks. "Are you stealing it?"

Lexi gives us a mischievous grin. She wheels the board down the road ten feet, along a small walking path and behind a hedge. We follow her. "Chill. I'm just hiding it," she says.

"You're crazy," Victoria says, laughing.

"Now, I need some paper!" Lexi says.

"Hey, we can rip a piece off the leftover sandwich wrapping," I say, sticking my hand into the plastic bag and tearing out a scrap of paper.

"Now we just need a pen," Lexi says. She looks around frantically.

Then I see a huge smile come across Vic's face. "I'll help you," she says.

Victoria walks over to the silver Lexus parked in the lot. I see her peek through the open passenger-side window. "Go see if anyone's coming."

Lexi runs down to the edge of the parking lot and looks up and down the beach as Victoria opens the car door.

"What are you doing?" Sydney says, shocked. "What if there's a car alarm?"

"No one locks their car out here, silly," Victoria says. "It's too safe."

My mouth opens as I watch Victoria crawl inside the front seat. I just see the back of her head and her legs kicking around as she rummages around the car's floor mats. Then we hear her call, "Got it!"

Victoria slams the car door shut and emerges holding a ballpoint pen in her right hand. She hands it off to Lexi.

"Wow, nice work!" Lexi says. "How did you know it was in there?"

"Old people always have useful stuff like pents in their cars," Victoria says, as though this is something everyone knows.

Lexi leans the paper against her upper leg. We all look over her shoulder as she writes, *Cute boys shouldn't get things so easy,* followed by her cell-phone number. Then she uses a stick to draw a bunch of arrows in the sand from where the board was left to where she hid it, leaving the note resting on top of the skateboard. "See, ladies. That's how you go after a guy," she says, licking her lips. "Now watch him come and get it."

CHAPTER EIGHT

Butterflies are visual creatures capable of seeing all the colors of the spectrum from red through violet, which makes finding other butterflies in flight relatively easy. If a butterfly has its choice, it will go for the more colorful flowers, those with purple, orange, or yellow blossoms.

That night in the backyard of Victoria's parents' estate, we sit at a round table eating two-pound lobsters. There's plenty of melted butter and fresh corn, as well. Rosalind hands out plastic bibs for everyone. "Don't be shy, girls! Everyone needs one! We'll have no lobster juice or butter stains on our outfits tonight!"

Victoria announces that I'm the guest of honor. I look down and blush. Then she gives a very sweet speech.

"It's funny the way life works," Victoria says, lifting up her glass of iced tea. "At first I was pissed at Nikki for laughing so loud and the security guard heard, but now I think it's kinda cool, 'cause look how we're becoming friends." Victoria smiles at me. "And I'm sure I'm totally speaking for all of us when I say it's been supercool having you here this weekend and getting to know you a little better. I'm sure as the weeks go on, we're only gonna become closer and better friends."

"Here, here!" Rosalind says, lifting up her Pellegrino. The five of us clink glasses. "Now, let's tear into these crustaceans," she says. "And if you can't finish it, don't worry. I'm sure Lexi can eat your leftovers."

"I know," Victoria says. "It's not fair. Her stomach's like a garbage can and she never gains weight."

It's been a few years since I last ate a lobster, so I scrutinize the way Victoria cracks open the claw. She notices I'm watching her and gives me a tip. "See, once you break it open here, just pull the meat out with your little fork. I like to save the huge tail for last."

I pull at the claw meat and it comes out in one piece. The first bite I take is magnificent. The meat is so tender. I've never eaten anything like this before.

"What do you think?" Victoria asks.

"Amazing," I say.

"They're from Nova Scotia," Victoria brags.

While Lexi and Sydney start quizzing Rosalind on which celebrities' babies she's delivered lately, Victoria speaks to me privately. "So good news. I heard back from Olivia. We got the info."

"What'd you find out?" I ask.

"Her younger brother, Derek, is taking Wing Chun with Connor every Tuesday night at eight o'clock. They've only met one time so far."

"What on earth is Wing Chun?" I ask.

"It's a type of martial art," Victoria says, and then takes a sip of her iced tea.

"Never heard of it," I say. "So we can casually bump into him on the street afterwards?"

"Even better," she says. "I'm gonna enroll you in the class."

I take a sip of water and almost choke on it. "But I don't know a thing about Wing Chunning."

"Look, you've seen *Charlie's Angels* before, right?" she asks.

"Of course."

"Just copy some of Cameron Diaz's kicks and punches. Anyway, the point is not that you're good, it's that you're near him. Use the time to flirt and bond over punching and fighting. He's gonna fall right into your arms."

"You think?" I say.

"Totes. Boys love it when you support their hobbies and stuff."

"Are you sure?" I say. "I'm just worried that I'm gonna fall on my ass."

"You're gonna do great. I've a really good feeling about this," Victoria says.

I pick up my buttered corn and take a bite. Connor's adorable face flashes through my head. When I'm done chewing, I turn to her. "All right," I say. "It's certainly worth a shot."

That night, Lexi squeals when the skateboarder from the beach calls her cell. His name is Keenan, and he comes by in his silver Audi around nine o'clock to take her to the movie theater on Main Street. I'm surprised that Victoria's mom doesn't seem to care that Lexi's going out on her own with some guy she hardly knows. "Just be safe," Rosalind tells Lexi as she runs out the door in a short skirt and black Michael Stars T-shirt. Sydney goes to bed early, and Victoria and I stay up eating dessert.

Victoria takes cookie dough, sticks it in the microwave for ten seconds just to warm it up, and then throws it on top of vanilla ice cream. She tells me how excited she is for me to Wing Chun with Connor on Tuesday night.

"I'm kinda nervous, though," I admit. Without the other girls around, it's much easier to open up.

"You shouldn't be. The way I see it, you have everything going for you. He'll adore you. Just be confident."

"It's just . . . I feel lame-o admitting this to you, but I feel a bit out of my element here, ya know?" I take a spoonful of the ice cream. "Like, I look around at the three of you, all so-phisticated and self-assured. I'm just not like that as much."

"Do you want to be?"

"Yes, of course," I say. "I mean, since the first day of school, I felt like you guys knew things I didn't know about life, fashion, boys. Maybe it's 'cause you grew up in New York City and I was raised in a much smaller town or—"

"But that's what I like about you," Victoria says. "I mean, between you and me, Lexi and Sydney have been my best friends since seventh grade, but I still feel like sometimes they're so critical. And I can't tell you how hard it is for me to put my guard down with most people. Look at my mom. She acts all perky most of the time. But when you guys aren't around, it's a whole different story. She's nicer to you guys sometimes than she is to me. When it's just me here, she does tons of work. It's like she needs to impress my friends, but she doesn't need to impress me 'cause I'm just her daughter. And I don't know if you've noticed this, but nothing she talks about is ever . . . deep or vulnerable. We've never talked to each other about the meaty stuff. I feel like we're constantly trying to live up to some idea of what we're supposed to be."

Victoria puts her spoon down in the bowl. I wonder why she's telling me all this stuff about herself.

"Anyway, tomorrow, I'll get the girls together and we'll teach you some of our insights, but promise something?" she asks.

"What's that?" I ask.

"Please keep that part of you we talked about."

"What part?" I ask.

"The part that never judges me as much as other people do," Victoria says. She takes our empty ice-cream bowls and loads them in the dishwasher. "All right, I'm wicked sleepy. Wanna crash?"

"Sure," I say. It has been a tiring day with a lot of newness to absorb.

Victoria fills up two glasses of water and hands me one. "Sometimes it gets hot at night, so keep this by your bed in case you get thirsty."

"Thanks," I say, taking the glass. We say good night. Then I go upstairs and crawl into my bed. I listen to the night sounds and can hear leaves rustling outside, and the sound of a girl snoring in another room. I figure it must be Sydney, as Victoria probably couldn't have fallen asleep so fast and her mom's master bedroom is on the bottom floor at the other end of the house.

That night I have a dream about Connor. He holds me in his arms, runs his fingers through my hair, and tells me he wants to take me to the Winter Formal. Then we fall asleep together in each other's arms. I love that I'm asleep within my own sleep, so it feels as if I'm asleep twice at the same time.

In the morning, I wake up to Victoria and Lexi knocking on my door. "Wakie, wakie, eggs and bakey," they say in unison.

I open my eyes and sit up. "What time is it?" I ask.

"Ten," Victoria says. She and Lexi plop down on the end of my bed. Victoria's wearing pink pajama pants and a white tank top, and Lexi's in boxers and a T-shirt.

"My mom already took off at the crack of dawn to head back to work at the hospital," Victoria says. "But we don't have to go back till our helicopter reservation tomorrow at four in the afternoon."

"Cool," I say. "Sooo," I look at Lexi. "How did things go with Keenan last night?

"They were pretty good," Lexi says. "We went to the movies, got tons of candy, popcorn, and sodas, and he paid for everything."

"Did you offer to cuddle?" I joke. "Like your sister said."

"I didn't exactly take my sister's advice."

"Tell her about after the movie," Victoria says, nudging Lexi's arm. It's clear she's already heard the tale of last night's escapades.

"We hooked up in the alleyway behind Ralph Lauren for almost an hour. He took off his shirt right there and I think he shaves his chest hair."

"Wow, how fresh and clean," I tease. "Is he a good kisser?"

"At first his mouth was closed too much, but then he got into it and used the right amount of tongue," Lexi says.

"That just sounds so gross!" Victoria says. "I hate the word *tongue*. You shouldn't use that word. It's unbecoming."

"Just delivering the facts," Lexi says. "And it was kind of romantic 'cause there was a full moon out. But I don't think I want to see him again."

"Why not?" I ask, squinting my eyes at her.

"'Cause afterwards when we were in his car, he turned on the overhead light to pick a song off his iPod, and from where I was sitting, I zoned right in on his eyebrows. That's when I realized he has a unibrow. I don't know why I didn't notice it before. There were so many little black hairs on the bridge of his nose."

"If you like him, you should still see him again. Give him another chance," I say.

"Just bring tweezers," Victoria jokes.

"No, I'm done," Lexi says, scrunching her lips.

"The kissing bandit strikes again!" Victoria says, raising her hands in the air like she's at a sports game.

"Oh, stop," Lexi says, playfully hitting Victoria's hands.

"See," Victoria says. "Lexi always finds the smallest faults with each boy she starts to get involved with. Then she ditches him and quickly moves on to the next victim. She never lets them get much past the first kiss."

"So you're already done with Keenan?" I say.

"Mr. Unibrow and I have been done for ten hours already," Lexi says.

Just then, Sydney appears in the doorway. "You guys are talking so loud it woke me up," she says, rubbing sleep dust out of the corners of her eyes.

"I'm surprised you didn't wake yourself up with your own snoring," Victoria laughs.

"So that was you!" I say to Sydney.

"Aww, you heard me, too?" Sydney says. "It's not my fault, though! I have a deviated septum."

"Oh, Sydney, don't be so sensitive," Victoria says.

Now that everyone's awake, we get dressed and head downstairs. There's a large bowl with fresh fruit salad laid out in the kitchen, as well as four bowls and spoons. Over breakfast, Victoria suggests that we swing by the town of East Hampton as soon as we're done eating. She says she wants to come through on what she promised me last night and teach me some of the Revelers' insights on life, fashion, and boys.

"I thought we could go to Main Street," Victoria says. "There are lots of cool stores and good people-watching."

"All right," I say. "I'm down."

Since I'm the only one with a permit, Victoria asks me to drive her parents' Porsche into town. The whole way, I'm petrified of crashing it. Finally, we turn down Main Street and I glimpse the lineup of high-end stores: Theory, Tiffany, Calypso, Catherine Malandrino, Scoop, Coach, Cynthia Rowley, and the Polo–Ralph Lauren store that Lexi kissed Mr. Unibrow behind last night.

As we walk around Main Street shopping, the girls teach me about how to be fashionable like them.

Victoria begins the day's lesson. "First of all, never wear everything perfectly. It will look like you tried too hard. For instance, don't tuck something in all the way. Keep one sleeve pushed up higher than the other. But your hair should always look perfect when you leave the house, and you should own two kick ass accessories. That's all you need. Then you can just throw on jeans and your two kick-ass accessories and everyone will assume you're rich but just don't want to flaunt it.

And what better place to pick up two great items, but here?"

They carefully select a pair of sunglasses at Prada for me. I look at the price tag. "They're really expensive," I say. My mom would be mad if I spent over two hundred dollars on these.

"But they look so good on you," the girls say, throwing me compliments.

I look in the mirror. The black frames do flatter my face, and I've never owned anything like them before.

"You have to get them," Victoria says.

I give in and take out the credit card my mom gave me. *I'll just pay her back*, I convince myself. *One of these days.*

For my second kick-ass accessory, Victoria makes me wait outside Tiffany with Sydney while she and Lexi run inside. "I just need to do a quick errand," Victoria says.

A few minutes later, Victoria emerges and hands me a Tiffany gift bag.

"Surprise!" she says.

"What's this?" I ask, my mouth ajar.

"The three of us each chipped in and got something for you," Lexi says.

"You just bought this for *me*?" I ask.

"I actually ordered it ahead of time so they could do the engraving," Victoria says.

"We wanted you to have it," Sydney says.

"Just open it already," Lexi says.

Inside the turquoise bag is a small blue box. I untie the white satin ribbon, pull off the lid, and look inside. There is a bracelet identical to the ones that Sydney, Victoria, and Lexi wear every day. I pick up the silver stretch band in my fingers and admire the ID plaque inscribed with a cursive, uppercase *R*.

"Now that you're officially a member of the Revelers, I guess you know what the *R* stands for," Victoria says.

I turn my wrist around and admire the bracelet. "This is so pretty," I say. "But it's too much money. I can't accept it."

"You have to. Think of it as a token of our friendship," Victoria says.

"But it's such a nice gift. I mean, no one's ever given me anything like this before. Can I at least contribute?"

"Shh," Victoria says. "Not another peep out of you. We insist."

"Just be gracious and accept it," Lexi says.

"I love it," I say. "That's really nice of you guys. How can I thank you?"

"Just put it on!" Sydney says.

I slip the bracelet over my hand.

"It fits you perfectly," Victoria says.

She's right—it does.

The rest of the afternoon as we walk around Main Street, the girls teach me more about their tricks of girl survival. Victoria pulls a pen and a small pad out of her Marc Jacobs bag. She hands them to me and says, "You might want to take notes." While the four of us browse through a small art gallery, Victoria begins my lesson. "To be stylish, it's important to watch tons of movies. Here's a list of movies you have to see if you haven't already: *Splendor in the Grass; The Godfather; The Royal Tenenbaums; The Empire Strikes Back; Sixteen Candles; Grease; Mary Poppins; Sex, Lies, and Videotape; Charlie's*

Angels; *The Goonies*; *Breakfast at Tiffany's*; early James Bond; *The Birds*; *Pulp Fiction*; *Citizen Kane*; *Legally Blonde*; *Mean Girls*; *Pippi Longstocking*. And when you're done with those, keep going and try to see as many more as possible. You can never see enough films in one lifetime.

"Also, I can't stress to you the importance of being informed about the art scene," Victoria says as we step deeper into the gallery. "Other than the old greats Monet, Matisse, Picasso—obviously—there are tons of new ones you should know. My dad's a big collector and he's taught me all about Dash Snow, Jeff Koons, Dana Schotz, Cecily Brown, Elizabeth Peyton, Gedi Sibony, and Vito Acconci."

After Victoria purchases a collage by Mark Wagner called *Fortune's Daughter*—it's a woman's naked body made of dollar bills—the four of us hit up a store called Shoe Inn. Victoria and Sydney try on leather bags, while Lexi gives me an earful.

"Whatever you do, Maggie, there are some essentials you must have in your wardrobe. Leggings or something spandex from Amer Appar."

"I've never heard of that store."

"It's my shorthand for American Apparel."

"Got it," I say.

"Flats, Converse, an Amer Appar hoodie, boots, oversized sweater, a cute hat for the winter, an LWD, and an LBD."

"I don't know what those are," I admit.

"Little White Dress and Little Black Dress," Lexi says. As we sit down and Lexi tries on a pair of shoes by Christian Louboutin that the saleslady called Bling-Bling Peep-Toe pumps, she continues. "Pick up one Juicy sweatshirt, but it *must* be worn sparingly to avoid being labeled a Juicy-whore like one of those Upper East Side, faux-blonde, Juicy-clad trophy wives you see in Central Park going out for a morning run."

"Roger that. Only one Juicy." I scribble it down. Man, oh, man. How on earth am I going to afford all that designer gear? There's no chance in hell. Even if I negotiate up my allowance, my cash flow will still be too piddly-diddly. Maybe I can find some of this designer stuff secondhand and extra cheap on eBay?

Lastly, we stop off at a clothing store called Calypso. While Victoria and Lexi play with the perfumes and gold necklaces by the cashier, Sydney models a flowing long skirt and teaches me her lessons.

"Cool foods to eat: edamame, Diet Coke, sushi, steak, and obviously anything gummy candy. Also, go for the high end and the low end—extremes rock. So it's either The Palm or McDonald's—never ever the Red Lobster. Also, check out certain Web sites every day. Transbuddha.com for short films, CollegeHumor.com for a little raunch, nytimes.com for current events, and Page Six on the NewYorkPost.com for the perfect dash of celebrity sightings. And when in doubt with music, just look to anything played on 103.1's Jonesy's Jukebox, and NPR's show *Morning Becomes Eclectic*."

As Sydney pays the cashier for a long pastel yellow skirt and a cute belt, I jot the names of these shows down in my pad. *When am I going to have time to do all of this?* Being stylish and sophisticated is more time consuming than I ever imagined.

~~~~~~~~

As I drive the Porsche back to the house on Georgica Pond, Victoria says she wants to throw a small party at her parents' place that night. "It's so rare they're both not out here," Victoria says. "Gotta take advantage of the sitch." She convinces Lexi to suck up her gross-out, call Mr. Unibrow, and invite him over with a bunch of his friends for a barbecue. The girls are excited to put on the new outfits they bought during our East Hampton shopping spree. Sydney has her new long skirt and belt, Victoria bought a new LBD, and Lexi sports her Bling-Bling Peep-Toe pumps. I decide to spice it up a bit myself, putting on a touch more makeup. Lexi helps put it on, throwing her own bronzer, mascara, and pink lipstick on me. I look in the mirror and like what she did.

"You have great eyes," Lexi says. "This just brings them out."

Victoria decides to serve beer. There's tons of Stella Artois in the refrigerator in the garage left over from a summer dinner party her parents threw for fifty people.

"Did you know as you get older there's a natural progression to the beverages you drink?" Victoria says. "As a baby, you start with your mother's milk. Then you move on to water, regular milk, apple juice, soda, beer, vodka, coffee, wine, and when you're ready to die, you're drinking cordials."

There's a bunch of steaks from Citarella in the freezer and we take them out to defrost. As Victoria and I get the grill ready and lay out plates and napkins, Lexi and Sydney bike down to the local vegetable stand to get fresh corn and lettuce and tomatoes for a salad.

Unibrow shows up at seven o'clock with three of his

buddies. One of them is kinda cute and takes an interest in me. His name is Wiley, and he helps me shuck corn and then wants to sit next to me while we eat. As the night progresses, the eight of us end up playing a game of Truth. You pick someone around the circle and ask them a question, and if the person doesn't want to answer it, they have to take a swig of beer.

When it's Victoria's turn, she asks Wiley, "If you could kiss one of us, who would you pick?"

Wiley stares down at the beer he's drinking, his hand circling the neck of the bottle. Then he says my name. I look down at the grass and blush. He seems really nice, but I'm not interested in him that way. He's missing the magic I felt when I was with Connor.

"Then I dare you to do it," Victoria says.

"But this isn't that kind of game," I say. "Up to this point, there hasn't been a single dare."

"Now there is," Victoria says.

Lexi and Unibrow start laughing. I see him try to put his arm around her, but she pulls away, keeping her distance.

"I can handle that," Wiley says.

He gets up from the table and walks over to me.

"A real kiss," Victoria says. "Open mouth."

My heart starts racing as Wiley bends down near my chair, leans into me, and presses his face against mine. I feel him part his lips and touch his tongue to mine. Just then, there's a flash of light. I pull away and look over. Victoria's snapping a photo of him kissing me.

My jaw drops in shock. "Why'd you do that?" I ask.

"It's just a joke," Victoria says.

"But, I didn't want . . ."

"Did you not like kissing my friend?" Unibrow asks.

I want to say that I don't want evidence of it around, but at the same time I don't want to hurt Wiley's feelings. "No . . . it's just that . . ." I say, flustered.

"Don't worry. I won't show it to anyone," Victoria says. "Relax."

The game moves on around the circle, but I'm stuck feeling annoyed.

"I'm sorry if I upset you earlier," Victoria tells me as we clear the dirty plates together. "We were just having fun."

"That's okay. It's fine," I say. I don't want to seem uptight.

"There's tons of pictures out there of me kissing different boys," Victoria says. "You're not the only one."

"Yeah, I'm just not used to it, though," I admit.

"Forgivesies?" she says, holding out her little pinky.

I link my finger with hers and we shake and move on.

The rest of the night, the eight of us have a really great time. Victoria blasts music from the speakers in the pool house, and we all jump into the indoor wave pool. Victoria, Lexi, Sydney, and I went to put on our bathing suits. But since the boys didn't bring theirs, they strip down to their boxers and dive into the deep end. We're all laughing, splashing around, and having silly races. I think it's after two A.M. when the boys finally leave and the four of us tumble off to sleep. "Keenan tried to kiss me again," Lexi complains as we climb the staircase. "But I wouldn't let him."

"He seems like a really nice guy," Sydney says. "I like the way he looks at you."

"And how he got you a towel when you were cold and came out of the pool," I say.

"That was really sweet," Victoria says.

"Humph," Lexi says as we reach the top of the stairs. "Not interested."

"You nitpick too much," Sydney says.

"Shush up," Lexi says, and smiles. Then the four of us say good night and head off to our rooms to sleep.

In the helicopter on Monday, my mind is spinning from the weekend. The strange kiss I had with Wiley, and everything Victoria, Lexi, and Sydney taught me about being stylish and sophisticated. I'm impressed by the extent of their knowledge on girlhood studies, but there must be a tidbit that I have to teach them. Though I have a strong feeling they don't think I'm aware of anything that they don't already know. I bet they believe they're more plugged in than almost every other girl our age. And maybe they are. The three of them seem much more worldly than anyone else I've ever met—my age or older.

I play with my new bracelet as I look out the window at the Atlantic Ocean below. *I'm going to teach them something new one of these days,* I promise myself. *It's just a matter of time.*

When we land at the heliport near the Hudson River and the West Side Highway, we grab cabs home. Lexi and I live on the Upper West Side, so we decide to split a cab. Victoria lives on the Upper East, but shares with us and then will have the cab cut through the park. Sydney's on her own, heading downtown to her parents' loft in the West Village. In the cab ride, we talk about how much homework we have to catch up on since we frolicked all weekend in the Hamptons.

When the cab is a few blocks away from my apartment, Victoria taps me on the arm. She's sitting in the middle, and I'm on her left.

"Remember, Maggie, we have a top secret Revelers meeting every Friday night at seven at my apartment. All four of us have to be there. No exceptions."

"Top secret?" I ask.

"Well," says Victoria. "You can tell people where you're going, but not what goes on at our meetings."

"Sure, of course," I say. The cab stops short at a red light and I catch myself with my hand on the partition.

"And another thing." Victoria turns back to me. "It's no biggie, but we all have to bring offerings to the meetings."

"What do you mean by offerings?" I ask.

"Like fun new stuff to write on the Wall," Victoria says. "We each have to come every week with three new truths to write on it."

"And there's all different levels," Lexi says. "Big *T*s, Medium *T*s, and Little *T*s."

"I'm not sure I follow," I say.

"The *T* stands for *Truth*," Victoria explains. "The big ones are the most monumental and can be very painful. The little ones are the most fun, and the mediums fall somewhere in between."

"So I just find out three *T*s of any size about kids in our class or teachers and bring them to our meeting on Friday?" I ask.

"Bingo," Victoria says.

"But isn't that kinda nosey?" I ask. I remember what I

read in the student handbook the first week of school. There was a part about ethics and the school's six key words. I think *caring* and *respect* were on the list. "Like meddling in other people's business?"

"No, not at all," Victoria says. "Everything we put on the Wall is for our eyes only. No one will ever find out. We protect the information. That's why we won't put any of this on a computer. People can hack into it. If this information got out, it could cause World War Three. It must be protected."

"Besides, it looks much cooler slapped right on a wall in front of you like a post-Modern collage," Lexi says.

"It's the age of communication, baby. Information is power," Victoria says.

I don't say anything. Instead, I move around in the seat.

Victoria studies me. "Are you really bugging out? I thought you were on board."

"No, I am," I say. "I just don't want to get in trouble at school." It's hard to get comfortable 'cause I'm squished against one of the side doors.

"Relax," Victoria says. "None of us do. We're in this together and no on else is ever gonna find out. Okay?"

"I know." I nod and look straight ahead. The cab pulls over to the side of the street. I open the door to get out.

"We had so much fun this weekend," Lexi says, her voice bright like she's trying to lighten the mood. "Thanks for coming out with us!"

"Yeah, thank you," I say, but I can't quite look them in the eyes. "Thanks for everything."

"The wave pool was a blast. And that bracelet looks so pretty on you!" Victoria says as I get out.

"I really love it," I say. I force a smile. "That was so generous of you guys."

"Anytime," Victoria says.

I walk around to the back of the cab, and the driver pops the trunk. After I get my overnight bag, I watch as the cab drives off. Victoria looks out the back window at me, smiling and waving. I stand on the corner with my duffel at my feet and try my best to wave back.

When I walk through the door of my apartment, I get in an argument with my mom. She's standing right there like she's been waiting to yell at me since Saturday.

"How could you not have mentioned you were going in a helicopter? Do you know how dangerous those things are? If something happened to you, I would not be able to go on."

"I'm sorry, but I didn't know until the last possible second, and if I didn't get onboard, they would've left me behind."

"So what?" My mom puts her glass of iced tea down too hard, and some liquid bounces out and lands on the wood surface. "Then you don't have to go, or you could have taken the bus out instead. I thought you had a mind of your own. Since when do you need to follow what everyone else does? Monkey see, monkey do. Maybe these girls have too much influence on you."

"You saw how hard it was for me at first. You're the one who plucked me from my last school and brought me here. Don't you want me to be happy and have friends?"

"Listen, Maggie. This is hard for both of us, and sometimes I need your cooperation here." She plops down wearily on the couch.

"Okay, I'm sorry. Next time, I'll let you know beforehand."

"Fine, but no helicopters."

I look away. There's something else I need to come clean about. "Mom, there's one more thing. I charged something to the emergency Amex you gave me."

"You *what?*" she asks, eyeing me.

I lift the sunglasses from where they're resting on top of my head and show them to her. She takes them from me and turns the frames around in her hand. "Prada," she says. "I don't see an emergency here. What's the emergency?"

"It's hard 'cause all the girls at school are so much more stylish than me. I just wanted this one little pair of sunglasses."

"You're looking in the wrong place. It's not Prada that's gonna make you feel good about yourself." She puts her elbows on her knees. "So what's the damage?"

"A few hundred dollars," I say sheepishly.

"A few *hundred?* Are you kidding me?"

I look down at the wood floor. "I guess that sounds like a lot now that I'm not in the moment."

"It makes me question what's becoming important to you," my mom says. "I guess I'll just take it out of your allowance."

"You can't!" I say. "I need my allowance. Do you know how expensive it is to live in the city? I think you should just minus it from my fall clothing budget. That's what Dad would do."

"I'm not your dad." I sense I'm getting under her skin. Her voice becomes quiet. "Look, fine. I'll take the cost out of your clothing budget. I don't even know what that is anymore. But next time before you make a big purchase, ask me first."

"I will," I say. "Thank you."

She hands the sunglasses back to me. "Do I at least get to see how they look?" she asks. I take the black frames and model them for her.

"They do look good on you," she says, then gets up from the couch. "Anyway, I'm gonna start making dinner. How about eggs?"

"For dinner?" I say. "But you usually only make that for breakfast."

"It's easy," my mom says, going into the kitchen. I watch her as she methodically cracks eggs open into a white bowl and mixes them with a fork.

CHAPTER nine

Butterflies search for mates in two ways: perching or patrolling.
When males and females meet, sometimes mating is quick, without
any ritual. Other times, pairs engage in ritualized aerial dancing,
flutter next to each other, brush each other's wings, or tap antennae.

It's a short week thanks to Berkeley's professional development day for the teachers. I'll bet Mr. Z had a blast stroking his intellectual curiosity. Maybe he came up with more freaky ways to illustrate his favorite philosophical principles.

Tuesday at school, I run around in my favorite jeans and a T-shirt, but this time I'm also wearing a pair of black Prada sunglasses on my head and a kickass Tiffany bracelet on my wrist. Any awkwardness from Monday's cab ride between Victoria and me seems to be gone. I get to sit with Victoria, Lexi, and Sydney in the back of the bus on the way to gym class. They invite me out to lunch with them, so I skip the sloppy joes in the cafeteria and go to a charming café called Yura.

I can feel the girls in my grade looking at me with a new sense of admiration. Olivia and Fredrika of the Snobby Indies actually say hi to me when I walk by them in the hall. In philosophy, Aspen and Brianna from Cheers and Beers grab the seats right beside me.

When I sit next to Anne Marie in homeroom, she asks me about my newfound status. "I see you're rolling with a new crew," she says. "Do you think you'll still want to talk to me?"

"Of course," I say.

"'Cause I understand if you don't want to. I mean, if our high school was an aquarium, I'd be a bottom-feeder. You know, like a catfish."

"That's so not true," I say.

"No, it's okay," she says. "I'm fine with that. I don't need to be popular like some other girls do. I've accepted who I am."

"Hey," I say. "You were my welcome buddy from day one. I won't forget my roots."

"I hope so," she says. "'Cause I kinda like having you around. Plus, I'm still hoping to convince you to join the bowling club."

"We'll see about that," I say. "Not sure I'm the recruit you have in mind. I'm queen of the gutter balls."

"With a little practice, I bet you'd be great," Anne Marie says.

I'm not so sure I want to be a great bowler, but I don't want to offend Anne Marie, so I keep that thought to myself.

I'm nervous all day for my Wing Chun class with Connor. During a free period, I head upstairs to the library hoping to check out a book on the topic. As I'm walking up the stairs, I remember my brother used to take karate when he was little, so I decide to give him a call on his cell. We're not allowed to use our cell phones in school, but I don't see any teachers, so I decide to sneak a call in before walking through the library doors.

He actually picks up.

"Jason, it's me," I say quickly. "Can you talk?"

"Just for a second," he says. "Chloe and I are about to grab a late lunch at Bertucci's. What's up?"

"Long story, but I'm taking a martial arts class tonight and—"

He starts laughing and puts down the phone. "Mags is taking karate," I hear him tell Chloe.

"No, not *karate*," I correct him. "This thing called Wing Chun. And can you not laugh at me?"

"Sorry, sis, it's just hard to imagine you doing that."

"Well, anyway, have you heard of it?" I ask.

"Is that from the eighties song?" he says. Then he starts to sing, *"Ba da da da, Wing Chun tonight."*

"That was *wang* chung," I hear Chloe correct him.

"Riiight," he says to her. Then he speaks back in the phone to me. "All right, so what do you want?"

"Do you have any advice? Like anything I need to know?" I ask, pacing the hallway outside the library.

"Yeah, let's see . . ." he says.

My heart races. I'm optimistic he's gonna drop some good advice.

"Don't get punched in the boobs," he says.

I roll my eyes. "Thanks, Jay," I say. "Really appreciate it."

"Oops, gotta run."

"Hey, wait," I say. "Did you get my messages? I left you two and you never called me back."

"I've been busy," he says. "Film classes have been taking up all my time."

"Have you talked to Dad lately?"

"Yeah, he calls me almost every other day."

I lean against the hallway wall. "Do you know what we're gonna do for Thanksgiving this year?" I ask.

"I assume I'm going to Dad's and you'll do something with Mom."

"So we're gonna do it apart?" I ask.

"Look, I just heard Chloe's stomach rumble. Gotta go."

"But what do you think—?" I try to get in one last question.

"I think I don't want them to kill each other. See ya soon, little sis. Be careful at that class. Bye." He hangs up the phone.

I can't help but feel a little hurt that Dad calls him but rarely checks in with me. He's dialed my cell only three times since I moved to New York a month and a half ago. It's like since my parents separated, my brother and I have been forced onto different sides. The whole situation royally pisses me off, but I try to push it out of my head.

In the library, I go online and research Wing Chun. I click on a Web page that says it's the only system of martial arts invented by a woman. There are several debates over its precise origin, but according to this one legend, the style of fighting was developed during the eighteenth century by a nun named Yim Wing Chun who was on the run from Imperial soldiers in China. While hiding in caves, she created this style of self-defense in order to protect her own life. Wing Chun assumes that the person is fighting an opponent who is bigger and stronger than them. The book also says that Bruce Lee started his martial arts career with Wing Chun and brought it to the big screen in his movies.

Interesting. Wing Chun could be useful if I ever need to defend myself. But all I need it to do tonight is get me closer to Connor.

Finally, nighttime comes along. I've called the Six Harmony Martial Arts Academy and am relieved to know I only have to wear a pair of loose pants, a T-shirt, and sneakers instead of the traditional kimono uniform, so I can just put on my gym clothes. Victoria texts to wish me luck.

FROM: Victoria

'Sup chica. Kick ass and take names, Wing Chun style.
You're a rock star! Connor's gonna love you.

I smile as I read her message, then quickly text her back.

TO: Victoria

I hope to hang tuff like a Charlie's Angel.—M.

As I walk up the stairs slowly to the second floor of the academy, I feel a lump in my throat. I know that as soon as I reach the landing, I might see Connor and I'll have to fake how absolutely surprised I am to see him. And who knows what he thinks of me after the bus incident when I acted like a mute.

As I reach the top step, I see a bunch of kids around my age, about seven boys and two girls lined up inside the studio waiting for class to start. I check out all the guys' faces one by one, but I don't see Connor. What the F? I mean, I spent so much time psyching myself up, and he's not even here. My shoulders slump over as I check in with the man at the front desk. I give him my name and he checks it off a list.

"It's the second class," he says, "but you shouldn't be that far behind."

"Thanks," I say. *It doesn't matter if it was the first one, I'd still probably dislocate my shoulder.* "How much do I owe you?"

"It's already taken care of," the man says. "A young woman called this afternoon and charged it."

"Oh, right," I say. It must've been Victoria up to her usual tricks. I'll have to thank her later.

I lean down and tighten my right shoelace, then enter the class. I walk into the room and all eyes are on me as I take my place at the end of the line. A moment later, I see a figure entering through the door. I look over hoping it's Connor, but no luck. It's the instructor, wearing black sweatpants and a dark T-shirt. He's tall with a toned body, light skin, a receding hairline, and an English accent.

All the students bow to the teacher. I copy what they're doing and lean forward.

Uh, yeah, hello, where the hell is Connor? Victoria said that he takes this class every Tuesday night with Olivia's younger brother, Derek. I look down the line and try to guess which one he is. I decide he must be the freckled blond kid with the same horse nostrils as his sister. Maybe the Wall doesn't work after all and I'm gonna be Wing Chunning it all by myself without my hottie.

The teacher's name is Sam Goodman. He begins by making us do something that sounds like "soo-nim-dow," which he says means "little idea."

Sam tells us all to stand upright with our arms straight down by our sides and feet together. *"Hoi-ma!"* he says, instructing the class to clench our hands into fists and pull them back toward our waists. "Now sink your weight down at your knees, and pivot your toes outward."

I try to do what he says, moving my legs into what I know as first position in ballet, but with my legs more bent.

"Then, while staying on your toes, pivot your heels outward sixty degrees like so." He demonstrates, and I try to copy him. The move reminds me of something Michael Jackson might do or something you'd see in an eighties music video. I stifle a giggle. I look down the line at the other students. They all seem to be doing it with ease. Maybe that first class really gave them an advantage.

Sam walks down the line checking out everyone's style. "Good work. Nice. Great balance." Then he stops in front of me. "Try to use your knees more. Come on, pivot out."

I try to follow his instructions, but just then, I spot Connor walking into the class late. His eyes open wide when he sees me doing my what probably looks like a mix between bad Wing Chun and sick MC Hammer moves.

He scrunches his eyes at me, confused. Then he walks over to the only available spot, which happens to be right next to me.

"Come on, concentrate," Sam says to me. "One more time."

I try the move one last time. As Connor watches me out

of the corner of his eye, I want to collapse from embarrassment.

"Better, better," Sam says. As he walks by Connor, he says,
"Don't be late next time."

"Sorry," Connor says. "I got stuck at practice."

The instructor walks to the front of the class and begins
to teach a new form. This one's called something that sounds
like "chum-kyew." "Put the hands in front of your body and
then drive the fingers outward!" Sam orders.

"What are you doing here?" Connor whispers as he does
the exercise.

I have my excuse all lined up. "Now that I live in Manhattan, my mom's making me take a self-defense class," I say. I
raise my hands out in front of me like Sam said. This move-
ment's a lot easier than the last.

"Wow. I can't believe you're talking to me."

Sam stands in the front of the room. "Fold your arms in
front of you. Then turn one hundred and eighty degrees."

We both fold our arms and then turn around.

"My throat hurt last week and I couldn't speak."

"Yeah, right," he says. "Next time a guy tries to ask you
out, instead of ignoring him, just say no. Let him off the
hook."

"I didn't mean to—"

"Quiet back there!" Sam yells.

After taking us through a few more forms, Sam calls us to
the front of the class in groups of two. He pairs the kids off
down the line, and naturally, I'm matched up with Connor.
Sam has each pair go one at a time and do "Sticky Hands,"

a series of movements that Sam demonstrates. You have to move your hands in and out of your opponent's face trying to deflect their energy. Then Sam picks which member of the duo would win if it were an actual standoff.

Connor and I are the last two to walk to the front of the class. We stare into each other's eyes, and the energy is charged as we do the exercise together. My hands start to sweat as I move my wrists around his arms. When I touch him by accident, I'm worried he will feel how slimy my hands are and be grossed out. Although I'm pretty bad, I'm somehow doing better Sticky Hands than Connor. When we're done with the matchup, Sam says I'm the winner. I look over at Connor, but he won't make eye contact with me.

After the class ends, he heads out the door. I hurry after him as he runs down the stairs. I'm finally by his side as we step out onto Seventh Avenue.

"Are you okay?" I hurry past a woman pushing a baby stroller to keep up with his stride. He's still not looking at me. "I'm sorry. I really don't know how I did better than you. It must've been a fluke."

Connor turns around and bursts out laughing. "Are you kidding? Of course it wasn't a fluke. I *let* you do better than me."

I study his face trying to see if he's telling the truth. "You did?"

"Do you know how terrible you were doing? I felt bad for you," he says.

"Oh, well, I never wanted to take this class anyway," I say. "And I'm never gonna come back!"

"I'm shaking with tears," he says.

I squint my eyes, exasperated. "Ew, you are such a jerk," I say.

"And you're a snob. Admit it," he says, throwing it back at me. "Last week, you were embarrassed to acknowledge me in front of your tan friend with the dark hair. For whatever reason, you didn't want her to see you talking to me."

"That wasn't it!" I throw my hands down by my side. "I mean, that was it. But it's not what it seemed!" *Damn, I wish I could tell him the truth, but that would be against Pledge Week rules.*

"Whatever. Who cares," he says. "You seem different from the night I met you." Connor takes off down the sidewalk.

I let out a loud breath of air. I can't take this anymore. If I don't say something now, I feel like all chances of fixing things with him will be lost. "Hey, Connor!" I yell after him. "Will you just go out with me already?"

He stops and turns around. "*You're* asking *me* out now?" he says. He walks closer to me. "Let's see. Ask me again," he says, standing within arm's reach of me now.

"Do you want to . . ." I search my brain for a good activity to suggest and remember my conversation with Sydney about cool foods and fun days of the week. "Like, grab sushi on Thursday night?"

He looks at me then looks up at the sky as if he's deep in thought.

I wait for a few moments. "So?" I ask.

He still doesn't respond. Instead, he turns his head to the side and looks away as if still pondering my answer. Then he gives me a bunch of silly smiling faces.

"Oh, I get it. You're making fun of me on the bus the other day." I run my Adidas sneaker along the crack in the sidewalk. "I guess I deserve that."

Suddenly, Connor doubles over, cracking up. "Of course I'll hang out with you," he says. "But, damn. You're such a saucy minx."

"What?" I say, blushing.

"Trouble with a capital *T*."

"I don't mean to be," I say, looking away.

"You just are," he says. "But I can handle it." He smiles at me, sideways and sly, with one side of his mouth climbing up his right cheek.

I can't help but grin back at him.

"What's your number?" he asks. I tell him, and he programs my digits into his cell phone. "I'll call you," he says.

"Bye," I say, and we go our separate ways. As soon as I turn the corner and am out of his sight, I jump up and down, stomping the pavement with excitement. And then, filled with the charge of the moment, I jokingly throw a karate chop into the air.

When I get home, I call my brother's cell. His voice mail picks up, so I leave a message. "Hey, Jason. It's your sis. Just calling to let you know I survived the class. You're probably out with Chloe, but give me a ring later." He doesn't call me back.

Thursday night, Connor and I go out to dinner at a restaurant called Tao on East 58th Street. It's a huge Pan-Asian joint filled with flirting twentysomethings. The waitress takes us to our seats deep inside the restaurant at the foot of a tall statue of Buddha.

"This used to be a movie theater," Connor tells me. "That's why the ceilings are so high."

I look around at the huge exposed-brick walls. There are paper lanterns the size of barrels hanging from the ceiling, which is covered in painted Japanese writing.

"I like it," I say. "There's nothing as spectacular as this back where I moved from."

We open our menus and look over the selections.

"So," I say as I read over the appetizers, "I'm done with Wing Chun."

He takes a sip from his water glass. "Is your mom okay with that?" he asks.

"She's disappointed," I fib. "But I told her I'd rent some self-defense DVDs instead on, like, how to kick a mugger's ass."

He laughs. "All right," he says. "Or maybe *I* could teach you some moves sometime."

We giggle.

"Okay. I have to admit," I say, closing the menu and putting it down on the table. "I've never had sushi before."

"Neither did I till last year," Connor says.

"I'm totally open to it," I say. "I just don't like the fishy taste."

"No fishy taste. Got it," he says, scanning the choices. "Okay. I know what we should get."

"It's all you," I say.

The waitress comes over and takes our order. Connor

orders a bunch of salmon, spicy crunchy tuna, and shrimp tempura rolls for us to share.

While we wait for our food, we start talking about what his life was like back in Lancaster, Pennsylvania, before moving to New York. He tells me about his grandmother who passed away a few years ago from ovarian cancer. He says that she and his granddad lived in one of the most beautiful houses in Lancaster County. I ask him to describe it, and I'm surprised by the way he does. Most guys would just give a quick two-sentence answer, something like, "It was a huge white house with a big lawn and tons of maple trees." Connor gets really into it, and there's something poetic in the way he talks that makes my eyes get all foggy. "My grandmother had so much grace. I miss her."

He tells me how hard it was when he first moved to New York, too. It took him a while to get used to everything. His parents got divorced when he was a freshman in high school, and he asks me about the situation with my folks.

"It's pretty messed up," I tell him.

"Do you think it's over for good?" he asks. "Or are they just working it out?"

Then, I don't know why—maybe it's 'cause I'm under the trance of his big green eyes, or I feel comfortable because he let his guard down with me first—but I tell him what I've never told anyone else before.

"There's just something I know that my mom has no idea about," I say. "Like, eight months ago, while my parents were fighting a lot but still living together, pre-split, I came home early from school one day and saw my dad drinking 7 & 7—I know, 'cause there was a liter of 7-Up on the counter and that bottle of liquor. And with him in the living room is this waitress who worked with me nights this past summer at the clubhouse restaurant. She was sitting next to him and they were kissing. It was revolting. I wanted to vomit. She's this skinny waif with blonde-streaked hair, long fingernails, and tattoos. There's a rose by her cleavage, a heart with snakes going around it on her arm, and one you can only see when she wears this midriff shirt that says BRING BACK JAMIE whatever that means. She wears tons of makeup, but her face is still hard looking and I heard she's a high-school dropout. And the worst part about it is she's only twenty-five."

"How old is your dad?" Connor asks.

I look down at the chopsticks next to my plate. "Forty-one," I say.

"That's a big difference," he says.

"Obviously Roxanna—that's the twenty-five-year-old's name—has a thing for father figures. I'd see her flirt with him whenever he came into the restaurant, and she'd always give him double roast beef for free on his sandwiches. I always felt like she was super impressed by my dad's intelligence."

"Man, that's rough. I'm really sorry," Connor says. "Did your dad see you catch them kissing?"

"They turned around and looked surprised. I ran up the stairs and over to my best friend Kelsey's house. I didn't come home for dinner that night and we never talked about it afterwards. My dad pretended like it never happened. But I know why he did it."

"Why's that?" Connor asks.

"That girl made my dad feel good about himself when he went in there to eat alone, and he probably felt great rescuing her 'cause from what I could tell, her life is a sad tale. Sorry," I say. "I don't mean to sound so angry."

"That's okay. . . ."

I look down and my eyes start to water. "The hardest part is having to keep this inside. It shouldn't be my problem. It's my dad's, but he made it mine. And my mom and I are super close, so I feel like I'm keeping something important from her. But if I told her the truth, it might destroy her."

"Yeah," Connor says. "I don't know if you should tell her right now. That's a huge decision. You've gotta think that over."

"I definitely am," I say. Then I decide it's best to lighten things up. This may be too much information on a first date. "So, when's your next game?"

"There's one next week. Want to come?"

I smile. "Sign me up."

The waitress brings over a platter filled with sushi. The shrimp-tempura pieces are so big, I can barely stick one in my mouth.

"No looking," I say, picking the piece up with my chopsticks. "Chances are it's gonna fall all over my face."

He covers his eyes with his hand and I take my first bite of sushi.

Then he takes his hand away and watches me chew. "Good?" he says.

"I kinda like it," I say.

After dinner, we walk outside. Connor takes a few steps up the block, then stops and looks at me. He walks a little closer, backing me up so I'm leaning against the outside of the restaurant. He puts his head closer to mine and touches my cheek with his hand. Then he lowers his lips down until they meet mine and presses them slowly against my mouth. Our first kiss starts off gentle and slow. But then he grabs the back of my hair in his hands and we start really making out. There are people walking by on the street and customers coming out of Tao. He catches me glancing over at them.

"Guess I'm the first guy you kissed since you moved here, huh?" Connor asks.

"Mmm, yes." I touch my lips with one hand.

"Should we stop?" he asks. "I don't wanna make you uncomfortable with the public display."

I look at his mouth and just want it back on top of mine. I pull him gently close to me and we kiss. I open my eyes for one last quick second and see two women in their twenties dressed in business suits laughing as they walk by. But now I don't care. *Stare all you want, ladies. Check me out. I'm exactly where I want to be.*

CHAPTER Ten

An important aspect of nature study is to record field notes.
Amateur naturalists make vast numbers of observations and have
made meaningful contributions to many areas of natural history.
Historically, pen and paper were every keen observer's primary tools.

Friday at school, the girls swarm around me on the gym bus wanting to hear every last detail about my date. I tell them how wonderful it was. How Connor's so good looking and manly, but also sensitive, funny, and sweet. And that we kissed in front of Tao.

"Did he have skills?" Lexi asks.

"It was great," I say. "But I felt kinda bad 'cause he asked if he was my first kiss since I moved to the city."

"What'd you tell him?" Victoria asks.

"I said that he was," I say.

"That's not the truth," Victoria says. "Don't forget about that steamy night in the Hamptons with Wiley."

"That was a dare," I say. "And it was hardly steamy."

"But it still happened. We have the picture," Victoria says.

"That kiss didn't mean anything to me," I say.

"Enough, you guys. Tell us what else happened," Sydney says, patting her hand on the seat excitedly. "Anything romantic?"

"He told me about his grandmother who passed away, and I told him about my parents and their messed-up situation."

"Wow, he's really opening up to you," Sydney says.

"What stuff about your parents?" Victoria asks. "You haven't even told us that stuff, and we're supposed to be your best friends now."

"Oh, it's just that I have a hard time talking about it, and it's never come up."

"Well, I hope you will tell us soon. Like, our meeting tonight might be a great time."

I nod my head slowly. "Okay," I say.

"It's just I believe BFFs should tell each other everything. Don't you?"

"Yeah," I say. *Or almost everything*, I think to myself, but I don't want to start a confrontation.

"The way I see it, friendship is all about trust. I mean, you can ask me whatever you want," Victoria says. "I'm like open real estate."

"You're right," I say.

"Cool," Victoria says. "Oh, and don't forget to bring three Truths to add to the Wall tonight. We're counting on you."

"I won't," I say. Although between Wing Chun and my date with Connor, I've been utterly distracted this week. But I still have until seven o'clock to come up with my offerings.

I spend the rest of the school day using the information-gathering techniques that the Revelers taught me. In English class, when the girl sitting next to me, Sonya Ridgeback, gets up to go to the bathroom, I lean over and read the note she was doodling to one of her friends in the back of her notebook. It says that she thinks her younger sister might have an eating disorder.

I sit in the hallway on a bench located outside the foreign-language office for my whole free period pretending to do pre-cal homework. Boy, do I get an earful when Mrs. De La Fuente, a Spanish teacher, exits the lounge in the middle of telling Mr. Broussard, a French teacher, how she's been trying to hide the hickey he gave her all day. *Bada-boom, bada-bing!*

Also, while hiding in the bathroom stall, I overhear Autumn Clarke and Jenna Steele yelling at each other over a guy named Mikey McBride who they both have a crush on. I noticed in the first meeting how Victoria liked when a Truth was grounded in a social theory, and I think this could be a superb example of two girls violating the Chicks Before Pricks Principle I read about in a magazine. The article said that a girl should always put her best girlfriends before boys because guys come and go, but friends are forever.

That evening at Victoria's apartment, Rosalind orders us filet mignon from The Palm and sends their old Russian cleaning lady, Yelena, to pick it up. She seems bright and cheery to see me joining her daughter for the weekly meeting.

As I walk downstairs into Victoria's swanky pad, I notice that the money collage by Mark Wagner that she bought in East Hampton is hung up at the bottom of the stairs. There she is, *Fortune's Daughter*, made of money, welcoming us to her lair.

Before we push the bookshelf back to the room with the Wall, Yelena brings the steaks down for us on four separate wooden trays. Each of them has a jungle animal hand-painted on it, and I get the one with the elephant.

I've never met Yelena before, so Victoria introduces us. She's a big-boned woman in her seventies, with a wide face, strong jaw, and a nose that looks like it's been broken a few times. She looks like a girl version of this French actor, Gérard Depardieu, who I watched with my mom in some old movie called *Green Card*.

"Nice to meet you," I say, smiling and waving. "Thanks for picking up our dinner."

She smiles back, but I have a feeling she didn't understand a word I said.

"Her vocabulary still isn't good," Victoria says. "My mom's thinking of sending her to an English as a Second Language class at The New School."

As soon as Yelena leaves, Victoria sticks her hand into the bookcase, pulls out the Picasso book, reaches for the knob, and opens the door so it swings back into the room.

We grab the oversized pillows from the leather couches and sit on them on the floor in front of the Wall. Then while enjoying our high-end meal, we take turns adding notes under kids' and teachers' names.

"Be sure to say out loud what you're writing while marking it on the paper," Victoria says. "And since it's your premiere time, Maggie, we give you the honor of going first."

I'm anxious while I take the proper color-coded pens out of a jar set on the floor and scribble my additions. As instructed, I speak while I write and tell them the three things that I prepared about Mrs. De La Fuente's hickey from Mr. Broussard, Autumn Clarke and Jenna Steele fighting over Mikey McBride, and Sonya Ridgeback's note about her sister.

When I finish, Victoria nods her head and says, "All right. Not too bad for a first timer."

I bite my lip. "You didn't like what I found?" I say.

"You did an okay job. See, those were Little and Medium Ts. Next time, try and dig even deeper. Go for the Big Ts. They're like gold."

"Here, I'll show her." Lexi grabs the permanent markers and adds her share. "Gretchen Smooke's brother is in jail for getting into an accident while drunk driving. Anne Marie's mom is addicted to prescription sleeping pills, and Dehlia Wong's boyfriend dumped her because she wouldn't sleep with him, and now she cries herself to sleep every night."

"The only thing that fixes heartbreak is time," Victoria says.

"Or a new love," Sydney says.

Next, Sydney contributes. "Ashley Moore has been taking acid. Last weekend, she snuck into an office building on the East Side and ran around the empty hallways tripping. She wants to take it seven times because supposedly that makes you legally insane. Although I heard that's a myth. Kelly Poloski's parents have an open marriage. Mr. and Mrs. Poloski can hook up with whoever they want to, *and* they swing both ways. Also, Anne Marie just got her dosage increased for her meds."

"Oh, then add that up by her name under the Kids in Our Class on Meds list," Victoria says.

"I didn't know Anne Marie was on meds," I say.

"If you read the Wall more closely, you would have," Lexi says. "She went on them three years ago after she didn't get a perfect report card freshman year and went off the deep end."

"We know what everyone's on," Victoria says, turning to me. "Prozac, Lexapro, Zoloft, Ritalin. There have been tons of articles written in the *Times* about kids our age being overly medicated. There's a constant debate over the upsides and downsides. Plus, now some doctors think it might be linked to suicide."

"There're twelve girls in our grade on anti-Ds—and that's out of forty-three," Lexi says. "It's all up there."

Now it's Victoria's turn to write. She uncaps a red felt-tip marker. "I feel really bad, but Kathleen McRoy has to get an operation for scoliosis. She's gonna miss three weeks of school."

"I really like Kathleen. She always helps me in Western Civilization," Sydney says.

"Yeah, she's the sweetest girl I've ever met," Lexi agrees. "Not like us."

"What are you talking about?" Victoria says. "We're nice. We're just nice with an edge. Anyway, it's my turn. Devorah Klinger was hospitalized over the summer for bulimia. And Tatiana Bisset's parents are divorced and her dad just got a mail-order bride from Russia."

"Holy shit," Lexi says. "That's wild."

"See, those are more like Big Ts," Victoria says proudly. "They're something to aim for. Now, you're up again, Mags."

"You're kidding, right? I already went," I said.

"But not under your own name. Tonight, we need you to help fill up all that empty space under 'Maggie Wishnick.'"

"What should I write?" I say.

"Start with the obvious things. Just moved here from Jersey. Has a crush on Connor Pederson. Pretended to like Wing Chun in order to meet him. Made out with him on first date after sushi at Tao."

I grab a gold pen and start to write under my name. It feels kind of weird jotting down these notes about myself in such a public way.

"And it wouldn't be complete if you didn't put up there the stuff about your family," she says. "You know, what we talked about today on the gym bus. The mysterious thing you told Connor but not us."

I hold my pen down by my side. "It's just super private," I say.

"All of this stuff is," Lexi says. "Look around. There are intimate things written about every girl in our grade up there, including me, Sydney, and Victoria. Why should you be left out?"

"Lexi, let me handle this," Victoria says. Then she turns to me. "I know how difficult this can be. It was hard for each of us when we first started. But stand back and look at what we're creating here, at all those names beside yours."

"It's just not easy to—"

"Whatever you're going through, the pain or torment, we're all experiencing it, too, in one form or another. Put it up there and you'll be one of us."

I feel the pressure of their eyes on me. They aren't eating

another bite of their filets until I do what they say. I start writing. As soon as I finish writing about Roxanna and my father, I want to break down and cry, but I hold back the tears. Seeing it on the Wall in front of me makes it seem so much more real.

"See, that wasn't too hard," Victoria says. Then she digs through her black Marc Jacobs handbag and takes out a photograph. "Put this up there, too," she says.

I take it from her and look at the image. It's the picture she snapped of Wiley kissing me in the Hamptons last Sunday night. The last thing I want to do is paste it on the Wall.

"Do I have to?" I ask, looking at the picture of me locking lips with some boy.

"Yeah, it's the rules," Victoria says. "Sorry."

"There are tons of crazy photos of the three of us up there, too," Sydney says.

"Come and join the party," Lexi says. "There's glue on the floor in the corner."

I walk over and pick up the orange container of rubber cement. Then I paint some on the back of the photograph and stick it on the Wall.

After the Revelers meeting, Victoria asks me to stay behind to get my opinion on plans for the Winter Formal. She wants me to listen to CDs from two potential DJs she might hire and tell her which one I think is better.

"Lexi and Sydney have already heard them and put in their votes."

We hang on the leather sofas downstairs and she sticks the first sampler into the stereo. As the music plays, she talks to me.

"I'm really happy everything seems to be working out with Connor," Victoria says.

"Me, too," I say.

"And I'm super encouraged by your effort today. Your Truths aren't quite up to par yet, but I know you have it in you."

"Thanks," I say. "To be honest, I left it to the last minute. Next week, I'll take more time."

"I'm sure you will." Victoria picks up a silver remote control and switches to the next track. "In addition to that, I have a small yet important mission for you."

"What's the mission?" I ask. There's silence for a second in between songs.

The next track starts up. It's a house-music beat. "I need you to quietly find out what Anne Marie is writing her essay about for the Golden Wreath competition. And bring it to the Wall."

"How am I supposed to do that?"

"That's where you have to get creative," Victoria says.

"But . . ."

"Come on. She's your buddy. She'll open up to you. You're easy to talk to."

"That will give you an unfair advantage," I say.

"I'm not gonna steal her essay. I just want to be informed. That's all. Come on, I helped you out with Connor. Who's your better friend? Me or Anne Marie?"

"You, of course."

"Then please, help me out. I'd be there for you if you needed me."

I look away, thinking about it.

Victoria taps me on the arm. "Come on, I want to show you something." We go into her room and she pulls out a file folder filled with ripped-out magazine articles from *Travel & Leisure* and a bunch of brochures from some travel agency. "As a graduation present, my parents are renting me a private yacht for the summer, and I can invite my best friends for a sailing trip. No parents or supervision. Just us and the captain and the crew. I was thinking of starting off at the Greek Islands. Also, there's a huge party scene going on in Croatia. Kids just hop from boat to boat raging in the Adriatic Sea. It's like the new Thailand."

She shows me one travel brochure after the next filled with pictures of lush landscapes, white-sand beaches, and charming coastal towns. Plus she printed out pictures of good-looking members of the Croatian National soccer team with their shirts off from their Web site.

"Sydney and Lexi already know about it and they're down. But I wanted to invite you to come with us, too."

"Are you serious? I've never been outside the U.S."

"I'm completely serious," Victoria says. And then something unusual happens. She slowly starts to crumble right before my eyes. Tears run down her cheeks. "I'm so scared," she says. "Aren't you? Of everything to come . . . graduation . . . moving away from home . . . our futures . . . being everything our parents want us to be . . . trying to be happy in this universe . . . not dying a failure . . ."

Victoria wipes her eyes with her hands. Her nose is running. I spot a box of tissues on her nightstand and hand her one. She blows her nose. It's a loud mess. "It's just if you could help me with this one thing with Anne Marie, I'd feel so much better."

I look down at the white shaggy carpet on the floor.

"I'll see what I can do," I say.

"You will?" Victoria looks at me, her eyes big and wet. "Oh, thank you! Thank you! I knew I was right about you."

The next morning, I'm doing homework at the desk in my bedroom when my cell chimes with a text message. I click on the inbox and jump up and down when I see Connor's name.

FROM: Connor
What are you up to tonight?

I wait five minutes so I don't seem overly anxious, and then type back.

TO: Connor
Still deciding. Hopefully something fun.

I want to leave things open for a possible invitation from my stud muffin, but I also don't want to make it sound like I was just hanging around hoping he'd call. While I wait for him to reply, I make a good effort to distract myself by reading a few more pages from a chapter of my astronomy textbook.

Oh, come on! Chime for me, Motorola! Chime! Chime, chime!

Finally it does.

FROM: Connor

Maracas Mexican restaurant at 8pm? They have karaoke on Saturday nights.

I wait exactly three minutes before typing back.

TO: Connor

I'm there!

When I show up that night, Connor's waiting for me outside in jeans and a soft, cashmere-looking sweater with the Abercrombie deer logo on the side pocket. His light brown hair hangs down into his eyes.

We grab a seat in one of the red half-moon-shaped booths and watch an elderly man on the stage belting out a pretty awful rendition of Guns and Roses' "Paradise City."

"He's pretty hipster," I say, snacking on the chips and salsa that the waitress brought over. "I'm impressed he knows G&R."

"So? Are you going to sing to me?" he says.

"Oh," I say, "I'm decent at holding a tune. Just mega shy about getting up in front of people. But maybe if you go up there with me?"

After splitting our entrées—a chicken quesadilla and a chicken burrito—Connor goes up and grabs a thick black binder from near the stage. He brings it over to me and we flip through the tome of songs listed by artist. "Let's see what they've got here," he says. He stops under the *T*s. "How about Tone Loc's 'Wild Thing'?"

"I think I can do that," I say.

He takes a piece of paper and fills out our name and the song.

When the MC, a heavyset bald guy in his thirties, calls our names, we get up on the stage and sing "Wild Thing" together. It's hard not to break out laughing, because we're absolutely terrible.

A group of guys sitting at a table in front of the stage starts booing us while we're singing. I can't believe it. Afterwards, Connor walks over to them.

"Hey, man, why you gotta do that?" he asks them. "It's not *American Idol.*"

"Chill out," one of the kids says. "We're just messing around."

"Yeah, but you're panning her while she's up on the stage. That's weak. This is karaoke. You're *supposed* to be bad."

"Dude, we're just having fun."

"I don't know how you can boo someone while they're up there having a good time, man. That's just not in my boo range," Connor says. Then he turns to me. "Come on, let's get out of here."

He pays the bill and we head out on the street. "Perfect excuse to leave," he says. Connor and I wander over from Greenwich Avenue to Sixth Avenue and walk uptown. Just a block north, near Ninth Street, we stumble across a small hidden alleyway, blocked off with a black wrought-iron fence.

"Did you know this was here?" I ask.

Connor shakes his head no. "Let's check it out," he says,

pushing the gate open. We walk past a few trees and a bunch of old-looking townhouses. On one of them, we spot a plaque and go over to read it. It says:

4 PATCHIN PLACE · ONE-TIME HOME OF "POETandPAINTER"
E. E. CUMMINGS (d. 1962) AND HIS WIFE,
MODEL AND PHOTOGRAPHER MARION MOREHOUSE (d. 1969)

Below that inscription, there is a quote from one of his poems:

"—do lovers love? why then to heaven with hell.
Whatever sages say and fools, all's well"

"That's what I like about walking around down here— you never know where you'll end up," Connor says. He looks into my eyes, smiles, then looks away and shakes his head.

"What is it?" I ask.

"Nothing," he says, but keeps smiling. He throws his arm over my shoulders and we walk back toward the gate.

After we leave the park, Connor hails a taxi. "What's your address?" he asks when we get in. I tell the driver West 64th and Broadway, and Connor starts kissing my neck.

I look up at the cab driver and feel awkward. "Do you think he's watching?" I whisper.

Connor shakes his head no. "He's used to this. I'll bet he gets five or six like us every night. That glass partition is an imaginary wall." Then he starts to kiss me again. But when

I glance up front again, I swear the driver is eyeing us in the rearview mirror. I squirm in the seat.

"Let me guess, it's your first yellow-cab-seat make-out ride, huh? Well, congrats. You're a real New Yorker now."

I laugh.

He leans in and starts to kiss my cheek. Then he moves his lips up to my ear. "You smell so good," he says, brushing against my earlobe.

"No, *you* do," I say.

"I think it's you," Connor says. His hand gently touches the bottom of my shirt. It tickles.

Just then, the driver taps loudly on the glass. "No sex in my cab," he says in a thick accent.

I blush, my mouth ajar. "Did he really just say that?" I whisper to Connor. "But we weren't even going—"

"Shh. Shh," Connor says. "I know."

We move apart in the seat and look out opposite windows. Then we glance at each other and laugh.

"I guess that guy had a few bad experiences," he says.

"You think? Maybe one or two?" I say, joking. "I can't believe people would actually do *that* in *here!*"

"Millions live in this city. They do a lot of crazy things," he says. Then he picks at the bottom of his sleeve. "So do you still wanna come watch me play soccer this week? There's a big game on Wednesday against All Saints Academy. We're playing at Asphalt Green. It's this turf field in the Nineties on York Avenue."

"I'm there," I say. "Plus, Victoria and Sydney like two guys from All Saints, so maybe they'll come with me."

"As long as you're cheering for my team."

"But of course," I say.

"So can I come up?" Connor asks.

"Kinda hard. I'm sure my mom's waiting up for me, and I don't normally bring guys home, especially this late. It would be mega awkward."

"Do you want to go over to my place then?" he asks. "My mom and her boyfriend definitely go to sleep early. They won't hear us come in."

I look at my watch. It's eleven thirty.

"I think it might be hard tonight. My curfew's at midnight," I say. "Next time."

"Okay, good night, you little minx," he says as the cab stops in front of my building.

"See you soon," I say, and get out of the cab.

After I close the door, he rolls down the window and pokes his head out. "Hey, Maggie! If I wanna rap more to Tone Loc, I know who to call."

I laugh and smile as the cab pulls away.

Upstairs in my apartment, my mom's waiting up for me, just like I thought she would be. She's sitting in front of the TV with an open bag of microwave popcorn on her lap.

"You look happy," she says.

"Oh, yeah, whatever," I say, playing it down, embarrassed.

"Did you have fun with Connor? And when do I get to meet him?"

"One of these days. We've only gone out two times. Get off my back," I joke.

"Well, whenever you're ready," my mom says as she tosses a few pieces of popcorn in her mouth. "Also, you need to get up by ten tomorrow. We're having brunch with Grandpa at Sammy's Noodle Shop at eleven."

"Chinese food before noon. Yuck," I say.

"It's his favorite place," my mom says. "Besides they have dim sum. And he's dying to see you."

Sammy's is abuzz with West Village locals ordering little dumplings from the waitresses pushing around the metal carts. My mom and I get there early and grab a table. A few minutes later, Grandpa Jack meets us in a pale-blue track suit. He gives my mom and me hugs.

"How's my gal?" he says, turning to me.

"Good." I smile. "Nice to see you, Gramps."

After we grab a bunch of spring rolls, pot stickers, and spare ribs from the various carts, my grandpa starts going on about how he's so happy we moved to Manhattan.

"Sarah, I tell you, you made a good decision," Grandpa says to my mom. "How could you live by yourself out there? It's so boring and unexciting." He runs his hand over his thinning brown-and-white hair, which is combed neatly back. "You have me in New York and your old friend, Karen."

"It was still hard to leave," my mom says. "We lived there for over twelve years. It was difficult to pull Maggie out of her school."

"That *farkakte* school," Grandpa Jack says. "Maggie's getting a much better education now. If only you'd moved here sooner. I never liked her going to school out there. It was a waste of her brain."

"I know, Dad." My mom sighs. "You're right." She scoops a tablespoon of duck sauce onto her plate. "We can't thank you enough for your generosity." I wonder if she really means it or if she's just saying it.

"I'm happy to do it. There's no one else I'd rather spend my savings on," Grandpa says, smiling at me. "And I mean that. You're my gal." He gives me a light jab in the arm.

"I hope to make you proud," I say. Then I take a bite of my shrimp pot sticker. I feel a wave of anxiety as I chew. Grandpa didn't make that much money in his life. He worked as an accountant and put any extra money he had into his savings account.

"Now, who's gonna be a member of the Clean Plate Club?" he asks, popping a whole pork dumpling in his mouth.

I take a bite of a spring roll, but then put it down on my plate. I never thought my m mom would feel funny taking money from her father to pay for my tuition, but now I think she might.

CHAPTER eleven

While there are approximately 20,000 types of butterflies in the world, the species called the Painted Lady is native almost everywhere. They are nicknamed the Cosmopolitan Butterflies, because they can be found all over the world, from Canada, Iceland, and the United States to Europe, Asia, and South Africa.

That Monday, I set out on the mission Victoria assigned me. For lunch, I skip going to Sarabeth's Kitchen with the girls, grab a PB & J from the cafeteria, and head up to the library. On the first day of school, Anne Marie told me the location of her favorite spot. I push through the glass doors and head right for it, passing the stacks of books and heading for the far-back-left corner of the library. The room is cast in a fluorescent glow. One wooden table is filled with five younger girls flipping through identical biology textbooks.

The place where Anne Marie likes to sit is where two stacks of books meet at a perpendicular angle, creating a small private square of carpet between the last stacks and the wall. As I turn the corner, I recognize her green JanSport backpack on the floor next to her army jacket, white laptop, and a stack of textbooks. But Anne Marie's not there.

"Looking for me?" I hear her voice. I turn around and see her worn black Chinese slippers walking my way. She's dressed in a vintage empire-waist cotton dress with an orange-and-yellow daisy print and carrying a stack of library books in her arms.

"Hi!" I say. I notice she has a fresh crop of zits on her forehead.

She sees me looking. "I know. I totally broke out. Can't help it. Whenever I get stressed, they appear like a mountain range on my forehead."

"Didn't even notice," I say.

"Oh, you're nice," she says. Anne Marie walks past me and sits down on the blue carpet, leaning against the wall. She stretches her freckled legs out in front of her.

"Okay if I join you?" I ask.

"But of course," she says. "As long as we don't distract each other and get some serious work done." She's separating the books she just carried back into smaller piles.

"That's what I'm here for. I have so much to do," I say, opening up my bag and taking out my astronomy textbook.

I sit down across from her and read the names of some books beside her. *The Human Body, Advanced Placement Bio, Statistics: Modeling the World,* and *The Sound and the Fury* by William Faulkner.

"Looks like you have a nice lineup there," I say. "What's on tap today?"

"You know, the usual. A test in AP Bio, a five-page paper in Literature of Madness, a chunk of Faulkner to plow through, a packet of homework for Honors Statistics. Plus this presentation I have to research for my Mandarin Chinese class on racial tension in nineteen-sixties Singapore. And add to that volunteering at the art class for kids with special needs at the YMCA, heading up a bowling club practice, remembering to feed my guinea pig, Diana Ross, and taking my multivitamins every morning, which make me nauseous."

"Wow," I say. "That's a ton on your plate."

"Oh, and speaking of the bowling club," Anne Marie says, looking at the titles of the library books she just brought over, "you should really come by. We need more members because two girls just dropped out to spend more time on their college applications. I know you said you're not a pro, but you saw our recruitment video at the first assembly, right? Just come on over and help us strike!"

"I'll think it over," I say.

Anne Marie picks up a library book called *Communal Riots of 1964* by Lay Yuen Tan and flips to the introduction. Then she takes a batch of white index cards out of her JanSport. I watch as she gets engrossed in the pages, moving her mouth slightly as she reads. I decide to get out some of my own books to at least look like I'm studying while I try to figure out how on earth to bring up the Golden Wreath.

I open my astronomy book to the chapter on the moon. While I stare at a picture of wrinkles found in the moon's basin, I try and psyche myself up. *Just go for it. Say something. Act casual.*

"Oh, you know, I overheard some teachers talking about that Golden Wreath award," I say.

"What about it?" Anne Marie says. She doesn't look up while she writes on an index card.

"Well, what is that award exactly?" I play dumb, hoping to get her to talk.

She stops writing, looks up at me, and smiles. "Only the most prestigious honor a girl can get at Berkeley Prep. You get to give the graduation-day speech. And the winner every year so far has always been accepted into their first-choice college. Plus, everyone admires you. You can't walk down the hall without kids and teachers shaking your hand, congratulating you. And a lot of the past winners have gone on to unbelievable careers. The Golden Wreath winner in nineteen ninety-eight went on to win the Booker Prize. Nineteen ninety-two girl clinched the Palme d'Or at Cannes. The nineteen eighty-one lady seized the Pulitzer."

"Wow," I say, impressed. "Are you going for it?"

"Let's just say I've been working on that paper for the last four years."

"What are you going to write about?" I ask.

Anne Marie looks at me, then back at her computer screen. "No offense," she says, "but it's top secret. I'm not breathing it to a soul. It's between me and Tina Turner."

"Tina Turner?" I ask.

"You know the Queen of Rock and Roll? Anyway, it's an inside joke I have with myself. Skip it," she says.

I'm kind of relieved she won't tell me the answer, because part of me doesn't want to know.

We sit there and study in silence for the rest of the period. When I get up to go to my next class, she says, "If you change your mind about the bowling club, come meet us this Thursday at Bowlmor Lanes. We always go back to my house afterwards for chips and salsa."

"I'll let you know," I say.

Victoria, Sydney, and I go to the All Saints vs. Chesterfield soccer game that Wednesday. Lexi can't make it because she's got a tennis match. As we walk along 90th Street, Sydney's talking a mile a minute on her cell to Ashleigh, one of the girls in the Fresh Melodies. The entrance to the sports recreation center called Asphalt Green is half a block away. We can see the bleachers filling up on the other side of the black fence.

"But you promised me that your dad would let us use it," Sydney says into the phone while strutting along in her camel coat and red Mary Janes. "If we don't do it soon, we won't have time to record our CDs before Christmas." She looks annoyed as she pulls at the blue wool Gatsby hat on her head.

Meanwhile, Victoria zeroes in on me. "Fess up. Whatcha got for me, girlie?" Victoria asks. She opens the black buttons of her black-and-white Marc Jacobs tweed coat that hangs just past the edge of her knee-length, charcoal-colored sweater dress.

"Nothing yet," I say. "She won't talk."

We walk through the open black gate. I notice how confident Victoria seems as she makes her appearance on the field—chin up, and swaying her long chestnut hair so it flips from side to side behind her.

"Then get crafty," Victoria says. "I need you to bring some juice to this Friday's meeting."

"I'll try my best," I say.

"You have to do better than that," Victoria says. "It's your mission."

The three of us continue along the edge of the green asphalt and over to the bleachers located closer to the middle of the sidelines. As we climb up the silver metal stands, I notice that they're already filled with rowdy prep-school kids and schmoozing parents wearing All Saints and Chesterfield school sweatshirts. We find room for the three of us in the top middle section, and Victoria sits down between Sydney and me.

Sydney snaps her phone shut, then tells us that she's so frustrated, because Ashleigh just reneged on her offer to let the Fresh Melodies use her dad's recording studio for free. "Now she's saying we can only use the studio if we give her a cut of all future CD sales. And that would be ludicrous."

A group of All Saints players huddle around their coach. They're dressed in maroon-and-white uniforms. I can see Victoria and Sydney looking for Jayden and Diego.

"There they are! Third and fourth from the end," Sydney says, pointing. "I love watching guys play sports."

"Diego looks so good in shorts," Victoria says.

"Oh, look! Jayden just bounced a ball off his head."

I can't be bothered with the maroon-and-whites. In my opinion, it's more interesting down by the left goal where the Chesterfield team, dressed in blue jerseys with orange numbers written on the back, are stretching. I notice Connor talking to some of his teammates while lifting one leg and extending his thigh muscle. I wonder if he saw me arrive.

The teams take their positions on the field. There's a coin toss and the game begins.

"Did you spot Connor?" Victoria asks.

"Yeah," I say. "Number eighteen. A forward."

"Cool, I see him," Victoria says. Then she turns to me. "So I don't mean to come down hard on you, but we're clear, right?" she asks. "This Friday, you're bringing me details on Anne Marie's essay."

"What happens if I can't find the info?" I ask.

Victoria looks out at the field. "Just get it," she says.

Anne Marie is happily surprised when I tell her the next day during homeroom that I'll be showing up for that afternoon's bowling club meeting. I get to Bowlmor Lanes in Greenwich Village at four o'clock. This bowling alley is the trendiest one I've ever been to before. It's buzzing with tons of young college students and is done up in a retro vibe with stools, counters, and banquettes in bright red, blue, white, and yellow.

When I walk in, Anne Marie is already organizing the girls into two teams. Besides Anne Marie and me, there are six other girls in the club—Anne Marie's two closest friends who are also members of the I-Have-No-Lifers, Robin Waldron and Grace Mills; two Warriors, Devorah Klinger and Ellen Gaines; one member of the Gay Asians, Susie Yamagata; and one member of Les Artistes, Leah Harrison.

Anne Marie and the two Warriors have all their own gear. The rest of us get shoes from the rental stand and pick out bowling balls. I find a red one that fits my fingers and is the right weight.

"Supposedly Richard Nixon played here," Anne Marie tells me as I'm lacing up my shoes. "So did Drew Barrymore and the Rolling Stones after a concert. This is *the* best place to bowl in all of New York City."

"In the late fifties, there were bowling shows broadcast on TV that were filmed here." Grace throws in a factoid while tying the laces on her maroon-and-cream-colored shoes.

When everybody is ready, we take over two lanes and put four people on each lane. I'm impressed by how good Anne Marie is at the game. She knocks down a bunch of strikes and spares. Also, she has perfect form. While I just walk up to the line and roll the ball, Anne Marie takes three steps, brings her hand back, and throws the ball as one leg swings behind the other.

At one point in between matches, one Warrior talks smack to the other because she bowled a better game. They break out into an imaginary sword duel, and I want to duck under the plastic seats and hide.

I bowl an eighty-five in the first game and a seventy-three for the second. It's nothing to brag about, but respectable among this crowd for a first-timer at their bowling club.

I'm really just putting my time in, though, because the real gold comes later when I'm back at Anne Marie's apartment for the after-game snacks. When we get there, she gives me a quick tour of the small two-bedroom she shares with her mom. Then her mother serves us big bowl of nachos with salsa and a plate of chicken wings.

Here I am on Anne Marie's home turf. There must be a lead somewhere. As the girls are busy chatting away and eating snacks, I excuse myself to go to the bathroom. It's right across the hall from Anne Marie's bedroom.

I stop and listen to make sure they are still engrossed in conversation. Then I open the door to her bedroom and walk inside. Everything is immaculately organized. Her closet is open and I can see all her sweaters folded neatly in piles and her shirts and pants on color-coordinated hangers: blue for tops, yellow for bottoms. I check out her desk. There's a stack of papers in a brown plastic tray. I look back at the door and then decide to go for it. I flip through the pages quickly, as Anne Marie's guinea pig, Diana Ross, watches me. It's a good thing guinea pigs can't speak, or I'd be busted. Past tests. An *A+* on a statistics exam. A paper for her Literature of Madness English class with another big *A+* marked on it. But nothing about the Golden Wreath.

I'm about to head back out of the room when something catches my attention. There's Anne Marie's old-school R&B funk and soul record collection in some crates lined up on the floor. I lean down and go through them one at a time, like flipping through a rack of posters, until I find a Tina Turner album called *Love Explosion*. The outside's blue with a spotlight on a young Tina, smiling wide, her hair airblown, wearing a purple, sleeveless leather jumpsuit. I reach my hand inside and sure enough, slipped between the record and the album cover are printed pages of notes on her paper. I read through them quickly. Then I put everything back where I found it.

Back in the living room, I have no appetite for chicken wings and chips. I listen to Anne Marie telling a funny story about her AP bio teacher and feel sick to my stomach as everyone laughs.

At the Revelers meeting that Friday, the doorman recognizes me and lets me get in the elevator before he even calls up to Victoria's apartment. Rosalind has Yelena pick up food for us from the Russian Tea Room. She brings the wooden animal trays down, but this time I get a leopard design on my platter. We sit on the floor on the oversized Luciano Marcato pillows we used last week. They're black-and-white images of a girl's face from the 1920s.

The girls take turns adding Truths to the Wall while we cut into our chicken Kievs and scoop up butter-soaked rice. I'm having a hard time eating, because I know soon all eyes will be on me.

Sydney starts by bringing sad news to the Wall. She found out that Nanette Beauchamp, one of the Snobby Indies, has a younger sister who was just diagnosed with Hodgkin's disease. Also, Luiselle Peña filmed a movie on her cell phone of her stripping and sent it to her boyfriend, who forwarded it on to a bunch of his friends. Sydney also noticed that Melody Ellman, a member of Les Artistes, is once again changing her style. As a freshman, she dressed as a prepster in only button-downs and khakis pants. Sophomore year, she was a hippie in bell-bottoms and tie dye, and junior year and the beginning of senior year she dressed like a Brooklyn hipster in mod outfits. But now this week,

Sydney noticed that Melody started wearing lots of black clothes with skulls. She also overheard Melody saying she's gonna dye her hair black with green roots, which surprisingly enough is technically not against the dress code at Berkeley Prep.

"Why do you think she changes her style so often?" Lexi asks.

"It's creepy," Victoria says.

"I think it's the I Am What I Wear Theory—because she can't figure out who she is," Sydney says. "She constantly has to try and reinvent herself by looking different."

"Ooh, I like that," Victoria says as Sydney writes both the Truth and the theory behind it on the Wall.

Next, Lexi grabs the markers and walks up to the Wall. She writes about how Gena Slettan is getting an operation to remove cysts on her ovaries. And that last weekend, Faith Fishman kissed her boyfriend *everywhere*, and now she's worried she has genital warts.

"I swear, it's true. She told me in the van to a tennis match," Lexi says.

"That's terrible," I say.

Then Lexi talks about how Isabella Newman just broke up with her long-distance boyfriend, Hunter, who is in college at Amherst. Lexi says that she isn't surprised Isabella and Hunter split, because she recently learned from her sister that in order for a relationship to have the best chance of survival, it must have three things—attraction, similarity, and physical proximity.

"Although Isabella and Hunter might still want to rip

each other's clothes off, they live over three hours apart and they are both going through a lot of different things right now. He has all the changes of being a freshman in college and she's a senior in high school," Lexi says with authority.

"My older cousin Dahlia is in a long-distance relationship with a guy who lives in Berlin, and they've been happily together for three years," Sydney says.

"I'm not saying it's true in every case," Lexi says. "Just most. Gosh."

Next, Victoria takes to the stage. She scrawls on the Wall in a red permanent marker. "Daphne Felder is lying and saying she's nineteen because she's dating a twenty-three-year-old investment banker. Dana Trivali shoplifts dresses from the sales bin at Betsey Johnson." Then she stops and turns to Lexi. "And I got this one for you," she says. "I know how Mr. Dumont is making your life miserable in geometry, so I got some goods on him. He didn't quit that last school he worked at in Grand Rapids, Michigan. The school asked him to resign because of his anger-management issues. He once threw a protractor across the room at some kids who were talking in class, and the pointy end hit a student in the face. The kid's name is Tony Renault. Next time you leave class, just whisper that name to him. I doubt he'll ever fail you on a test again. He'll want to keep you happy so you don't talk."

Lexi smiles wide. "Brilliant," she says. "You've just saved me from a world of pain. Mr. Dumont is a total lunatic."

"Isn't that blackmail, though?" Sydney asks.

"I think it kinda is," I answer.

"No way," Lexi says. "I'm just holding up a mirror to his face."

Victoria turns to me. "Okay, I can't take it anymore. You're up, babycakes."

I stand up slowly, pick out a marker from the jar, and walk over to the Wall. "I feel kinda mean saying this, but Grace Mills has backne."

"What's that?" Sydney asks.

"It's a term my friend Kelsey and I used back in Jersey. Basically, it's when people have zits and whiteheads, but instead of on their face, it's on their back."

"Nasty," Lexi says.

"Also, Risa Thorne, the Warrior, is dating the number one-ranked player on RabbitWars.com."

"Whatever," Victoria says. "Get to the good part. And, by the way, in the future, no need to focus on Risa Thorne. We have enough stuff on her already."

I look over at the Wall. "But there's only, like, three other things listed under her name."

"That's plenty," Victoria says. "Come on, girlie, bring on the Big Ts. Did you get the goods on Anne Marie?"

"Yeah," I say.

"So . . . ? What are they?" Victoria asks, cutting to the chase.

"It's just . . ."

"What? Did you not find out?"

"No, I did," I admit. "But I've been doing some thinking, and I've decided I don't feel right telling you this. It's not fair 'cause it obviously gives you an upper hand for the

Golden Wreath. And it means a lot to her, too, you know."

Victoria laughs and looks at Lexi. Then she turns back to me. "You're kidding, right?" she asks me.

"No, I'm serious," I say.

"Maggie? I mean, whose side are you on?" Victoria says.

"We're your real friends," Lexi says.

"I like spending time with you guys," I say. "And it's really cool being a part of the Revelers, but I need to pass on this one mission. I'm sure I'll be able to do a ton more, but this one just goes against my principles."

"You didn't join this group for nothing, did you?" Lexi asks.

"Think of all you've gotten so far. You don't have to sit alone anymore at school. You're in with the most powerful group at Berkeley," Victoria says. "And don't forget about the bracelet." Instinctively, I lift my arm and cover the silver ID bracelet with my other hand.

I notice Sydney has been quiet up to this point. She's looking down at her plate, stirring the rice in circles over and over again with her spoon.

"Maybe you should just let her off the hook," Sydney says softly.

Victoria and Lexi turn and give her a dirty look. "We're not going through this again with you like we did with Tracey," Victoria says.

"It just seems like she really doesn't want to sell out Anne Marie," Sydney says.

"Sydney, could you please be quiet? I'm handling this. Thanks," Victoria says. "Look, Maggie," she says, her voice softer now. "I really don't want to play hardball with you. You're a nice girl. It's not my style and it doesn't make me feel good in the morning. I just need you to cooperate here and tell me what you found out."

I'm a bit taken aback by the gravity of Victoria's tone. "What if I don't?" I ask.

Victoria lets out a loud exhale. Then she gets up and walks over to me. "There are some things we know that I'm sure you wouldn't want to get out," she says.

"What are you implying?" I ask.

Victoria shrugs her shoulders and purses her lips.

I think back over all the things I've told them in the last month, mostly the stuff about my family and Connor. They could tell my mom about what my dad did behind her back. They could show Connor photographic proof that I kissed another guy, even though I told him that he was my first kiss since I moved to New York.

"Come on. Just tell us this one simple thing and we can go back to the way things were," Victoria says. "I really want to work things out with you peacefully."

If I just tell them about Anne Marie, my life will be simpler. I'll be protecting my mom, Connor, and myself. The alternative seems too risky. I'm not sure I'd be strong enough to handle full-on warfare with Victoria Hudson.

"Fine," I say, but I don't feel good about it. "She's doing more than writing a paper. I saw her notes and she's creating a full-fledged multimedia extravaganza with a Power Point presentation and a short video she's filming herself."

"Interesting," Victoria says. "I hadn't thought about going in that direction. More than just a paper. I'm happy you told me."

"But you said you wouldn't copy her," I say.

"Don't you worry your pretty little head," Victoria says. "Mission accomplished." She leans over and gives me a hug. "I'm sorry I had to be so hard on you. But awesome job. I really appreciate it."

Somehow I feel better and worse at the same time.

The next Monday morning, Anne Marie sits next to me during the weekly assembly, but I can barely look her in the face. I'm a forgery of a human being. It was too hard to stand up to Victoria Friday night.

When I glance over at Anne Marie to say hello, I notice her eyes are puffy. Mine were the same way the morning after my parents told me they were pulling the plug on their marriage and starting the separation drip. I've found there's usually only one way to achieve those swollen eyelids. It involves crying your brains out until all the water from inside you is emptied and you wake in the night dying of thirst.

As Jacqueline Moore, the president of student government, calls up students and teachers to make announcements, I watch Anne Marie yank a notebook out of Stevie, her Jan-Sport. It says *AP Calculus* on the front, and she flips through the pages covered with equations.

"Aw, dammit," she says, hovering over her lap and leaning one hand on her forehead.

"You all right there?" I whisper.

She blows air out her nose. "Huge test next period and I

was on the phone with Robby until two in the morning, so my concentration is way off," she says quietly. We keep our voices low so we don't get in trouble for talking during the assembly.

"That's really late. Is everything okay between the two of you?" I ask.

"Peachy," Anne Marie says. "Except for the fact that he might want to end things 'cause I've been too stressed out lately and that apparently I'm no fun anymore. He says every time we're together I'm distracted thinking about all the buckets of work I have to do."

"Doesn't he understand it's just the time of year? Tell him to cut you some slack and things will get easier."

She wipes the corner of her right eye with one finger. "I convinced him to give me a chance, but he said if it doesn't get better soon, he wants to end things."

"Ouch," I say. "I'm sorry."

"I love him so much. He's been my honey for over a year now, and I don't know what I'd do without him."

"I'm sure the two of you will work things out."

"I hope he will. 'Cause when I cry, I cry hard."

I haven't seen Anne Marie like this before, and I try to think of a way to cheer her up. "Maybe what you need to do is get some good new music. Then after school, when you're home studying, you can take a ten-minute break and just dance around like crazy to let go of all the tension."

"I did see this one Persuaders album at Subterranean Records with my brother last weekend. It's called *Made to Be Loved*. I think I might get that."

"Do it!" I say. "You deserve it."

Anne Marie nods her head. "Now I'd better get back to this worksheet on the Sierpinksi Triangle Fractal. I appreciate the advice, though. You're a great friend."

"Thanks. Anytime," I say, but have a hard time getting the words out.

CHAPTER TWELVE

It has been proven that wing pattern mimicry aids butterfly survival.
Some nonpoisonous species have developed similar wing patterns
to those of noxious species that predators avoid.

The next week at school, I go through all the motions with Victoria, Sydney, and Lexi. I sit with them on the gym bus and we get lunch at Sarabeth's together. But there's a part of me that's starting to question the Wall. In the beginning, they acted as if their intentions were so high and mighty, but now it seems like they just use the information to their own advantage.

And I find myself wondering about what Victoria said to Sydney on Friday night. *"We're not going through this again with you like we did with Tracey."* What did she mean by that?

The last week of October, Mr. Z gives a pop quiz in philosophy and I get a B-minus. He hands me back the paper at the end of class and gives me a disapproving look. "Better get it together, Maggie," he says, shaking his head. I grab the quiz from him and hurry off. *What a jerk,* I think to myself. *I deserved at least a solid B.* My grandpa's face flashes through my mind. I see him looking at me, his eyes filled with disappointment.

We hold our Revelers meeting on Thursday night because Friday is Phase, the school's talent show. Lounging on pillows, we assume our usual positions in the hidden room. Tonight, Rosalind ordered food for us from Rosa Mexicana. There's a huge tub of fresh chunky guacamole, warm, soft tortillas, chicken fajitas, and chips and salsa on the floor in front of us.

I bring something to the Wall I heard about one of the Orange Shoppers, Alicia Butler. While applying bronzer to her already carrot-colored face in the school bathroom on the sixth floor, she was yapping away loudly to her best friend, Mia Bernstein. Apparently, Jenna's little sister, Regan, goes to the Chancellor School. There's a girl in her little sister's class who's making Regan's life miserable.

"Why?" Victoria asks. Then she takes a bite of a guacamole-covered chip.

"This girl stole Regan's makeup case, and Regan told on her," I say. "I guess the girl got in trouble, and now she's pissed."

"If you ask me, you're just asking for whole lotta trouble when you run crying to the teacher," Lexi says.

"But we *didn't* ask you," Sydney says.

"Can you let Maggie finish, please?" Victoria says, rolling her eyes.

"Anyway, the mean girl and her group of best friends started sending Regan mean IMs and text messages, and writing harsh stuff about her online like, "Regan's fat" and, "Everyone hates Regan." So now, starting this week, Chancellor just put this new policy in place that says students can be expelled or suspended for what they call 'cyber bullying.'"

"Stupidest thing I've ever heard. Aren't they aware of the First Amendment?" Victoria says. "Last I checked, as American citizens, we're guaranteed the freedom of speech. Even teenagers."

"Vic, we've debated this a bunch of times already. It's still a gray area." Lexi turns to me. "My dad had a similar case at his law firm, and he told me that most private schools and universities have their own sets of rules, and when we enroll we're expected to abide by them."

"Yeah, I know. I've read the student handbook," I say. "It's filled with regulations."

"Since we're only sixteen and still minors," Lexi says, "we have fewer rights, and my dad said our school's supposed to be serving *in loco parentis*, which means, like, in place of our parents in Latin or something."

"Total bullshit," Victoria says, getting fired up. "The Constitution says no laws can be made that cut into our freedom of speech." She angrily stabs a tortilla chip into the guacamole, and it breaks in half.

"Maggie, maybe you should keep going before there's a meltdown," Lexi says.

"It's just something I'm incredibly passionate about," Victoria says. "If we don't fight for our own rights, who will?"

"Go, go, go," Lexi whispers, motioning me to keep writing.

"Daisy Burbridge's dad got arrested for money laundering and he's gonna have to go to jail for three years."

"Ooh, nice one!" Victoria says. "Good work."

"And although it's hard to tell, Clarissa Barclay-Smith has alopecia, that disease where all of your hair falls out, so she wears a wig."

"I've been wondering how she's had so many good hair days in a row," Lexi says.

"Why don't I go next?" asks Sydney. She takes a sparkly purple pen and steps up to the Wall.

"Juliette Yuen from the Gay Asians, who is one of the straight members, is brokenhearted because she found out her ex-boyfriend has a new girlfriend. He changed his status on his online profile from 'single' to 'in a relationship.' He did it this Monday, and ever since then she can barely pull herself away from the computer. She's become a major online spy and stalks him on any site where she can find him."

"That happened to me once," Victoria says. "My ex, Jake, called me yelling one day when he saw I'd erased our inside jokes from my page."

"I took down my account this summer," Lexi says. "There were too many freaks trying to be my buddy."

"I just heard that all those sites actually increase jealousy among human beings because everyone's checking up on everyone else to see who has the best life," Sydney says. Then she continues with her Wall report.

"Mrs. Erasmus, the biology teacher, has psycho panic attacks whenever she sees smoke, and she thinks she can't breathe. Also, Penelope's dad performed some cosmetic surgery on another student's mom, and let's just say it didn't go too well. . . ."

Lexi goes next. "Monica Florez's mom freaked out on her for getting a tongue ring and she can't go out at night for two months."

"Why on earth would any girl get that?" Sydney says, then sticks out her own unpierced tongue. *"Bluck!"*

"Some guys think it's hot," Lexi says. "Like when you wiggle the silver thing around, it, like, turns them on. Also, Krystal Alba's older sister moved out to Los Angeles and starred in a soft-core porno movie. You can find it on the Internet. And Claudia Delvecho's dad is misogynistic and told her that she belongs in the kitchen and he'd rather spend time with both of her older brothers than with her."

"That is so wrong!" Victoria says. "I think Claudia should disown him ASAP." She jumps up, grabs a pen, and writes on the Wall.

"Whitney Lefkowitz has mono, so don't share any sodas with her. And Mr. Z goes to the Berkshires every weekend to stay in the house he bought with his wife, but she passed away. He takes care of these feral cats that his wife sort of adopted—he makes them this special concoction of canned mackerel and bread crumbs and leaves it in the backyard. It's like he thinks his wife was reincarnated as one of the cats or something. Apparently, his neighbors are totally pissed that he's still attracting this nasty bunch of cats to the block."

"Wow," I say. "Hold on a second. Is that true about Mr. Z?"

"Everything up here is true," Victoria says.

"How did his wife die?" I ask.

"A car accident," Victoria says.

"Oh, wow . . ." I say. "How painful."

"Maggie, please don't get emotional on us. You have to be tough like a news reporter. Can you imagine how border-line those TV anchors would be if they let everything get to them?"

"It's just—"

"We're trying to dissect what it's like to be a girl today at Berkeley Prep in the most honest way possible. A lot of what we write up here, people like our parents and teachers don't like to face. They turn their heads and like to pretend the world is prettier than it really is. But the fact is, what's on the Wall is what's really going on. And you can't blame us just because we have the guts to face it."

The next night, I am burnt out from my schoolwork and ready to break loose at Phase. It's also my parents' wedding anniversary. My mom and I don't talk about it in the morning, but when she comes back from work, she goes straight into her bedroom without saying hi. I hear the front door slam and her shoes squeaking as they walk down the hall. I go after her and stand outside her shut bedroom door.

"Mom?" I say, and knock lightly. "I'm getting ready to head out."

I hear the sound of her blowing her nose. Then she says, "Come in, honey."

"I just wanted to say good-bye. I'm going to the school talent show in a few minutes."

She smiles at me, but I can see her eyes are red. "That sounds like a lot of fun. Are you going with that boy you like?"

"Connor? Yeah, I'm meeting him outside Berkeley."

"Have a great time," she says, still smiling. "You have enough money? Let me give you some extra cash."

"No, I'm fine, Mom," I say. Then I start to walk out, but stop in the doorway. "Do you need anything before I go?" I ask.

"No, I'm fine. Don't worry about me," she says. She starts to change into her long white nightgown, even though it's just past six o'clock.

"Okay. Just call me if you need anything. Love you," I say, then I walk out the door.

As I enter the school's theater holding hands with Connor, I see that the auditorium is overflowing with girls from Berkeley Prep and tons of guys from the nearby all-boys schools. There are only a few teachers lingering in the back as mandatory chaperones. I notice Mr. Z standing by one of the rear doors laughing with the Spanish teacher, Mrs. De La Fuente. *Don't get drawn in by her dark eyes, Mr. Z. She's already getting down and dirty with Mr. Broussard.* He looks over at me, but I quickly turn away. He doesn't deserve a smile, just like I didn't deserve that B-minus.

The auditorium is swirling with energy. It's like no one can sit still. I watch a few Orange Shoppers dressed in tight black pants, tank tops, and pearls run up and down the aisle to greet their friends with big hugs. A couple of broad-shouldered football-player types in baseball caps and two Cheers and Beers girls sit on top of an upright piano pushed against the wall. A group of Snobby Indies leans over the side of the balcony waving to this good-looking guy with black spiked hair sitting below. All of the formal decorum that usually fills the theater during student-government assemblies is chucked out the window. It's Friday night with barely any teachers around, and we can finally let loose.

Connor and I sit together in the third row. Victoria sits down on the other side of Connor. Next to her is her guy, Diego, then Sydney, and her man, Jayden. He puts his tan arm over Sydney's shoulder and looks at her sweetly with his striking blue eyes. Diego is more Jim Morrison than ever. His hair has grown in around the front and sides and hangs down in his face. He's wearing a worn black T-shirt with a few small holes by the collar. It looks like the kind of shirt you'd pay a hundred dollars for to have it come special with all the rips. He definitely has that Bad Boy from Park Avenue look going for him.

Jayden brought his cousin Mason to the show tonight. As Mason tells us how he took the train in from Scarsdale where he lives, Lexi makes sure to grab the seat next to him. Mason is super tall with blond hair, blue eyes, and a goatee. I can hear him telling Lexi about how he loves basketball and spent last summer playing with a team of high-school kids in Israel.

Victoria makes sure to lean over and introduce herself to Connor. "Hey there. My name's Vic. I'm one of Maggie's best friends." She smiles and flips her long hair to one side.

"Heard a lot about you," Connor says.

"Only good stuff, I hope?" Victoria asks. She searches his face for a clue. It's like she's testing to see if I've said anything bad about her behind her back.

"Of course," Connor says.

Victoria flashes a big grin. "I'm so excited I finally got a chance to meet you. I watched you play in the Chesterfield/All Saints game, but you took off afterwards."

"Don't remind me," Connor says. "We got our asses kicked."

"I thought you played great. Anyway, we should all hang out together sometime."

"Sure," Connor says, and grins.

"Wow," Victoria says. "You have the best smile on the planet. Maggie, how do you look at him without melting?"

"You're really flattering," he says, laughing and looking down at his sneakers.

"It's hard," I say, and force a smile.

Just then, I feel a kicking on my chair and turn around. There's Connor's best friend, Teddy, sitting in the row behind us with his arm around Nikki. "Whaaat's up, Maggie?" he says, playfully jabbing me on the arm.

"Caused any more trouble lately?" I tease him.

"Always," Teddy says, playing with the bottom of his button-down shirt. I wonder if he's gonna pull it up a few inches to flash his Napoleon rock-hard abs, but he doesn't. "You taking good care of my boy, C-Dice?"

"Yeah, I hope so," I say, blushing and turning toward Connor. "Is that your nickname? C-Dice?"

"Never heard it before," Connor says.

Nikki sits forward and sticks her head between Connor and me. "Teddy comes up with new ones for everyone all the time," she says. "I'm already Nikirama, Nibinski, and Niki-Baby."

"Don't forget about N-Roni." Teddy kisses Nikki on the top of her head. Then he points at me. "I heard my man has it for you *baaad*," Teddy says.

"All right, that's enough," Connor says, whacking Teddy's black visor. I can see Connor blushing as he looks away. I can't help but smile to myself.

"Chill, bro. Everything is satisfactual," Teddy says.

Just then, the house lights dim. Connor looks at me and takes my hand in his. The audience bursts into applause, followed by wild screams and whooping cheers. As the lights on the stage come up in a glow of red, two Snobby Indies—Olivia and Fredrika—swagger onto the stage in short dresses with fishnet stockings and tons of black eye makeup, looking like they just stepped out of a goth-glam music video. The two of them volunteered to MC tonight's event, and now is their chance to gobble up the limelight. They stand in front of the podium and throw their arms up in the air like drunk presenters at the MTV Video Movie Awards.

"Welcome to the forty-seventh annual Phase!" Fredrika says. "Get ready for a Phasalicious ride!"

"Tonight we have some great performances lined up! So without further ado, let's get this party started. Dope on a rope!" Olivia screams out.

"What does that mean?" I whisper in Connor's ear.

"No clue," he says.

The show begins with the Ballet Folkloric doing an interpretive dance of the legend of the Chupacabra, a mythic creature like a gargoyle that lives off the blood of farmers' livestock. Next comes the Potty Rings performing a funny

yet totally dorky skit titled "If Harry Met Hobbits." Then
the Anime Club shows a film they created, an original short
film using their own anime drawings about a group of best
friends who are plaid skirt–wearing schoolgirls by day and
superheroes in the moonlight. Some girls from *Salon #33*, the
literary journal, read their poems aloud while one of them
plays the congas. Also Devorah Klinger of the Warriors gets
onstage and sings "I'm a Yankee Doodle Dandy" while wearing a top hat and marching around with a cane. Victoria turns
to Connor and me and covers up her mouth while cracking
up. "Only a Warrior could come up with something so lame,"
she says to us.

Then the Fresh Melodies get onstage and sing renditions
of "Mr. Brightside" by The Killers and "Clocks" by Cold-
play. Sydney has a solo during their rendition of The Bangles'
"Walk Like an Egyptian." She has a great voice, and I'm impressed to see her up on the stage. I wish I had the confidence
to go up there in front of everybody, but I have no idea what
I would do on the stage anyway.

The talent show ends around eleven o'clock. As we all
walk out of the auditorium, Connor pulls me aside. "I have an
idea. Go home now for a bit and then come by my place later
tonight," he says. "I'll tell the doorman to let you up. Then
take the elevator to the fifth floor. The apartment's Five-A.
My mom and her boyfriend will already be asleep. Walk ten
feet to the right of the front door and then knock on the wall.
My pillow is right on the other side so I'll hear you, then I'll
come let you in."

"You mean sneak out?" I say. "And then sneak in?"

"Only if you're into that," he says. "I don't want to pressure you." He starts to backpedal.

I put one hand on his lips to shush him. "I can get there around twelve thirty. I need to go home first and check in with my mom so she thinks I'm asleep in bed."

"Sounds like a plan," he says, and tells me his address. It's on Central Park West and 89th Street, which is about twenty-five blocks north of my apartment, but no longer than a ten-minute cab ride.

We step out of the building and onto the sidewalk, where the audience is breaking into smaller clusters.

Victoria, Sydney, and Lexi announce that they're heading out with Diego, Jayden, and Mason to some tiny dive bar on Second Avenue in the Eighties where Jayden is friends with a bartender who won't card them.

"Gonna head home early," I tell the girls.

"But why?" Victoria asks. "You and Connor should come out with us. Besides, you have another half an hour till your strict curfew. Which is way too early, by the way."

"Yeah, Sydney and I don't have to be home till three," Lexi says. Mason pinches her side playfully, and she throws him a flirtatious smile.

"And I don't even have a curfew as long as I call my parents and let them know where I am," Victoria says.

"I'll work on it," I say. "But tonight I'm feeling a bit under the weather. My throat hurts."

"Oh, I hate that," Victoria says, and seems genuinely concerned. "Do you need anything?"

"Cherry Halls are great for sore throats," Sydney says.

"Or gargle with warm salt water," Lexi offers.

"I'm sure my mom has a big stock of lozenges and salt at home," I say. I can feel Connor tickling my back lightly with his fingertips.

"That sucks that you have to go," Victoria says. "Connor, do you want to stay out with us?"

"No, that's cool," Connor says. "I'm gonna make sure Maggie gets home okay."

"Right on. We'll be at What Ales You if you change your mind. Ta-ta," she says.

Victoria, Lexi, and Sydney give me pecks on the cheek good-bye. I say "Later" to their guys, and then Connor and I head up the block to Park Avenue. He hails me a cab and I climb inside.

"See you soon," I say as he shuts the door behind me.

When I walk into the apartment, I head into my mom's bedroom. She's sleeping with the television still on. I tap her gently on the shoulder and she stirs. Her eyes open.

"I'm home," I whisper.

"What time is it?" she asks, and then turns her head to look at the clock. "You're back early."

"Just a few minutes," I say. "Besides, it was a long night." I notice a ball of used Kleenex on her nightstand. "I'm gonna go crash right now. Super tired." I kiss her on the forehead. "Night. Sleep well."

"Sweet dreams," she tells me.

As I leave her bedroom, I let out a sigh. Back in my room, I check out Tahiti sitting at the bottom of his glass bowl. At night, when it gets dark, he hides his body behind a fake green plant in the bottom of his bowl. Sometimes he is so still it makes me think he's dead, so I tap on the glass and wake him up. Then he starts to swim in a frenzy and I throw him some Bio-Gold fish pellets. This is exactly what happens tonight.

"Tahiti, Maggie W is about to have her first sneak-out. Wish me luck." I brush my hair back into a ponytail, then decide to leave it down. I chill in my room for about fifteen minutes, until I hear my mom's TV shut off. Then I stay still for a few minutes of total quiet after that. When I'm sure it's totally safe, I grab my purse and peek my head into my mom's room. After I see that she's fast asleep, I walk very quietly to the door. It's funny how there are all these small parts on the wooden floor that squeak and I've never noticed them before. The hardest part is turning the knob, stepping out into the bright of the hallway, and then closing the door ever so quietly behind me. As soon as I have it closed tight and locked, I run to the elevator banks and press the lobby button ten times.

I hurry out to the street and hail a cab. Since I can't call my mom, I decide to call my brother. He doesn't pick up his phone, so I leave him a message.

"Jason, it's Maggie. Don't ask. I just need you to have this information." I look up at the glass partition and whisper the medallion number into the phone so the driver doesn't think I'm a total weirdo. "My taxi driver's name is Frukhânage Miller, and his medallion number is 3C56. Don't mention this to anyone. Especially Mom. Unless something strange happens, like an emergency, and you have to. Okay, bye."

The cab driver lets me out right outside Connor's apartment

building. As soon as I walk inside, I see a nice-looking young doorman in his twenties standing by the back elevators. He's dressed in a charcoal-gray-and-gold-trimmed uniform.

"Hi," I say, "I'm a friend of Connor Pederson's. I'm supposed to tell you. . . ."

The doorman smiles at me. "Five-A. Take the elevator up to five and then make a right."

"Thanks," I say sheepishly. I'm kinda embarrassed that I'm showing up at this hour. I wonder if the doorman thinks I'm a slut.

As soon as I get off the elevator, I walk over to 5A and then estimate ten feet to the right. I knock gently on the wall and then wait, keeping my eye on the door. Nothing happens. What if I've somehow screwed up and this is the wrong apartment? Or maybe he went to sleep and doesn't hear me. I decide to tap a little harder. After waiting a nerve-racking minute, the door finally cracks open.

I step inside and there is Connor. "Shh," he says to me, then grabs my hand and leads me down a hall to the right and into the first doorway. As soon as we step inside and he shuts the door, he turns on the light.

"Welcome to my room," he says.

I look around. There's a khaki comforter with navy-blue stripes, a poster of Bob Marley dribbling a soccer ball, a futuristic, sleek stereo, a bureau with an Old Spice deodorant on it, and a desk with a computer, piles of paper, and blank CDs. There are cleats and sneakers thrown all over the place and dirty soccer clothes and T-shirts on the floor. I like that he isn't super neat because I'm not neat, either.

I walk over to Connor's bookcase, which is filled with

books like *On the Road*, *The Odyssey*, *The Electric Kool-Aid Acid Test*, and *The Invisible Man*. Plus, I notice a yearbook that says *The Wheatland School* on the binding.

"Ooh, can I look?" I ask, reaching for one with a maroon cover.

"Sure," he said, "but that one you just grabbed is from seventh grade back in Lancaster."

"Perfect," I say. I plop down on the edge of his bed and he sits down next to me. He's changed out of the clothes he wore to the concert into a white T-shirt and Adidas black-and-red running shorts.

"There's just one thing," he says. "I was really awkward then. Like, skinny as hell with huge glasses. And my mom took me to get a perm."

"A *perm?*" I ask, raising my eyebrows.

"She thought my hair would look better with more body. I let her drag me in there one time, but never again," he says, laughing. "And I mean, never!"

"I have to see this," I say, flipping through the pages.

"Here, let's just put me out of my misery," he says, flipping to the individual pictures of the seventh-grade class. He sticks his finger below the shot of him.

His face looks angular and skinny. There's an awkwardness to him that he no longer has. And his hair is very kinky.

"Nice curls," I tease him.

"Get off my back," he says, jokingly pushing me.

My eyes wander to the bottom of the page where there's a handwritten note from some girl named Paige. There are lots of hearts drawn around her signature.

"My old girlfriend," he says. "We actually dated until

right before I moved to New York, if you can believe that. I'm probably one of the few high-school kids who has a three-year relationship under his belt."

I laugh. Then I search the names on the page quickly for hers. I find it on the opposite side. She's a very pretty Puerto Rican–looking girl with a big smile, straight brown hair just past her shoulders, and thick bangs.

"Did you break up because you moved away?" I ask.

"Not exactly," he says. Then he closes the yearbook. "Can we put this back on the shelf?"

"Sure," I say. But I want to know more about mysterious Paige. "Do you mind if I ask what happened?"

"It's been done for a couple years." He leans back in the bed.

I lie next to him, but on my side. "I'm still really curious," I admit.

"Basically I found out that she lied to me. And once I knew that, it was just really hard for me to believe her again."

My eyes move toward a small cactus on his windowsill. I feel guilty about not being straightforward with him the night he asked me if I had kissed any other guys since moving to New York. It also feels like I'm keeping a whole part of my life from him. Of course he knows about my friendship with Victoria, Lexi, and Sydney, but I wonder how he'd feel if he ever found out about the Wall or what we did at our Friday-night meetings.

"To me, trust is the most important thing. It's hard to find and it can be impossible to replace." He kisses me on the chin and works his way up slowly to my lips. "Don't you agree?" he says quietly.

"Yes, completely," I say, then take a deep breath and kiss him back.

When I leave Connor's at around three in the morning, I take a cab back home. It's too late to call my brother with the cabbie's information so I just hope I won't be abducted, and luckily I'm not. I open the front door to my apartment by turning the knob ever so slowly and push the door open carefully so it makes as little noise as possible. It's a relief to see that all the lights are still turned off, and my mom is still fast asleep in her bedroom. I tiptoe like a ninja back into my bedroom and I'm out before I can even change into my pajamas.

november: OPPOSITION

CHAPTER THIRTEEN

*Butterflies are surprisingly territorial. There are reports of butterflies
buffeting each other with their wings so strongly that it's audible,
and the damage from such encounters might affect their ability to fly.
The frequent interplay between "contesting" butterflies at a
territorial site is a matter of possession: Who was here first?*

The Golden Wreath essays are due on the first Friday of November. If you're applying, you sign up to present what you wrote to the committee of judges after school that day.

There's a piece of paper with time slots posted outside the principal's office. Victoria is signed up for the first appointment, 3:30 P.M., and Anne Marie is signed up for later in the afternoon, 4:45 P.M. Other girls have signed up, as well, including Nanette of the Snobby Indies; Anne Marie's best friend, Grace Mills; Devorah Klinger of the Warriors, who sang "I'm a Yankee Doodle Dandy" at Phase; and Kelly Poloski, the girl from the Cheers and Beers whose parents have an open marriage.

The day before, Victoria, Lexi, Sydney, and I go for mani/pedis at Nails 'n' More, a salon around the corner from school on Lexington Avenue. We grab peanut butter Tasti D·Lite so we can get our nails done during lunch period. Victoria wants to make sure everything is perfect for the presentation tomorrow, and that includes having her nails painted Soho Nude.

The four of us lean back in gray massage chairs and soak our feet in basins of water. A Chinese woman with orange-highlighted black hair to her shoulders scrubs at the dried skin on my soles. She's wearing a name tag that says JENNY, and she helps me pick out the color Long-Stem Roses.

"It's no secret the competition's really between Anne Marie and me. We're ranked at the top of the class. Kelly, Nanette, Grace, and Devorah are no threat," Victoria tells us. "And I'm happy I have the first time slot, because it's been proven that judges usually remember the first and last contestants more than whoever falls in the middle. Devorah has the last time slot, but she's just a big dork. She's must've fried her brain playing Rabbit Wars if she thinks she even has a chance."

"I guess that's why people remember their first loves and their most recent exes most," Lexi says. She fiddles with the remote for her massage chair.

"Speaking of the last one, did you ever call Mason back?" Sydney asks. "Jayden keeps asking me."

"Haven't you heard? He's already lipstick roadkill," Victoria says. Then she grimaces and says to the woman clipping her toenails, "Ouch, that hurts."

"Oh, sorry," the Chinese woman says, and goes back to clipping.

Lexi plays with the zipper on her light blue hoodie. "He called and left a voice mail inviting me to hear some band play in Scarsdale. *As if.* On a first date, the man should always come to the woman. The woman should not go to Scarsdale."

"But he seemed like a nice guy," I say. "Maybe you should give him a chance."

Lexi shakes her head. "No way. He's off the list."

"What did he do that was so bad?" I ask.

"For starters, he used a double negative," Lexi says.

Sydney shakes her head. "You're too particular, Lexi. You're never gonna meet a guy that's perfect."

"Lay off, Sydney. We went out to that bar What Ales You after Phase and ordered appetizers, remember? He told me in between bites of his cheddar potato skins, 'I can't get no sleep when I eat late at night.'"

"I bet he said it deliberately," Victoria says, flipping through the book-review section of *Vanity Fair.* "To be cute."

"*I can't get no* is not cute," Lexi says. "Puh-*lease.*"

"Did you ever think that maybe it's a way to protect yourself?" I ask Lexi.

She turns to me. "What?" she asks.

"Like by being so critical, you never have to get close to any of these guys you meet."

"That's silly," Lexi says. "Nice try, but wrong."

"Just throwing it out there," I say. "I mean, both Keenan and Mason seemed like up-front, respectable, good guys. I think it's worth giving at least one of them a shot. I mean—"

"I can handle my love life on my own," Lexi says, cutting me off.

"Just looking out for you," I say.

There's an awkward silence. Then Lexi says, "Vic, your

toenails look so pretty. I'm really excited for your big day tomorrow."

"Are you nervous?" Sydney asks.

"Not that much. I've practiced my routine so many times already."

"Your routine?" I ask.

"Yeah, I can't just do a silly paper or I'll have no chance. So I came up with an entire one-woman show. I'm gonna dress up in an authentic toga and throw my own Greek festival celebrating Berkeley Prep for the judges. It incorporates music, dance, food, and academics. I'll lead the judges through my favorite aspects of our school, and end it by telling them how I hope to lead our class into the future on graduation day with the graduation speech."

I want to say that I'm surprised, but the sad part is I'm not. Of course Victoria was gonna try and raise the ante in the Golden Wreath competition. Anne Marie was creative and probably the first to think of doing more than just a paper. Now Victoria is aiming to top whatever Anne Marie planned with a Greek festival. I bite my lip as I sit there in silence.

"Vic practiced for me last night and she was off the charts," Lexi says. "It made me laugh and brought tears to my eyes."

"Sure you weren't at *Cats*?" Sydney asks.

"Stupid joke," Lexi says.

"You sound like an audience member being interviewed for a commercial outside some Broadway show," Sydney says.

"I'm just trying to be supportive of our friend," Lexi says.

"So am I," Sydney says. "But you just sound ridiculous."

While Sydney and Lexi bicker back and forth, I sit there

fuming until I can't take it anymore. "You said you weren't going to copy Anne Marie," I say.

Victoria turns to me. "What?" she says. "How am I copying her? Is she planning a Greek festival, too?"

"That's not what I mean," I say. "Obviously not. But you wouldn't have done that if you didn't know she was making a Power Point presentation. That's what got you thinking to take it up a notch."

"Maggie," Victoria says. "Come on. This is my own original idea. The info you found out simply motivated me, and I thank you for that. I'm sorry if this is upsetting you. I'm just trying to do the best I can, that's all."

I look down and shake my head.

"Please, I don't want to fight with you. I worked really hard on this. And I just need my friends backing me right now." Then she switches gears. "You seem kind of on edge. Is everything okay? I mean, are things cool with you and Connor?"

"Yes, they're great," I say.

"Okay, good," Victoria says, smiling at me.

Jenny finishes with the Long-Stem Roses on my toes, and I stand up. "I'm gonna have them start my mani," I say, and then head off on my own to the nail station.

As I sit down in a chair and soak my nails in a ceramic bowl filled with warm water, I hear Victoria talking to the woman painting her toes. "Here. Put the four of these on this Amex."

The next day during philosophy, Mr. Z performs another bizarre experiment. He sets a bunch of thick white candles down on his desk. Then he turns off the lights and pulls down the shades. I watch as he takes out a match and holds it to the wicks of the candles. As the flames burn, they cast shadows on the far wall.

"Now, stand up and turn your backs to me," he says. "Just watch the lights flickering in the back of the classroom. Keep your eyes glued to the reflection of the blaze. Watch how the darkness dances and shivers."

"Are we having a séance, Mr. Z?" Molly laughs. She's a member of Cheers and Beers.

"Shh. Stay quiet," Mr. Z says. "Focus. Now imagine that you're chained to a cave wall and the only thing you know is that there's a fire way down below you. You can't see it, but there are some activities going on by the fire, and whatever is happening below casts shadows on the wall."

Mr. Z makes the lights flicker and move around. In silence, we watch the movements.

"Although you can't detect what is below, you can see the shadows those activities create as they're reflected on the wall. This is Plato's famous cave allegory. He said that this is what our human experience is. We are all chained to the cave and only get to see the shadow of things. Or in other words, we can only see that which is perceivable to our senses."

Mr. Z turns the lights back on and has us take our seats. "Yet what's important is the shadow that each of you is seeing as you go about your daily lives, because that is what becomes your reality. You never get to see what's really happening down by the fire. So pay attention to what you are able to see, hear, touch, taste, and smell."

I think I like today's experiment a little better than the one where he mutilated a hat. Still, Mr. Z looks so wild while he talks, and I'm distracted once again because the Golden Wreath Presentations are going on right now. I keep daydreaming about Victoria performing a Greek festival for the judges. I hope she trips and falls on her toga and makes a fool out of herself serving grape leaves so Anne Marie emerges the rightful champion.

That evening at the Revelers meeting, however, my hopes are trampled. Victoria greets me with a big hug. As Sydney, Lexi, and I gather around, she brags that she "rocked out," during her presentation.

"I made the judges wet when I turned on the Greek music and started doing my speech while they munched on the grape leaves that I brought in."

I can only pray she's delusional, I think as Lexi and Sydney heap on the praise.

Before we begin writing on the Wall, Lexi updates us that she dropped the name of Tony Renault to her geometry teacher. Since then, he has given her an A on the lab she turned in and an A-plus on a pop quiz. She imitates the face Mr. Dumont made when she whispered the name of the boy he hit with a whirling compass.

Also Lexi says she scored Sydney free space at Ashleigh's dad's recording studio after all, so she can make a CD with the Fresh Melodies. "Be at the Sound Lounge this Sunday at ten A.M. Tell the security guard you're there to meet Ashleigh's dad's assistant, Chandra, who will take care of you."

"Are you serious?" Sydney says, jumping up and down. "But how did you convince Ashleigh to let me use it?"

"Screw Ashleigh," Lexi says. "I arranged it directly with her father."

"How?" Sydney asks, her mouth wide open.

"You know the new hot young thing on her dad's record label—the Christina Aguilera lookalike? I went out to dinner with my parents last night at Per Se, and I saw her dad with that singer at the restaurant, and they were doing more than eating dinner."

"Are her parents still married?" I ask.

"Oh, yeah," Lexi says.

"When his little diva went to the bathroom, I walked right over to him and introduced myself as one of his daughter's dearest friends from Berkeley. Then I asked him for the favor of setting you up with space to record, and he seemed happy to oblige."

"You little tart," Victoria says. "I love it."

"This is beautiful!" Sydney says. "If everything goes smoothly, we'll be able to make copies and sell them in time for Christmas and Hanukkah this year. Plus, I'll be able to give a portion of the proceeds to the Red Cross in time for the holidays."

After Sydney does a celebration dance, we take turns delivering our Truths to the Wall. The new group offerings include: Valerie Nissenblat was thrown out of her last school for having an affair with a teacher, Coco Barton's family's apartment is a pigsty and is filled with cockroaches and mice, Shelly Manzo has an appointment to get liposuction over winter break, Amy Jasko does cocaine with her older brother, and Georgina Sommerfield has endometriosis.

Tonight I can't wait for the meeting to be over. Hearing all these secrets is starting to disgust me. When I walk through Berkeley's halls and match the faces to the names on the Wall, sometimes an unbearable sadness comes over me. The outsides of these girls and teachers hide so much of what I now know is going on inside them. It's almost too much to take in at once. While walking down the stairs from French to pre-calc, I'll bump into classmates and be reminded of things like how Daisy Burbridge is losing her father to a jail cell because of money laundering, Juliette Yuen from the Gay Asian's is cyber-stalking her ex-boyfriend who broke her heart, Clarissa Barclay-Smith is hiding her alopecia with a blonde wig, Nellie Brooks is struggling with ADD, Tatiana Bisset's dad just ordered a Russian mail-order bride, and Nanette Beauchamp's younger sister was just diagnosed with Hodgkin's disease.

When the meeting ends, Victoria takes Lexi upstairs to show her some antique chair her parents just bought and Sydney comes over to me. "Are you all right?" she asks.

"Oh, yeah, I'm fine," I lie.

"All right, good, 'cause I wanted to invite you to a class with me tomorrow. It's called Laughing Yoga." Sydney explains, "It was invented by some guru in India. You're supposed to laugh a lot while doing yoga stretches and breathing exercises. I think it'd be so fun to try with a friend."

"I don't know, Sydney," I say. "It sounds kinda New Agey."

"No, it'll be fun. Come on," Sydney says. "Just try it once! You're the only one who might. There's no chance Lexi or Victoria would say yes. They're not as open-minded about this kind of stuff." After pleading with me for a few more minutes, she finally convinces me to go with her. Maybe it'll be fun. Besides, it might be a good chance for me to find out more about some of the Revelers' mysterious history.

The next day, I meet Sydney by the subway stop on Broadway and West 66th Street and we walk over to Yoga Works together.

"Hey," I say as we cross the intersection. "There's something I've been meaning to ask you, but it's been hard to find the right time."

"Go for it," Sydney says, looking back at a man selling roasted peanuts from a cart. "*Que bueno.* That smells *sooo* good."

"What did Victoria mean when she said you shouldn't do with me what you did with Tracey?" A man carrying a bag of laundry passes quickly in front of me, and I have to dodge out of the way.

"I think you've asked me about this before," Sydney says. "I'm not talking about it. Please don't pry." We hurry along past Kiehl's and a MAC makeup store.

I speed-walk to keep up with her. "It just sounds so mysterious. Did something happen between you guys and her? Was there a fight?"

Sydney puts her head down and smiles at me. "Maggie," she laughs. "You're too much."

"I'm just dying to know."

"Lighten up. We need to get ready to laugh our heads off."

We walk into the yoga center, and I decide to drop it. At least until class is over.

As we stand in the studio, the instructor, a very petite woman in her fifties with a dancer's physique and shaggy brown hair to her chin tells us to say out loud, "Hoo-ha. Ha. Ha. Ha," over and over again, while clapping our hands together. "What we're doing here is combining laughter with yoga breathing."

Sydney whispers to me. "If this is crazy, I still think it's adventurous of us to try it."

"I'm prepared for a little nutso," I say.

"'Kay, good," Sydney says. "'Cause I think you're about to get a nice dose of it."

The instructor walks around the room clapping with us. Then she tells us to try a new exercise. "Now, everyone walk around the room and make eye contact with each other. When you pass a member of the class, bow and then shake their hand."

Sydney and I bow to each other, but when we do we start giggling naturally. We can hear other students in the class start cracking up, too, and before you know it, as we're moving around the space, the room is filling up with genuine laughter.

For the next twenty minutes, the teacher has us do a bunch of exercises, including standing in a circle and throwing our arms up in the air while saying, "Yeah!" and sticking out our tongues and making silly faces while holding our hands near our ears with scrunched-up fingers.

Sydney walks up to me and makes a silly expression where she rolls her eyes up and distorts her entire face by moving her nose and mouth as far left as it will go. Then I stick my teeth out to mimic a rabbit's overbite while holding up my nose so it looks like a pig's. The whole time I'm trying to figure out how to get her to talk to me about Tracey.

"Your body can't tell the difference if laughter is real or

fake. It still creates the same wonderful physiological effects," the teacher says.

To end the session, we lie down with our backs on the floor. Then we kick our legs around and wave our hands in the air.

The teacher leaves us with this final thought. "Kids laugh an average of four hundred times a day. Adults laugh about seventeen times a day. Now go out into the world and bring all this happiness with you."

As Sydney and I leave the room, I'm surprised that my stomach muscles feel sore—I guess it must be from laughing for so long. I had no idea laughing could actually be exercise. We walk out onto the street and I follow Sydney toward her subway.

"That was a blast," she says. "Thanks so much for coming with me."

"No prob," I say. "I just . . ."

"What?" she says.

"I just wish you'd clue me in. I don't get why this whole Tracey thing is such a big secret."

"If I told you and it somehow got back to Vic or Lexi that I did, they would retaliate."

"But I swear, whatever it is will stay between us. If you need to know, out of the group, you're the only one I truly feel comfortable with right now."

"Really?" Sydney says, bringing her hand up to her neck.

"I feel like we're on the same page sometimes, like during Lexi's antics."

Sydney rolls her eyes. "She can be so bossy sometimes."

"Can't argue there," I say.

"But other times, she can surprise you and be really nice, too," Sydney says. "And we've been friends forever."

"I'm sure," I say.

Sydney twists the end of one of her long blonde ringlets. Then she turns to me. "Tracey didn't move to Japan. Her parents still live at the Dakota on West Seventy-Second Street, and she's off at boarding school in Vermont. She couldn't take being part of the Revelers anymore, so she quit. It made her too upset and guilty, especially when she turned in Big Ts. But you can't quit without repercussions. So when she stood up for herself, Victoria punished her by calling Tracey's parents from a blocked number. Victoria made her voice deeper and pretended she was an anonymous parent calling to warn them about their daughter's bad behavior."

"Like what?" I ask.

"She told her mom that Tracey stored condoms in her top bureau drawer; kept naked pictures of her boyfriend at the time, Chance, under the third row of cashmere sweaters in her closet; had a bag of weed tucked into her pair of tall black BCBG boots; and shoplifted, just for the thrill of it, countless pairs of jeans and lace camis from the Olive & Bette's boutique on Columbus Avenue. At first, her mom didn't believe a word of it, but then she went into Tracey's room and found everything just as it had been described—the Trojans, marijuana, nudie shots, and tons of clothes with the tags still on—and went ballistic. She pulled Tracey from Berkeley Prep after the year ended and sent her to a strict disciplinary school."

"Oh my God," I say. "That sounds horrendous." I cover my mouth with my hands.

"Yeah," Sydney says. "I tried to stand up for her, but I

ultimately failed. That's why Tracey won't talk to me anymore."

"Wow, that's crazy," I say.

"Stay on Victoria's good side, and everything's rosy. If
you don't, she'll find a way to get you. Besides, the way I see
it, graduation is in June. That means only seven more months
until we're free. But you can't tell Lexi or Vic I told you this.
You have to swear."

"I promise," I say.

As Sydney and I say good-bye, I'm haunted by twisted
scenarios of what Victoria might do to me if I got on her bad
side.

When I get home from the class, I miss my simpler life
back in Montague and find myself thinking about my dad.
Thanksgiving's in only a few weeks, and I'm dying to know
what we're doing. I really hope that we can spend it together
as a family like every other year. It doesn't seem like my parents are talking much, so it's up to me to make that happen. I
shoot my dad an e-mail.

Hi Dad,

How's everything up in Montague? Have you caught any largemouth bass lately? Everything is going good at school. You
should definitely come visit soon and I can show you Berkeley
and we can go eat at one of the yummy restaurants near
our new apartment. I know how much you love food. There's
this once place, Isabella's, that I think you would like.

Maggie

P.S. What are you doing for Thanksgiving this year? Do you think maybe we can all have it back at the house?

I feel a bit jittery as I hit the SEND button. Hopefully, he'll answer soon. I can't wait to hear what he says. Later that afternoon, I check my inbox and find his response.

Maggie,

I caught a two-pounder in Bass Alley last week on a rubber worm. It gave a great fight. I've been looking around for a new comfy chair for the living room. Every man needs one of those bad boys to lounge in while watching television. I've been busy translating a new edition of *Don Quixote*. Moose sends his love.

Dad

P.S. I thought hard about your question. We'll give it a try, but just for the day. I don't want her staying over.

I am so excited that he wrote me and actually wants to have Thanksgiving with all of us this year. I can't wait to tell my mom the news—even if Dad doesn't want her spending the night.

Over a game of Scrabble on our Special Silver Onyx Edition board, I bring up Dad's e-mail. "Mom, guess what? Dad asked if we want to have Thanksgiving in Montague this year. All four of us. Isn't that great?" I spell out the word *Taser* and get double points.

"Slow down," my mom says. "What did you say? Did *he* invite us?"

"Yeah, over e-mail," I say, and pick out five new tiles from the black velvet pouch.

"He came up with this idea of his own free will?"

"Well, I suggested the idea. But I think it would be great."

My mom places her tiles on the board and spells out *haiku*. "Are you sure he meant you *and* me?" she asks.

"Yeah, he said so. We haven't all hung out together in ages, and it would be so nice. I can't imagine doing it apart."

"You know, I won't have seen him in almost three months. And we always did have wonderful Thanksgivings together."

I write down the word's points under her name. "See? Exactly," I say. "Oh, and one last quick thing. Dad wants to make sure we come for the day and leave that night."

"We haven't even gotten there yet and he wants us to leave?"

"Mom, come on," I say. "Can we give it a shot? Maybe it's better just for a short time anyway. That way there's less chance the two of you will fight. Come on. Say yes. Please, please, please, please!"

"I can tell this is something you'd really like to do. . . ." she says. "I guess we can give it a try and hope for the best."

"Oh, Mom. Thank you!" I say.

"Maybe it'll work," my mom says. "Your father always did make a good gravy. Tell him I'll bring the sweet potatoes and dessert."

"Will do," I say, and pass my mom the velvet pouch. As she picks out five new letters, I run into my room and shoot a quick reply to my dad: *We would both love to come! Mom is bringing the sweet potatoes and dessert.*

Connor and I spend the night before Thanksgiving together watching the huge helium balloons being blown up behind the Natural History Museum. It's cold out, so I sport my cashmere gloves and a cute wool hat.

As we walk past a fifty-foot-tall Snoopy, Connor trips on the uneven sidewalk. "Man, how did you get stuck with me?" he says, catching his balance so he doesn't quite hit the pavement.

"You're not too bad," I say. "Only funny, super intelligent, cute, spontaneous, and——"

"Keep it coming," he says, joking.

"A smooth kisser," I add, then lean in and touch his lips with mine.

"Not too shabby," he says. A group of screaming little kids run by carrying soft pretzels.

"So?" I say. "How would you describe *me*?"

"Maggie Wishnick is this girl I met one night at a garden party who almost lost her balance and flew back on her head."

I start cracking up. "So embarrassing." I keep laughing and pretend I'm falling into his arms. "Can you imagine if I ended up on the other side of the bench?" I imitate a huge somersault with my hands.

He laughs. "Guess what?"

"What?" I say, still giggling.

He leans into my ear and whispers, "I'm so happy I met you."

I turn and look at him with big eyes. "What did you say?" I ask, not sure I heard correctly. Or maybe just wanting to hear it again.

"I think you got it," he says.

I look away because I can't stop smiling. We walk in silence for a few steps, past a helium-filled Betty Boop. As we pass the top of Betty's dark curls, I turn to him and ask, "Will you go to the Winter Formal with me?"

"Let me think about it," he says. Then he grabs my arm. "Absolutely."

CHAPTER FOURTEEN

Every fall, thousands of black-and-orange monarch butterflies embark on a long journey south to their wintering grounds in Mexico, covering the trees there with their bright shimmering wings. The monarchs, one of the few species of butterflies to migrate like birds, do so in a leap-frog fashion, with each successive generation eventually surpassing its parents in their southern track. What makes the migration even more amazing is that each butterfly makes the trip just once.

For Thanksgiving, I leave special food in Tahiti's fish tank so he won't be hungry while I'm gone. It's an orange tablet in the outline of a fish that decomposes slowly and releases pellets on an hourly basis.

My mom and I take a bus from the Port Authority up to Middletown, New Jersey, which is just a town or two away from Montague. I notice that the roots of her hair are dyed and she's more dressed up than usual, wearing a long black skirt and white knit sweater.

Jason picks us up in Dad's white Camry and drives us back to the house. He got in the night before from Tufts. It's a thirty-five-minute ride, so we have a chance to catch up.

Mom sits in front and runs her fingers through the top

of his messy, thick hair. "It's so good to see you!" she says. "When are you coming to visit us in the city?"

"Maybe I'll come down with Chloe sometime. She keeps saying she wants to go ice-skating at Rockefeller Center. I swear, girls are always trying to drag you to ice rinks and pumpkin patches."

"That's 'cause they're both really romantic places," I say.

"What do you know about that stuff?" my brother says, throwing me a quick glance over his shoulder.

"Hasn't she told you?" my mom says. "Maggie has a boyfriend. And from everything she's told me about him, he sounds like a doll."

"What kind? A Cabbage Patch Kid?" my brother says.

"Shut up, Jason!" I say.

"Just teasing, Miss Sensitive," he says. "So what's the story? Are you in love? Are you gonna get married?"

I roll my eyes at him. "None of your business. Did you get Chloe pregnant yet?" I ask.

"Enough already! Stop it, both of you!" my mom says. "This is supposed to be a nice family time."

"Yeah," Jason says. "Keep it nice, Maggie." He looks at me in the rearview mirror and gives me a devilish smile.

As we drive along familiar roads past wide pastures and farms filled with grazing horses, I think about Connor traveling with his family back to Lancaster today for dinner with his aunts, uncles, cousins, and grandpa. Victoria's family is having about twenty guests over to their place on Fifth Avenue, so that huge table in their dining room will finally be put to use. Sydney and her parents flew down to Boca Raton, Florida, to be with relatives, and Lexi went with her folks to her aunt's house in Westport, Connecticut.

Out the car window I see the Elks Club, Clove Deli—where I used to buy those egg-and-cheese sandwiches on Sundays—the BBQ Ribs House, and Ralph's Pizza Joint. Now that I'm used to New York City pizza, I can't believe I actually thought that place made a good slice.

Finally, we make the familiar turn into the Highpoint Country Club, passing the security guard's outpost and a small pond filled with ducks. As always, I'm reminded of the irony of its grandiose name. This country club is a blue-collar condo community. My parents bought one of the homes when it went into foreclosure back when I was little. It's hard to make a steady income translating books and company documents from Spanish to English, and my dad always thought that living here cheaply made good financial sense. This way he could keep his translation job and still have time to work on his own writing.

I feel nervous as we drive along the main road that goes around the periphery of the lake. I haven't seen my father in almost three months now. Neither has my mom. I'm worried about how they will act together.

We pull up to the house, and I help my mom carry the Fairway shopping bags filled with sweet-potato-dish ingredients and a chocolate mousse cake. My dad is taking care of the turkey and the stuffing. It's almost like the first Thanksgiving when the Pilgrims and the Indians came together and peacefully shared wild game and their own crops. But in this case, I'm not sure who's the Pilgrim and who's the Indian, my mom or my dad.

As we open the door to the house, I smell the turkey

roasting in the oven. Moose sprints around in circles and then runs over and licks my hand. I pick him up and scratch his poodle belly.

"Dad, we're back!" Jason hollers down the stairs.

My dad's playing the piano in the basement. The piano stops abruptly and I hear the sound of Dad's eelskin slippers shuffling along the downstairs floor and up the stairs. It's so good to see him and I run over and give him a hug. Jason turns on the television and starts to play video games. My dad takes out a liter of 7-Up and pours himself a glass. It reminds me of the 7&7 I saw him drinking that night with Roxanna, but I push it out of my mind. My parents seem amicable, smiling at each other, on good behavior. Although there's some tension in the air, at least there are no plates flying. I throw myself on the couch and watch my brother play Halo on the Xbox while listening to my parents' conversation.

"I see you've made some nice changes. Finally got that La-Z-Boy chair, huh?" my mom says. "It looks better than I would've imagined." I doubt she really means it, though. That chair was the kind my dad always wanted to get, but my mom opposed because it didn't go with the rest of the furniture.

"It's comfortable to doze off in at night," my dad says.

"I see you moved around the artwork a bit, too," my mom says. "I'm surprised to see our wedding picture is still up."

"My friends are surprised, too," my dad says.

"Why do you . . . ?" my mom says.

"It reminds me of the good times."

This is suddenly uncomfortable, and I want to get out of the house. Besides, I can't wait to see Kelsey, so I excuse myself so I can go meet her before our big meal. We meet outside the clubhouse and she runs over and gives me a hug. The restaurant is open, serving a thirty-dollar all-you-can-eat Thanksgiving buffet special.

It's only noon and not too crowded yet, so the hostess lets Kelsey and me sit at one of the square wooden tables for four people even though we're just ordering iced teas. The windows look out at the country club's pool area, which is covered in tarps in preparation for the winter season. I wonder if Roxanna is working today. I brace myself, just in case.

Kelsey looks great. Her shiny brown hair is longer than the last time I saw her, and parted in the middle, as usual, so it hangs like curtains alongside her big brown eyes. She's as energetic as ever and talks quickly as she fills me in on the latest. "I've written three new songs on my guitar since you left, and volunteering at that veterinarian office is going great. Except I positively can't stop crying whenever they put anyone's pets to sleep. It just cuts me through the heart. But last week, this doberman gave birth to a bunch of puppies and it was so exciting! I can't tell you how little and cute they were. Anyway, what's up with you? I'm sure your life is a million times more exciting than mine now."

Just then, I see my dad's plaything walking out of the kitchen. Her blonde-streaked hair is pulled back in a ponytail, and she's wearing her uniform—black dress with a white apron. When she spots me, she straightens her apron and then walks over.

"Back in town, I see," Roxanna says. She's holding a pad in between her two-toned, long fingernails.

"It's a major national holiday," I say, but I can barely look up at her. I play with the sugar packets in the middle of the table instead.

"Yes, everyone likes to come home for Turkey Day," she says. Her face looks even harder than when I saw it last, and she's wearing way too much green eyeshadow. "Your mom and brother around, too?"

"We're *all* here," I say. One look at the rose tattoo near her cleavage makes me want to puke.

Kelsey doesn't know about what happened, so she's oblivious to how much I hate Roxanna.

"I hope you don't have to work all day," Kelsey says.

"I don't mind," Roxanna says. "It's better working than sitting around with my parents. They're not big into the holidays."

I'm done chitchatting with her and would like her to leave pronto. "We're just getting two iced teas. Thanks," I say. "And I'm really thirsty, so if you could get them now, that'd be great."

"I'll be right back with them," she says briskly, and takes off.

"God, I feel so bad for her," Kelsey says, leaning into the table. "She dropped out of Montague High after freshman year when her older brother ran away. They still have never heard from him. That's who the Jamie is on her tattoo. This girl who works at the vet's office clued me in."

I watch Roxanna's back as she fills two plastic glasses with ice. "It's still not an excuse to be a waste," I say.

"Ouch," Kelsey says. "That's harsh."

"I just mean she should never have chosen to drop out," I say. "It's like she gave up on herself."

I know it's not kind to delight in other people's misfortunes, but I can't help but see some cosmic irony here. Maybe if she didn't go after married men—like my father—and get in the middle of other people's lives, she would have a happier world of her own.

Roxanna drops off our drinks, and I turn in my seat so she doesn't fall in my line of vision. I tell Kelsey all about my new school and the latest with Connor. "It's crazy how fast-paced the city is. Lexi and Sydney, the new friends I've told you about, can stay out till three A.M. Can you believe that? And this one girl, Victoria, doesn't even have a curfew." I play with my Tiffany bracelet while I talk.

"It sounds like you're having fun," Kelsey says. She looks at the bracelet. "Ooh, is that new?" she asks.

"Yeah. Victoria, Lexi, and Sydney got it for me. It's no big deal." I try and play it down because I don't want to hurt Kelsey's feelings or make her feel left out. But I can see it doesn't work, because Kelsey looks down and plays with her fork.

"It's really pretty," she says.

"It's all right," I say. "So tell me about the latest. Has Felix Mack had any more One Night Boob Stands? Do you have any crushes? How's my favorite teacher, Mrs. Shellenberger?"

Kelsey dives into one story after the next about Montague High. We only have a short time together, so we talk mega quickly. That's one of the things I love about our friendship.

We can speak a zillion miles an hour and still understand every word that comes out of each other's mouths. When it's time to get back to our homes, we hug good-bye and promise to see each other soon over winter break.

Back at the house, the turkey needs a few more hours to cook. My dad suggests that the two of us go out for a quick fishing run in the boat for old time's sake, while my brother and mom catch up in the living room.

The white aluminum rowboat is turned on its side in the backyard. We unlock it from the tree it's tied around and drop it on its bottom together. It makes a loud thud as it hits the ground. Then we push it down the shore into the water. Dad gets in first, balancing his weight while carrying the two rods and the orange tackle box to the front seat. I give the boat a push off and jump on board. Dad hands me the oars.

"Take us to Bass Alley," he says. It's an area of the lake we nicknamed because we often caught largemouth bass there. I row the boat around the bend and into the small inlet that runs between the shoreline and a small man-made island. Whenever we go fishing, I like to row at least part of the way in an effort to tone any excess flab on the undersides of my arms.

"Quieter," he says. "You're rowing too loudly and scaring the fish." When Dad gets bossy like that, it starts to take all the fun out of fishing.

He hands me a rod, a plastic magenta worm, and a few small silver weights to add to the end of the line. This has been our lucky combo in the past. Drop the line down to the bottom with a plastic worm, and the bass seem to bite.

We throw our lines over and wait in silence as the boat drifts slowly on its own.

"Maggie," he says. "I wanted to take you out fishing today so we could have some time alone. Also, I have a present for you."

"Thanks, Dad." I raise my eyebrows as he reaches into the tackle box and takes out a plastic bag.

"I didn't want to give it to you in front of your mother," he says, handing me the package. "I'm sure she wouldn't approve, so I snuck it out here with us."

I take it in my hands and feel around the edges. "Let me guess," I say.

"Just open it," he says, urging me with a wave of his hand.

I reach inside the bag and pull out a paperback book. "*How to Get a Rich Man,*" I say the title out loud. My dad has a track record for giving me self-help books. The last three he gave me were *Your Erroneous Zones,* which he called "brilliant"; *Ten Stupid Things Women Do to Mess Up Their Lives,* by Dr. Laura Schlessinger, who he warned me was a little strict; and *Why Am I Dancing Alone?,* a title that caught his eye while he was standing on line at Wal-Mart.

"I think you're really gonna enjoy this new one," he says, playing with the gold frames of his aviator sunglasses. He's not wearing them ironically like a hipster—these glasses really *are* from the 1970s.

I look at him and smirk. "Dad, are you serious?" I ask, teasing him. "I mean, aren't you supposed to marry for love?"

"There are many men out there in the world," he says, reeling in his line and picking off a clump of algae stuck around the hook. "I'm only saying, when you pick the man you marry, why not pick a rich guy?" He recasts his line. I listen to it make a plopping sound as it hits the water.

"That just sounds so shallow. I mean, isn't that bad to say?"

"I don't know if it's bad or good. It's just the truth. Maggie, listen to me," he says. "There are certain burdens and pressures that come along with not paying bills. Especially when you have kids and one's in college. You'll understand more when you're older. All I'm saying is money makes life easier. It takes away from the strain of it all. If you have a husband one day, and money is tight, you will see how hard it can get. I want you to be happy. And I only hope things will be different for you."

At this moment it hits me what my dad is really saying. He isn't just talking about my future; he's talking about his relationship with my mom—how their not having a lot of money made them unhappy. It's funny, but Victoria's parents are filthy rich and from what she says, they're really happy together. Maybe money *does* buy happiness. But I think there was a bigger problem to my parents' relationship than just money. It always felt like there were too many secrets between them. And they were never able to talk openly about the really important things until it was too late.

When we get back, my mom's pulling the sweet potatoes with marshmallows out of the oven. Then Jason takes out the stuffed turkey and pours the natural juices from the bottom of the pan into a big glass bowl. I help candy walnuts over brown sugar in a frying pan and watch the boiling cranberries. My dad steps in at the last minute to do his yearly gravy-making and turkey-carving.

We've had all the furniture in the living room since I was a little kid. It's probably way out of date, but there's something so comfortable about the worn white couches, and the oak dining-table set in front of the portrait my dad commissioned to have painted of my mom, my brother, and me when I was three years old. Although he's not religious, he liked to call it "Madonna and Children."

The thing that weirds me out is that the dinner goes remarkably amicably. My mom and dad seem to be getting along just fine. It almost feels just like the old days for a few hours. I see glimmers of warmth between them as we spoon sweet potatoes, cranberries, stuffing, and turkey onto our plates. At one point, my father picks Moose up onto his lap and feeds the dog a few pieces of turkey. Then he gently scratches Moose's white furry head.

But at six thirty, I'm reminded of how things are different. We've just devoured the chocolate mousse cake when my mom puts her napkin down on the table and says it's time to go. We have to catch the last bus back into Manhattan. When I give my dad a big hug, I feel a tightening in my chest. It's hard to leave all over again. Then I watch my parents say an awkward good-bye. My dad gives my mom a perfunctory kiss on the cheek while, with one hand, it looks like he's pushing her away.

As soon as we walk out the door, my mom lets out a loud sigh of relief. Then my brother—the middleman—drives us back to the bus station and drops us off. My mom's really quiet on the ride back into the city. She has a far-off look in her eyes. I'll bet it was hard for her to leave, too.

When I get back to school the following Monday, there

are only a few more days until the end of November. Banners are posted all over the school announcing the Winter Formal, and tickets have gone on sale in the lobby. I pick up two and put them safely in my wallet.

Later in the week, Victoria, Lexi, Sydney, and I go shopping for our Winter Formal dresses. By now all of us have lined up our dates. Sydney's going with Jayden, Victoria's taking Diego, and Lexi, after some encouragement from the three of us, has decided to give Mason another chance. We head over to Bloomingdale's and have fun trying on tons of options before deciding on the winners. We don't talk about the Golden Wreath or the Wall, and for a day I feel like the four of us are just regular friends, not members of a secret society—not people who know a lot of secrets about other people's lives.

DECEMBER: CULMINATION

CHAPTER FIFTEEN

The predators that target and consume butterflies include birds, lizards, snakes, small rodents, spiders, dragonflies, ants, wasps, and a number of bugs and beetles.

The Saturday of the Winter Formal, Lexi, Sydney, and I head down to Chelsea Piers early in the morning with Victoria. A bunch of members of the Social Committee, including Fredrika and Eliza, meet us by the entrance to the yacht. The boat looks like a two-tiered wedding cake with black-tinted windows, and the name *Lady Windridge* is painted on the front. A representative from the yacht charter company greets us and leads the group of us on board.

She shows us the interior of the main level where the room is being set up by the catering company Victoria hired for the event. The waiters, dressed in black pants and sleek black T-shirts, are setting up about a hundred gold chairs around several scattered round tables. I start to help one of the waitresses cover one of the tables in the magenta tablecloth, but Victoria pulls me away.

"No, no, don't. They were hired to do that," she says quietly.

"I really don't mind," I say.

"Please. All I need from you right now is to help me supervise."

As other members of the Social Committee show up, Victoria begins giving out orders: "Make sure the right amount of beverage glasses were dropped off and they're all clean." "Go over the menu with the servers and make sure they know what all the appetizers are called." "Put fresh flowers in all of the bathrooms."

The plan is to get all the details set up so we can go back home, get dressed, and have our dates meet us in a black stretch limo that will sweep us up, one apartment after the next. I spend the day running after Victoria and checking to make sure everything is up to her exacting standards. When the DJ arrives to set up his spin tables, Victoria gives us the okay to run home and get ready.

Although she seems consumed by managing all the small details, I know what's truly on Victoria's mind. Tonight Mrs. Hanover will announce the winner of the Golden Wreath Award. I notice a pep in Victoria's step, and she seems in extra high spirits. I know she thinks she nailed it.

I split a cab with Lexi and shoot to the Upper West Side. Then I hurry upstairs to my apartment to change. I jump in the shower, put makeup on, and straighten my hair with the flatiron. Then I slip on my new dress. It's pale baby blue, and made of chiffon. In the center of the neckline is a small jeweled brooch that looks like it's made of diamonds.

"Look at you!" my mom says as I come out of my bedroom. Then she gets tears in her eyes.

"What's the matter?" I ask.

"You're all grown up. I can't believe how old you are," she says.

I laugh and try to lighten the vibe. "I hope I don't look *too* ancient," I say.

My mom takes out her camera and starts snapping away. Then the buzzer rings and Connor comes upstairs to pick me up. I can't wait for him to see me.

He looks great in black pants, a white button-down shirt, and a striped green tie. My mom is so thrilled to meet him and keeps snapping photographs of us together until I have to tell her to calm down. *Chill, Mom, chill.* Still, I'm privately happy that now I'll have tons of pictures of Connor and me dressed up together.

The buzzer rings again, and it's the doorman telling me that the limo has arrived. Connor and I hurry downstairs. We're the last couple inside, and everyone looks wonderful all dressed up. Victoria's in a Catherine Malandrino ruby-colored silk dress with a tie at the waist, Lexi's wearing a Tory Burch ivory dress with gold sequins, and Sydney's in a Marc Jacobs black dress with a large cream-and-red-colored flower pattern.

As soon as the limo pulls up outside Chelsea Piers, we climb out. A photographer waits for us at the entrance to the yacht, ready to snap a quick picture of each arriving couple. He makes every pair pose in front of the New York City skyline. I think I blink during my photo with Connor. It's probably gonna look like I have tiny eyes and a huge mouth. Damn. Hell. Crap. Suck.

Connor and I take our first steps into the main dining room. The DJ is blasting dance music and a few couples are already shaking it up on the floor under rose-tinted spotlights. The tables are all set up with the magenta tablecloths, and white and pink flowers.

I spot Anne Marie milling about with a group of her friends. She's dressed in a vintage green baby-doll dress and beside her is a guy who I assume is her boyfriend, Robby. He's a nice-looking dork with glasses, a head that's way too large for his body, and a thick chunk of hair that looks like a shiny black cat is balancing on his head.

As soon as Anne Marie sees me, she runs over shaking her head. As she gives me a big hug, she whispers in my ear, "Oh, Maggie, he did it last night. Can you believe it? He ended things," she says, then pouts her lips.

"Robby broke up with you?" I ask.

She nods her head.

"But who's that guy you walked in with?"

"That's him. He already paid for his ticket, so he decided to come anyway. But just as friends. He wants to be free for the rest of senior year." She leans her head on my shoulder. "I don't know what I'm going to do."

Connor's watching us talk back and forth. "Connor, this is Anne Marie," I say.

"Nice to meet you," he says.

"Sorry to interrupt," Anne Marie says. "I just really needed to talk to Maggie."

"That's cool. I'm gonna go say hi to Teddy. I'll catch up with you in a few minutes," he says. I sense he's giving us privacy so Anne Marie can spill her guts out. *What a thoughtful date,* I think. And how cute his butt looks as he walks away.

"Look, who knows? You guys might get back together," I say.

"I don't think so. He said he's been wanting to do this for a while." Anne Marie shakes her head in disbelief.

"Then you're gonna meet someone else wonderful. This year or even next year at college," I say, trying to cheer her up. "Think of all the smart, nice university guys out there."

"But Robby was my best friend. All day today, I could barely eat. I cried all morning in the shower. Grace had to come over and stick me into this dress. I didn't want to get out of bed."

"I'm so sorry," I say. "It's his loss. He's gonna miss you one day and you're gonna have moved on and—"

"I just hope that tonight brings good news," Anne Marie says. "If I don't win the Golden Wreath, I don't know what I'll do. Not one album I played today made me feel a bit better." Her eyes start to tear. "My brother made me peppermint tea to cheer me up, but that just made me cry more 'cause it was so sweet of him."

If she doesn't win the Golden Wreath, Anne Marie is destined for a one-two punch in the gut. And I'll be partly to blame.

I touch her shoulder. "I know it's not easy breaking up. My one boyfriend back in Montague dumped me, but it's like what I read in Dr. Laura Schlessinger's *Ten Stupid Things Women Do to Mess Up Their Lives*: 'Never forget that one day you will love again.'"

"I truly hope so," she says.

Just then, Grace Mills walks up beside us. "Anne Marie, come on. People are starting to sit at the tables and I want to make sure we get a seat next to each other."

"I'm coming," Anne Marie says, taking a deep breath and forcing a smile. "Thanks for listening, Maggie. I talked Grace's ear off today already, so it's good to talk to someone else."

"Anytime," I say. "I hope you feel better."

"Me, too." As Anne Marie walks away, she gives me a small wave.

Connor and I sit down at a table with Victoria, Lexi, Sydney, and their dates. I keep playing with the salad fork in my place setting. "Is everything all right?" Connor asks me, rubbing his fingers along his tie.

"Yeah, why?" I say.

He puts his hand on my leg and rubs my knee. "You just seem like you're trying to bend metal."

"This actually could make a nice bracelet." I put the fork down. Then I turn to Sydney. "Hey, Syd, do you know what time they announce the Golden Wreath winner?"

She shakes her head. "Not sure," she says. "But it's gonna be soon."

Lexi overhears my question from across the table. Mason's resting one arm on her shoulder and rubbing his blond goatee with the other.

"Mrs. Hanover's doing it during the entrée course," she says.

"I can't take it any longer," Victoria says. "I'm shaking 'cause I'm so excited."

The DJ puts on a slow jazz song, and Connor asks me to dance. I head to the dance floor with him, but it's hard for me to enjoy leaning against his chest while we sway to the music. My mind is tossing and turning over Anne Marie's fate and my responsibility. I keep lifting my head to look for Mrs. Hanover.

"Do you not wanna dance?" he asks.

"No, I do," I say. "Why?"

"You keep doing this weird, spastic head thing," he says.

"I'm sorry," I say. But he's right. I wish I could spot Mrs. Hanover and see a clue just by looking at her face. Like the winner's name would be written across it in lipstick.

The waiters start serving the appetizers. Connor and I return to the table for a salad of mixed greens with goat cheese and sliced pear, but I can barely eat it. I just cut the pears up into small pieces and leave them on the plate.

When the waiters serve the entrée—a choice of farm hen with string beans or skirt steak with mashed potatoes—I finally see Mrs. Hanover across the room sitting at a table full of teachers. Just then, she puts down her fork and knife, pushes out her chair, and walks up to the DJ booth. She has a quick little chat with the DJ, and when he finishes playing the last song, he stops the music and hands her the microphone.

Mrs. Hanover taps it to get everyone's attention and says, "Hello. Hello."

The room quiets down, and all eyes turn toward where she stands in her black pantsuit with a long pearl necklace.

"How great to see such a large turnout this year!" she says. Then she praises the Social Committee's fine work creating a magical and delightful evening. After I've bitten the top of my manicure off, she finally gets to the meat and potatoes.

"As I'm sure all of you know, tonight we announce the winner of the Golden Wreath." She holds up an actual wreath that looks like it's made of gold-tinted, woven, metal branches. "This year, it was an incredibly hard decision, but after much deliberation, the members of the committee have decided on a fine young lady who we believe embodies the spirit of the Berkeley School."

I look across the table at Victoria. She squeezes Diego's hand while watching Mrs. Hanover with expectant eyes. In a corner table on the opposite side of the room, I see Anne Marie next to Robby. Their seats are pushed apart. Her hands are clasped together in front of her chest as if she's praying.

Mrs. Hanover raises the microphone closer to her lips. "So without further ado, I have the honor of introducing this year's Golden Wreath Girl . . ." She makes a dramatic pause and then says, "Victoria Hudson."

My body sinks into the chair as Victoria pole-vaults out of her seat. She throws a hand up in the air and clenches her fist. "Yes!" she whisper-screams. "I win! I win! I win!" Lexi jumps up and gives her a big hug, and Diego kisses her on the cheek. As Victoria runs up to Mrs. Hanover, I glance back at where Anne Marie was sitting before, but now she's gone. So is Robby.

I stand up and Connor looks at me.

"Where ya going?" he says.

"Be right back," I say.

He scrunches his eyebrows, confused.

I lean in and whisper in his ear, "Need to check on Anne Marie."

He opens his mouth as if to say, *Aha,* and nods.

I watch Mrs. Hanover place the golden wreath on top of Victoria's perfectly blown-out hair as if it's a tiara on the head of a newly crowned Miss America. Victoria takes the microphone and begins to make a thank-you speech.

I head out the side door and onto the deck of the boat. I walk around searching for Anne Marie and finally find her sitting on a small bench near a decorative anchor. Robby's crouched beside her.

He looks over at me. "I don't know how to make her stop shaking," he says. "And she won't talk to me." He scratches his thick black hair.

"Can I talk to her alone?" I say.

"If you can get through to her," he says.

"I'll try my best," I say.

Robby nods and stands up. "I'll be back at the table waiting for her," he says, and then takes off.

I sit down on the bench next to her. "Hey, Anne Marie," I say.

She looks up at me with tears rolling down her face. Her cheeks are flushed. "My whole life's falling apart. First Robby and now this."

"He still cares about you. He even came out here to comfort you," I say.

"That's just 'cause he's worried I was gonna jump off the boat."

"You wouldn't do something like that, would you?" I ask, half-jokingly.

"No," she says. "Well, maybe if there were sharks."

"Well, I don't think there are sharks in the Hudson River. I'm so sorry, Anne Marie. I wish there was something I could do," I say.

"Now I have to go home and tell my mom that I lost. She's gonna be so disappointed that I'll bet she leaves me behind on the cruise she's taking winter break. This time it's to Puerto Rico."

"You think she'd do that? That really sucks. Just because you don't have that wreath, you're still one of the smartest girls in our class. Doesn't she see all the work you do?"

"It's never enough. She wants me to be what she could never become herself. That's why she pressures me but not my brother. It's right out of Messed-Up Mom 101."

"She's way too hard on you. Maybe you could have one of your teachers explain to her how perfect you do in a class or—"

"I know you're trying to help, but would you mind going back in? I need to be by myself," Anne Marie says.

"Talk to me," I say. "Maybe I can make things better—"

"Just go. I want to be alone. I'm sorry." Anne Marie stands up and runs away. I wait, thinking she'll come back. When she doesn't, I go after her and try to find her, but I can't. She's disappeared somewhere on the yacht. She probably found a hidden corner, like her secret library study spot, where no one can bother her.

Connor finds me outside, and I explain to him that I was trying to cheer Anne Marie up after losing the Golden Wreath Award.

"That's gotta kill," he says. "Breaking up and losing this big award within twenty-four hours."

"She's not doing well," I say. "But she doesn't want to talk."

"Maybe it's best just to give her some space," he says.

Connor drags me back into the party. The dance floor is now on fire and everyone's grinding, shaking their hips, and jumping in the air. In the center of it all is Victoria dancing in a circle with Lexi, Sydney, Diego, Jayden, and Mason. Victoria spots me and calls me over with one finger.

I grab Connor's hand and lead him through the dance floor over to a smiling Vic.

"Aren't you going to congratulate me?" Victoria shouts in my ear over the music.

"I can't hear you over the music," I lie.

"Aren't you going to congratulate me?" she says again, louder.

"Oh, yeah, congrats. You got what you wanted," I say.

"Isn't it fabulous? This is the best day of my life," she says, and then shakes her hands to the music like she's holding invisible maracas.

I dance with Connor the rest of the night, but I can't stop worrying about Anne Marie. She's even MIA during the apple pie à la mode.

As the dance winds down, Victoria gathers our crew and says, "Great news! I called my parents to tell them I won the award, and it turns out they decided to go to the Hamptons at the last minute because my dad's weekend meeting got canceled. Which means we have the apartment to ourselves! After-party!"

I've never seen her so happy before, beaming like a blushing bride. Connor asks her if he can bring Teddy and Nikki, too. Victoria agrees. "The more, the merrier!" she says.

As the Winter Formal ends and we get off the boat, I keep my eye out for Anne Marie. I finally spot her hurrying through the crowd and out into the parking lot alone. I tell Connor to wait for me by the dock, and I run to catch up with her. When I do, I notice her arms are folded in front of her, and she looks like she's trembling.

"Anne Marie, please will you talk to me?" I ask her. "I'm worried about you."

She keeps walking and won't turn around.

I walk faster to catch up with her. "Please?" I plead. "It's gonna be all right. Everything will get better, I promise. You're too hard on yourself."

"Tonight . . . crushed . . . me," she says. And then she turns and runs toward a cab. She waves it down and jumps in. I quickly lose track of which cab she's in as it takes off into the night.

CHAPTER SIXTEEN

*Victorians were known for their butterfly collections, in which
specimens from all corners of the world were neatly arranged under
glass. Throughout history, the butterfly also made frequent appearances
in art as a sacred symbolic image of transformation, awakening, courage,
and hope. In both science and art, butterflies remind us that positive change
is possible, and that we have to be mindful of our surroundings,
because if we destroy nature, we destroy ourselves.*

Our limo takes us back to Victoria's apartment on Fifth
Avenue. As we arrive, a few other white and black stretches
pull up. A crowd of about fifteen kids storms into Victoria's
building. We can't all fit into one elevator, so we break into
smaller groups. A few boys volunteer to go to a nearby bodega
to pick up beer from the Japanese man who sells to minors.

As Victoria opens the door to her apartment, she gathers Lexi, Sydney, and me around her to strategize. "Since
there's no lock to the downstairs section of the apartment,
we need to take turns watching the door. We can't risk anyone seeing the Wall. I'm gonna leave a note on the door above
the staircase, but you can't trust a note to ward people off.
So we need guards. Maggie, can you please do the first shift?

Sydney will relieve you, and then Lexi. Take turns every twenty minutes."

"Are you going to do a shift, too?" Sydney asks.

"No way. I'm making sure beer doesn't get on any of my parents' antiques." Victoria straightens the golden wreath on her head. I wonder if she's going to wear it all night.

Victoria makes sure I am standing in my position by the door before anyone else is allowed inside the apartment. She hands me a note that says, NO TRESPASSING! and some Scotch tape, and I stick it up on the door.

I've been on duty for two seconds when Connor walks up to me. "Let's go check out the badass view," he says.

"I can't," I say. "I promised Victoria I would watch this door for twenty minutes. She doesn't want anyone down-stairs."

"What's down there?" he asks, leaning in and kissing my neck.

"That's where Victoria's parents store some of their valu-able artwork."

"Like van Gogh?" Connor asks.

"Nah, when it comes to paintings and photos, they're more into modern stuff."

Just then, Teddy and Nikki walk over to us. "C-Dice!" he says, barrel-punching Connor in the chest. "You're the man!" Then he turns to me. "Magatini, you look lovely this evening."

"Even I get a nickname now," I say. "Why, thank you."

Just then, I notice Grace Mills walk through the front door. She must've gotten wind of the party after Victoria shouted it out at the top of her lungs on the dance floor.

I wonder if she knows anything about Anne Marie. While Connor chats with Teddy and Nikki, I try and wave Grace down. The music's playing pretty loudly, so when I call her name she doesn't hear me. I see her duck into the living room. I could run to her and be back in a jiffy. I lean into Connor. "Guard this door with your life. I'll be back in thirty seconds. And don't let anyone—I mean, *anyone*—down there."

"I'm on it," he says.

"Why can't we go down there?" I hear Teddy asking Connor as I hurry off.

I run into the other room and grab Grace's arm. "Have you talked to Anne Marie?" I ask. "Is she okay?"

"She left me a voice mail saying that she just wants to go to bed. Don't worry, she gets like this sometimes. I love her to pieces, but she can be super emotional. She's gonna be fine."

"You think so?" I ask.

"Oh, yeah. I've seen her like this before."

I relax a little. "Okay, thanks," I say. Then I dart back into the other room.

Connor's still by the door talking to Teddy and Nikki.

"Anyone try and go down there?" I ask.

"No one," he says. "It's all good. Except I missed you." Connor pushes me against the wall and we make out for a minute. This is the only time I let my eye wander from the NO TRESPASSING! sign. I swear.

As we pull back from our lip-lock, Victoria grabs my arm. "Connor, give us a minute," she says.

"Sure," he says. "I'm gonna grab us drinks."

"I'm having a little freak-out session," Victoria says, talking quietly in my ear. "I need you to go downstairs and double-check that I locked the bookcase. Since I wasn't expecting to have people over, I'm not a hundred percent sure. Even though the Wall's hidden, I'm not taking any chances."

"No prob," I say.

"The key's hidden behind the Egyptian goddess picture on the fireplace mantel. I'll stay up here and make sure no one breaks any of my dad's antiques."

I leave Victoria on guard at the top of the stairs, turn on the lights, and walk down to the bottom level. I take a quick look around to make sure no one is down there, and then I pull the Picasso book out of the shelf. I feel back for the doorknob to see if it turns, and it does.

I reach behind the framed photo of Ma'at on the mantelpiece and find the key. I lock the door to the secret room, slide the Picasso book into place, and put the key back. I start to head back up the stairs, but that's when I think I hear a noise coming from behind the couch. I walk over slowly and look behind it. No one is there.

I run back up the stairs, turn off the light switch, and slip back through the door.

"It wasn't locked," I say. "But now it is."

"You're the best," Victoria says. "Make sure Sydney relieves you in five. You deserve to have fun, too."

I stand there alone waiting for Connor to come back. The party is filling up. A pack of Orange Shoppers arrives showing off their new spray tans and over-the-top Vera Wang gowns. A Snobby Indie runs past me chasing her date, who is wearing a pair of girls' underpants on his head. A Cheers and Beers girl is standing on a chair shooting cheese from a can into her date's mouth. A bunch of Les Artistes girls are banging away at the piano and singing show tunes.

Even though it's cold outside, Victoria opens up the terrace doors and turns the heat lamps on. I see one of the Snobby Indies, Olivia, take her boyfriend out to the balcony. "Look at this view," she tells him. "It's dope on a rope."

Across the room, Lexi and Mason are making out by an antique clock. *Wow*, I think to myself. *That may be a second kiss. Impressive.*

I wish Connor would come back with our drinks.

I spot Sydney and Jayden complimenting each other's dance skills at the formal tonight. "You were sooo good," she tells him. "No, *you* were," he says. Then they rub noses. It's revoltingly cute. She looks over at me watching them and smiles, embarrassed. Then she runs over to me.

"Go frolic," she says. "It's my turn."

"Thanks," I say. "I'm gonna find Connor." I head to the kitchen, where there's a crowd of kids trying to get to the sink, which is filled with ice and beer bottles. Then I spot Connor walking to me with two glasses of something clear. He hands me one. "That took forever. You off antique duty for a while?"

I smile. "Most certainly," I say.

He grabs my hand and leads me through a bunch of Cheers and Beers girls dirty-dancing with their guys in the living room. We step out onto the terrace. It's cold outside, so we find a good position under one of the heat lamps and he holds me in his arms. The amazing view of Central Park expands before us, and we try and pick out each other's apartment buildings from the West Side skyline.

There's a moment when Connor stands behind me and

puts his arms around my waist. I feel his face against my ear. He gets real close so I can hear the sound of his breath. "I think I'm falling for you," he says.

My heart beats so fast. I can't believe what I just heard. No one's ever said that to me before. I take a moment to let it sink in. Now I just need to get my mouth to open so I can say it back. I turn around so I'm facing him and look into his eyes.

I take a deep breath and am about to say it when, suddenly, there's a loud scream from inside the apartment. It sounds like a girl's voice. I grab Connor and run to see what's going on. No one's dancing anymore, but a bunch of kids are heading toward the door downstairs. Sydney is holding her hands in the air, trying to push people back. Nikki's screaming at the top of her lungs, "Everyone! Come look what we found! Hurry! Hurry! You gotta see this!"

Olivia and Fredrika push past Sydney. A bunch of Cheers and Beers girls run through the open door, too. Victoria appears, pissed as hell, chasing after them down the stairs. Lexi tries to get kids to move back, but she gives up and storms after Victoria. Sydney and I hurry behind.

When I get to the bottom of the stairs, I see what looks like a crime scene. The door to the secret room is open. Teddy and Nikki and a zillion other girls from our class are looking at the Wall.

Victoria's hollering, "Get the hell out! You're trespassing on private property!" She's forcibly pushing girls and boys out of the room. I see her give a hard shove to Grace Mills.

Lexi's down there, too, fighting people back. "You're not allowed down here. My dad's a lawyer and we're gonna sue you."

Sydney and I hurry over and try to get people out of the room, but the odds are against us. It's four against over twenty. I see Connor's face in the crowd, pushing his way toward me.

"What's going on? Are you okay?" he asks me. Then he gets shoved into the secret room with the Wall. I feel like I might vomit. "What is this?" he asks, squinting as he takes in all the writings.

Teddy stands beside him. "Nikki and I were just hooking up downstairs. We didn't mean to . . ."

Connor touches my arm with his hand. "Maggie, explain to me what's going on."

Before I have a chance, Victoria shouts at Teddy and Nikki. "How the hell did you get down here?"

"When Maggie and Connor were . . ." Teddy says.

Victoria glares at me. She looks like she wants to slap my face. Teddy notices and changes his tune. "We were just looking for some privacy. It's not her fault."

"But then Maggie came down and we saw her get a key out from behind some picture frame and play around with that bookshelf, and we were like, what the hell is she doing?" Nikki says. "So when she left, we got the key ourselves, and Teddy found a doorknob to this secret room. And there's all this stuff written about us." She turns to Victoria. "I can't believe you said that I pluck my eyebrows too thin and that I want to get a breast reduction." Then Nikki starts snapping photos of the Wall with her cell phone.

"I'm up here, too!" Olivia says, pointing to her name on the Wall. "I thought we were friends. Why are you guys saying all this shit about me?"

"Look, they have a list of what medication everyone's on," Fredrika says.

"Ah! I can't believe you discussed my backne," Grace says.

"It's none of your business if I made that movie on my cell phone," Luiselle says.

Grace Mills is standing by the Wall. "How did you know what Anne Marie did for her paper?" she asks. "She wouldn't even tell me."

I see Connor hovering by my name and run over, but it's too late. "Why does it say all this? I didn't know you went to Wing Chun just to find me. You said it was 'cause your mom wanted you to take self-defense. And why did you put up all this private stuff we talked about . . . ?" Then Connor spots the photo of Wiley kissing me in the Hamptons. He runs his finger along it and then turns to me. His eyes narrow.

"I can explain," I tell him.

"Who is this guy? You said you didn't . . ." he says.

"That happened before we got together," I say. "I can explain."

"But you said I was the first guy you kissed since you moved here. This is really weird. I mean, who is this guy? Did you cheat on me?"

"Connor, I can explain everything."

"I can't believe you've been keeping all of this from me. I didn't think you were like that."

"Please, please, listen to me. I didn't have a choice. Just hear me out—"

"No, this is too weird. I'm sorry. I just can't deal with you right now." Connor takes off out of the room. I try to follow him, but Victoria holds her hand up and blocks me.

"Where do you think you're going?" she says. "You royally messed up and now you're gonna pay."

"Get out of my way." I shove her arm and run up the stairs out of the apartment. I don't even look back to see if she's following me. Then I take the elevator down and run through the lobby out onto the street. I spot Connor getting into a taxi and slamming the door shut. I yell his name and hurry into the intersection after him, but the cab pulls away. Just then, I hear a car's loud honk. I turn and freeze as a white Volvo slams on its brakes and stops just a few feet before hitting me.

"Get out of the middle of the street!" the driver screams at me.

My body shakes as I hurry back onto the sidewalk.

Although it's past my curfew, I head over to Connor's apartment building in a cab. There's no way I can sleep knowing he's angry with me. After I try calling his cell for the twentieth time, I text him: *I need to talk to you. I can explain. Please listen to me.*

But I get no answer. When I arrive at his building, the young doorman's on duty again. He recognizes me and lets me to go ahead upstairs.

As I take the elevator up, nerves are shooting around my stomach. I'm pacing back and forth inside, and my teeth feel like they're chattering. When I get off on the fifth floor, I walk to Connor's door and take ten steps to the right. Then I knock on the wall softly. I look to the front door expectantly, hoping it will open, but it doesn't. I try knocking harder. "Please, please," I say to myself. I sit on the floor in the hallway staring at the front door for ten minutes, but it stays sealed shut.

I take the elevator back down to the lobby.

"Have a good night," the doorman says as I walk past him.

"Right, thanks," I say, heading out of the lobby.

Back out on the sidewalk, I look up at the apartment building. I count up to the fifth floor and find Connor's room with the familiar cactus in the window. The light is still on.

CHAPTER seventeen

The monarch butterflies almost exclusively migrate to the Oyamel forests of Mexico's Transverse Volcanic Belt. These are the only places in the world where you can actually hear butterfly wings beating. The locals call the returning migration of butterflies las palomas, *which means "the doves" or the "souls of lost children."*

Sunday, I hole up in my room. I feel terrible and I have no appetite. My mom caught me coming home forty minutes past my curfew last night. Although she yelled at me then, she gives me a calmer lecture this morning about how I need to be more considerate and respectful.

All day long, I get prank calls on my phone from blocked numbers. Girls' voices leave angry messages on my cell telling me how much they hate me. I also get text messages, but I don't recognize the digits and I'm not about to respond. One says: *We're gonna get you back.* Another says: *You're a fat bitch.* The one nonconfrontational message I get is from one of the Orange Shoppers who wants to pay money for a personal tour of the Wall because she missed the Winter Formal and Victoria's after-party due to strep throat. Is she out of her mind? The Wall isn't some ride at Disneyland.

My mom senses something's wrong with me, and she comes into my room.

"Does it have to do with Connor?" she asks, sitting down in my desk chair.

"That's just for starters," I say.

"Are you in a fight with your friends?" she says.

"Something like that," I say. "I'm not in the mood to talk about it, Mom."

"Well, I'm here if you need me," she says. "I don't like seeing you this way."

"I'll be fine," I say.

Around four in the afternoon, my cell phone rings for the millionth time. I pray it's Connor, but when I check the caller ID, the screen says SYDNEY. I decide to answer.

"Hello?" I say.

"Hey," she says. Her voice sounds groggy.

"Today's been horrible," I say. "I've gotten a ton of bashing phone calls. Have you been getting them, too?"

"Yeah," Sydney says. "But that's the least of it. Did you hear what happened?"

The tone of her voice sounds ominous. My body tenses. "No . . ." I say.

"Anne Marie tried to kill herself."

I freeze. "What?" I say, shocked. "How? When? Is she okay?"

"Apparently, she got into her mom's sleeping pills."

"No . . ." My eyes tear up.

"It happened early this morning. She left some strange message on her ex-boyfriend's cell phone at five A.M. When he got it, he called the land line and told her mom he was worried that something might be wrong with Anne Marie."

"Is she okay?"

"Her mom got to her in time, but it sounds like it was a close call."

"I can't believe that she tried that. I knew she was upset, but I had no idea she'd go that far."

"People can surprise you," she says.

I can't speak for a few moments while I digest what happened to Anne Marie.

"Maggie?" Sydney asks. "Are you there?"

"Yeah," I say. "I just feel so bad about Anne Marie."

"Me, too," she says, then we're both quiet again.

"Last night was a nightmare," I say finally. "I keep replaying it in my head, and hope to wake up."

"Tell me about it," Sydney says.

"Have you spoken to Vic or Lexi?"

"Yeah, they just called me. Vic is going to Lexi's house in an hour to discuss how to handle things in case we get in trouble with school. I think Lexi's dad is giving them legal advice. They asked me to go, but I said no."

"I didn't get invited," I say.

"They're both pretty pissed. I guess they blame you for what happened."

"What'd they say?" I ask.

"Just that they want to kill you for not seeing Teddy and Nikki go downstairs."

"It must've been the two seconds I turned away to kiss Connor. Teddy's Connor's best friend. I didn't think he would do that."

"Teddy's really sneaky. Remember what he did the night of the back-to-school party?" she says.

"Yeah, but I thought he was harmless. . . . I'm really sorry I messed up," I say. "Do you really think we're gonna get in trouble at school?" I ask.

"Depends how much the word gets out to teachers. Right now, with the amount of calls we're getting, I think our entire grade knows. And don't forget, Nikki took photographic evidence with her cell phone."

"What do you think is gonna happen to us? I'm worried we might get kicked out. I don't know how I could ever look my grandpa in the eye again if we get expelled."

"No point in guessing," Sydney says. "We'll find out soon enough."

When we hang up, I can't stop thinking about Anne Marie. I should've been there more for her. If only I'd found her on the boat wherever she was hiding, maybe I could've helped. Or if I'd run after her while she got into that cab. But when I spoke to Grace Mills at the party, she made it seem like Anne Marie had acted this way before and it was nothing to be too worried about.

And what about Victoria and Lexi? Do I really have to watch my back now? Is this going to turn into some sick sequel to *Heathers*?

I get up out of bed and walk around my room. There must be something I can do to make things better. I change from my pajamas into jeans and an aqua cashmere cable-knit sweater, then I look down at the bracelet around my wrist and take it off. I walk into my bathroom and think about throwing it in the toilet, but can you flush a piece of metal? I don't think so. Instead, I go to the hall closet, pull out the toolbox, and take out a hammer. Then I put newspaper down on the kitchen floor and start smashing the bracelet. There's something that feels wonderful about trying to crack it apart.

My mom hurries out of her room when she hears the banging. "What are you doing?" she asks.

"Hammering my Tiffany bracelet," I say, looking up at her.

"Are you losing your mind?" she asks.

"A little," I say. I make one last hard hit and then look down at the smashed-up piece of jewelry. "I feel a little better now."

"Baby, can you put down the hammer?" my mom says.

"Oh, yeah, sure," I say, handing it over to her. "That was just a one-time deal."

She eyes me strangely. "You're really starting to worry me."

"Mom, I can handle it. Trust me. I'll be back in an hour. Gotta run over to Victoria's."

I hail a cab outside our building. As soon as I get in, I call my mom. She picks up. "Hi, Mom. Rajeev Adams. 3B15. Gotta run."

As the cab pulls up outside Victoria's building, I pay the driver, then climb out. The doorman recognizes me and waves me past.

I hope Victoria is still out at Lexi's house and that her parents are still in the Hamptons. I take the elevator upstairs and Yelena answers. She smiles shyly.

"Hi," I say. "Is Victoria here?"

She can barely understand me. "Be back very soon," she says, smiling.

"Thanks," I say. "I'll wait downstairs for her."

I hurry to the bottom level of the apartment before she can stop me. The door to the secret room is still open from last night. I guess there's no reason to lock it anymore. My heart is beating very fast as I stand back and look at the huge scrolls before me. I undo the bottom tacks. Then I take a chair from the other room and stand on it so I can reach the top tacks. As I undo them, the slabs of paper fall to the floor. I lay them on top of each other and roll them up as if they were oversized posters. There's a sound from the staircase. I freeze for a moment and look over.

"Hello?" I say loudly. There's no answer. I let out a sigh of relief. I'd better hurry. Who knows when Victoria might come through that door?

I look at the naked wall for a moment. You can still see where the tacks were stuck up there, and there are a few small markings and smudges. But compared to before, the room looks empty and clean. It's strange, but as I hold the Wall rolled up in my hand now, the papers feel warm. It's as if the writings that covered these pages still hold some of the heat from the people whose secrets they kept.

I carry the papers in my right hand and start heading back up the stairs. The roll is three feet wide and weighs less than a textbook. It's astonishing how light hundreds of secrets can be.

When I reach the top of the landing, I see Yelena cleaning the kitchen floor with a Swiffer. She's distracted and doesn't notice me as I start to head for the front door. I put my hand on the knob and am about to open it when it swings back on its own. Standing before me is Victoria. Her eyes meet mine, and I see a fuse in her pupils start to burn.

"What are you doing?" she asks. Her gaze moves down roll of papers in my hand. "You did not!" she says. Her eyes narrow into little slits. "What are you doing? Give me that. How dare you break into my house and go through my things."

"I had to," I say.

"Give me that now," she says slowly. "It's not yours to take down—it's mine. My family started the Wall. It's my tradition."

I step back and she follows me. "I can't give it to you," I say.

She puts out her hand. "Seriously, Maggie. Just hand it over."

"The Wall can't stay up anymore."

Victoria lunges toward me and reaches out to grab the rolled-up Wall. I duck out of her way just in time, and she misses it.

"Be careful," Victoria says, her voice softening. "You're gonna ruin it. Please be gentle. Just put it down and we can talk about it." She's moving slowly toward me and backing me into that salon room with the Roman busts.

"There's nothing to talk about. We have to end this. Can't you see how much pain it's causing?" I move behind one of the sculptures.

"Maggie, please. I've put so much into this. Years. Don't ruin it. I'll take it down and put it in the time chest early. No one will ever see it again for thirty years."

"No, it can't be preserved. These secrets aren't ours to

keep. You just use them for manipulation, but these are people's lives that you're messing with."

Victoria bolts over toward me. "I was stupid to let you be a part of the Revelers. The only reason I picked you is 'cause I saw how desperate you were to be liked. It was obvious you'd do anything I told you to do." She shakes her head sadly. "You were so insecure and lost."

As I run around one of the busts, she dives after me and grabs again at the rolled-up Wall.

We freeze for a moment in a standoff.

"You never deserved to be one of us. I made a mistake about you. You're not cool enough. You're not good enough. You don't deserve to go to Berkeley. You should go back to that crummy white-trash town you came from."

She pulls at one side of the Wall with one hand, while I yank the other. It feels like a careful tug-of-war over a fragile piece of art.

"Shut up. You don't know what you're talking about," I say.

She pulls harder, and the paper starts to tear.

"Don't you see that you don't belong here? You can't keep up with us. You're never gonna amount to anything! I gave you so much. What a waste. You're an ungrateful wench. Now, let go!"

The paper rips even more. I can see there's no way I'm getting out of here with the Wall. I run my hand along the tear and rip it all the way across.

Victoria gasps as I tear a large section in half. She makes a last effort to push me and grab the scrolls, but it's too late. I'm ripping them to shreds and scattering the pieces on her salon floor. She's still trying to pry my hands off what's left of the Wall, while I keep tearing and ripping away. I can see the names of some girls from our grade staring up at me from the gleaming floor. I spot a chunk with Anne Marie's name and grab that section—and a few more—then shove them in my pocket.

Victoria looks like she wants to claw my eyes out. "Get out!" she screams. "Get out of my house!"

I start moving back toward the foyer. She stands there in the center of the shredded Wall. "I will never forget how you betrayed me. *Ever.* Even when I'm thirty or fifty or a senior citizen. Watch your back. I put a curse on your head. On everything you ever touch. And you never deserved Connor. He could get someone much better than you. I always thought he was out of your league. And your pathetic family. And poor mom. I feel so sorry for her walking around like a schmuck while you keep from her that your father was chasing some other woman's tail."

I stop and turn around. And then something opens up from a place deep inside me. There's no way I'm holding back.

"You have nothing better to do than keep track of other people's lives. You hold on to all this material bullshit because it's the only thing that makes you feel like you have worth. Your mansion in the Hamptons, your huge Fifth Avenue apartment. Your stupid Dior red bikini. If you didn't have all that expensive crap floating around you, distracting you, you'd have to see how ugly you look without all of it. You need to control everything and everyone because you're so scared if you don't, people will see that deep down you're a miserable person, and they'll leave you. Obsessing over other people's private problems only makes you feel better about your own miserable life."

"If you don't get out this second, I'm calling the cops," Victoria says.

I'm done here, so I leave.

When I get back to my apartment, I burst into tears as soon as I see my mom.

"What's the matter?" she says, her eyes wide with concern. "Sweetheart, whatever it is, we can work it out."

I collapse on the couch, and she sits down beside me and rubs my back. I feel like the moment that I've been dreading is here. Now that the Wall is exposed, if I don't tell my mom everything that's been on my mind about her and Dad, she may find out some other way, which will only make it all the more painful for her. Even though the Wall is destroyed, I'm not sure how much the girls from my school saw and what parts Nikki took photos of.

"Are you and Dad ever getting back together?" I ask.

"Mags, I don't have an answer for you. Your father and I have just started talking about this ourselves. It's complicated, but as soon as we have a definite answer, you'll be the first to know."

I look up at her and wipe my face with both hands. My eyes sting, and I feel a little like I might throw up. "Mom, there's something I have to tell you," I say slowly.

She looks down at me and runs her fingers through my hair. "What is it, honey?"

"Those girls I've been hanging out with this year. It's more than what it seems. Ever since we became friends, I've been putting stuff up on this wall at Victoria's house about all the kids and teachers in the school. It's been, like, a secret society."

My mom pulls back and leans away from me. "I don't understand," she says.

"We kept this massive collection of writing in her apartment—things about other people, like truth or gossip or whatever—and no one knew about it except us and her mom."

"Her mom knew? Why didn't you tell me, too?" she says, shaking her head.

"Vic's mom helped start the whole thing. That's how come she was in on it."

"Her mom began this wall writing about kids in your class? Isn't that a bit bizarre for a parent?"

"Mom, it's more complex than that." I sit up and lean against the side arm of the couch. "But what you need to know is . . . what I have to tell you is that I put stuff on it about my own life, too."

My mom looks at me with a serious expression. I see some lines around her mouth that I've never noticed before.

"Things about how much I like Connor, things I found out about girls in my grade . . . and a little about you and Dad."

Her mouth opens in surprise. "What kinds of stuff did you write about me?"

I squeeze the back of my neck with one hand and turn away. "You know, just stuff about you guys fighting and breaking up this summer."

My mom looks up at the ceiling and her bottom lip quivers. I see her eyes fill with tears. "Well, that sounds fine, honey. I mean, if you've been feeling sad about things, I'm glad there's been a way for you to express yourself. And if you haven't felt comfortable talking to me, then at least you have this place to go. . . ."

"But there's more," I say. I look down at my lap and start to cry. "I put stuff on the wall about the separation. Even stuff that I've never told you."

She just looks at me without saying a word.

"I'm so sorry, Mom. I'm a horrible daughter. I just didn't know how to tell you. I didn't want to hurt you and . . ." Tears start rolling down my face.

"What is it?" my mom asks.

"I saw him . . ." It's so hard to get the words out. "I can't say it."

"Maggie, just say it. You can tell me."

"I saw him with the waitress from the clubhouse."

"Dad? What waitress?" she says. "Are you talking about Dad?"

"And Roxanna. The young slutty one. With the tattoos."

"And what were they doing?" my mom asks. There's an edge to her voice, and it sounds like she's losing patience.

"They were kissing on the sofa in our house."

It looks as if the air is being sucked out of my mom's body. She freezes and then turns away from me.

I reach out and put my hand on her shoulder. "I didn't know if I should tell you, but I had to now. Last night after the Winter Formal, the wall that we wrote on at Vic's house was exposed. I was afraid someone would tell you, to get back at me, and I wanted you to hear it from me. It had to come from me first."

"Kids in your grade saw this? They know this before I even know myself?" She looks down and covers her face in her hands. "Lovely," she says softly. "How really lovely to know. . . ." I hear the sound of her sniffling from under her hands. "This is just delightful."

"Mom," I say. "I didn't mean to . . ."

She gets up from the couch and walks toward her room.

"I'm so sorry. I didn't know how tell you."

"I'm going to my room," she says softly. "Don't wake me up."

CHAPTER EIGHTEEN

*If a butterfly breaks its wing, it can be fed a sugar and water solution
and kept in a butterfly case. But chances are, if a wing is broken,
there are other injuries as well.*

When I show up at Berkeley on Monday, there's a strange vibe
in the halls. I hear a lot of girls arguing, and as I walk to my
homeroom, I'm greeted by angry glares. I even see a few kids
crying.

At student assembly, the seat that Anne Marie usually sits
in next to me is empty. I wonder how she's doing. All I want is
to see her in one of those little vintage dresses yanking books
out of her Stevie.

Sydney catches up with me after assembly. "This place is
a mess," she says.

"Is this all because of us?" I ask.

"Pretty much," Sydney says. "Word has spread far and
wide. Girls are pissed about the stuff written about them.
And some are mad at their friends for hiding secrets and lying. This is even nastier than I thought it could be."

We walk down the hall of Golden Wreath Girls and I can

imagine the latest edition, a framed photo of Victoria smiling down at us.

As if she's reading my mind, Sydney says, "I heard about what you did with the Wall. Ballsy."

"From Victoria?" I ask.

"No, from Lexi. They're both ape shit, especially Victoria. But I doubt Victoria will ever talk to me again."

"I'm sure she will. I'm the one she hates," I say.

"You're not the only one anymore," Sydney says. "Let's just say Vic didn't exactly go for it when I stood up for you."

"You did?" I ask.

"I told her not to blame it all on you. We had it coming," Sydney says. "The Wall has been a risk factor since day one, and I said I agreed that it had to come down." Sydney twirls one of her long blonde curls around her finger. "I want you to know, whatever happens, I'm on your side. I learned this mistake once the hard way. I really don't want to lose another real friend. What do you think about that?"

"*Que bueno,*" I say.

She smiles and says, "*Fantástico.*"

During philosophy, Mrs. Hanover shows up at my classroom. She apologizes to Mr. Z for disturbing his class and then turns to me. "Maggie, I need you to come with me," she says. "And take your things."

I feel a lump in my throat as I stand up from my desk, throw my book in my backpack, and walk over to her. The whole class is staring at me, and I have a feeling that they're guessing the same thing that I am: *My world is over.*

As soon as we get out into the hall, she says, "The principal wants to see you." I remember how she welcomed me on the first day of school with a big smile and the student handbook. Today there is not a glimmer of warm hospitality.

As I follow her into the elevator and down to the first floor, my mouth gets dry. I'm having trouble swallowing. "Is everything okay?" I ask.

"I can hardly say that," Mrs. Hanover says, shaking her head with disapproval.

She leads me into a conference room near the principal's office. The room is a small stark rectangle with a long wooden table, chairs, and bright fluorescent lights. The perfect place for a police interrogation.

Lexi, Victoria, and Sydney are already there. The jig is up. News of the Wall has spread beyond the students up to the teachers and administrators.

"Principal Hudgins will be here in one minute and we will begin," Mrs. Hanover says in a serious tone.

I look around the table. Lexi stares down at her lap and refuses to catch my glance. Sydney acknowledges me, and bulges her eyeballs as if to say, *Holy shit, what are we in for?* And Victoria eyes me coldly and looks away. I stare at the wood pattern in the oak table.

Principal Hudgins walks into the room. She closes the door behind her and takes a seat next to Vice Principal Cutter.

"When I arrived at school today, I heard a very distressing story from Mrs. De La Fuente about events that transpired this weekend. I learned about the party following the Winter Formal at Victoria's apartment, where a number of girls uncovered a room filled with stories about the students and teachers at Berkeley Prep. Would any of you like to respond to this?" she asks, looking around the room.

Lexi chimes in. "My dad told me not to say anything without him present. It's not in our best interest."

Principal Hudgins folds her hands in front of her on the table. "In the last ten minutes, I've personally placed calls to each of your parents. Lexi, Sydney, and Maggie, we reached either your mother or father directly. Victoria, we left a message on your parents' contact numbers, but I'm sure we'll hear back soon."

"If you're lucky," Victoria says. "They both have busy days. One of my mom's patients, a *Sports Illustrated* swimsuit model, went into labor in the middle of the night. And my dad has a meeting with Landmarks West."

"I'm sure when it comes to the future of your education, they will make time to speak with me. I will be meeting with all of your parents as soon as possible to discuss how best to handle this situation," Principal Hudgins continues. "Some things that I heard were written on your wall sound quite cruel and personal. I'm sure you all are familiar with our code of ethics in the student handbook? Each of you signed a form promising that you would read it. Honesty is right up there with respect."

"But everything we wrote down there was true," Victoria says. "We have the right to speak our minds. It's the law. I mean, since when did I get kidnapped by a Communist regime?"

"Shh, Vic. Remember, anything we say they can use against us," Lexi whispers.

"We have the right to express our feelings," Victoria goes on. "We wrote on my own private property outside of school grounds. Are you going to start controlling the television shows I'm allowed to watch at home, too? What books I can pick up in my own house? What music I can listen to? It's not fair that you have any control over me after I leave this place."

"Victoria, we will speak about this with your parents," Mrs. Hudgins says. "In the meantime, you should pack up your lockers and go straight home."

"And stop by the main office to check out with me," Mrs. Hanover says.

The four of us stand up from the table and push our chairs in.

"Oh, and one last thing," Mrs. Hudgins says. "Victoria, I regret that in light of the current situation, the administration will be reevaluating whether you should keep the Golden Wreath Award. Your recent actions have certainly put that into question."

"But I already won it," Victoria says. "You can't take it away."

"The award must go to the senior girl who most embodies the spirit of Berkeley Prep. I have a strong feeling that will no longer be you."

After our meeting, I hurry up to my locker on the fifth floor. I don't want to cry at school, but my eyes keep filling with tears. My nose starts to run, and I wipe it with the back of my hand. I can't believe how much trouble I'm in.

The hallway of the fifth floor is deserted except for two

Warriors wearing sweatpants and talking smack to each other over some computer game. They don't even seem to care when I walk by.

My hands start shaking as I open my locker and pile textbooks into my bag. Just then, I hear a door to one of the classrooms open. I turn around and see Nikki walking down the hallway. It's in the middle of a period, so I assume she must be going to the bathroom or getting a drink of water. She gives me a cold glare and then looks away.

I wipe my face and try to pull it together so I can talk to her. I turn around just as she's about to pass me. "Nikki," I say.

She stops and looks over. "What do you want?" she says. Her lips are tense and she puts one hand on her hip.

"I want you to know that the wall we wrote on is gone. The writings have been destroyed."

"Why should I believe you?" she asks.

I reach into my backpack and pull out a bunch of pieces of it that I took as evidence. Each scrap has writing on it. "Here," I say, going through the scraps and finding the one with her name on it. "It's the part that had stuff written about you."

She takes it and looks down at the paper. Then she shakes her head. "Do you know how furious a lot of girls in our class are at the four of you?"

"After the messages I got this weekend, I have a pretty good idea," I say.

"I'm glad you took it down," she says. "But it already hurt a lot of people, including me."

"I know, and I'm really sorry." I look down at the small

scraps in my hand. I know what a big mouth Nikki has and in this case, I think that might be to my advantage. "Will you spread the word that the Wall came down? Make sure all the girls in our class know."

Nikki looks at me. I see her thinking it over. "I gotta go," she says. Then she takes off.

"Please tell them," I say as she disappears into the restroom.

After signing out with Mrs. Hanover in the office, I head straight home. My mom is there waiting for me. After she got the phone call from the principal, she took the morning off.

"I guess the school found out pretty quickly," she says.

I sit on my bed and nod in silence.

"Maggie, I appreciate your being straightforward with me yesterday and telling me about what's been going on. I suppose you now realize how unwise it was of you to get involved in this, and now we have to deal with the consequences of your school finding out. I mean, this was a big chance for you and—"

"I know, and I already feel terrible enough. Can we please not tell Grandpa?" I ask. "I'd be mortified if I hurt him in any way."

"I've already thought about this. If you don't get expelled, we can keep this between us."

"Thank you so much," I say. Then I think, *Could I really be expelled?*

"But I had to call your father and tell him that you're in trouble with Berkeley."

"What'd he say?"

"He's worried about you and is driving down to New York tomorrow so he'll be here for the meeting with your school on Wednesday morning."

"Dad's gonna be at the meeting, too?" I say.

"Yes, he's still your father, even if he's not my husband anymore," my mom says.

It makes me sad to hear her say that, but also a little relieved. I'm sorry my mom is losing my dad, but I don't want to lose him, too.

When Dad arrives on Tuesday night, he goes straight to the Beacon Hotel on 75th and Broadway. After he gets settled in, I meet him in the lobby and he gives me a hug. We decide to go out to dinner at a nearby restaurant called Isabella's that's across the street from the American Museum of Natural History.

For the first half of the meal, I do a wonderful job distracting my dad by asking about his latest fishing outings on the lake and what Moose has been up to. He tells me that he's been trying to teach himself to cook, and that he even bought a rotisserie machine for chicken.

It's not until he's halfway through his skirt steak and I am partially done with my grilled chicken salad that he brings up the incident that led to his visit. "So, I've heard you've turned into a big troublemaker," he says, cutting into a piece of rare meat.

"Dad, I didn't mean to cause so much harm," I tell him. "I feel really bad, but one of the girls keeps talking about the First Amendment. Doesn't that guarantee freedom of speech? I mean, can't we say what we want?"

"Of course. But when it involves other people, you have to be more careful. Honesty requires a delicate balance between what should be said and what is best to keep to yourself."

I take a sip of my iced tea while I listen to him.

"Once you get to be an adult, you become responsible for yourself, but now you're still growing up. So schools and parents are partially responsible for what you do and say. We want to guide you in the right direction." My dad straightens the frames of his gold-rimmed glasses.

"As if teachers and parents know what that is," I say sarcastically, then take a bite of my salad.

I think about my dad's liaison with the waitress in Montague. That was something he chose to keep secret from my mom. But didn't she have the right to know? Who was he to decide to keep that from her? In my opinion, it seems like adults are honest when it's convenient for them, and they hide things when it serves their best interests.

"I wish there was a rule book I could give you, or an equation," my dad says. "But part of growing up is learning that the world can't be seen in black and white. It's filled with gray areas. People like to box stuff up into neat little squares. It makes things easier to lump everything into one compartment or another. But it's not that neat and clean." I notice my dad playing with the gold band on his ring finger. "I mean, just look how you can love someone and miss them immensely, but also dislike them and resent them at the same time. And these complexities never end. Even when you're a wise old man like me."

After the waiter clears our plates and brings the bill, I

ask my dad if I can come visit him over winter break in New Jersey.

"Of course," he says. "You can come anytime." And then he says something that surprises me. "You're the one who decided to leave."

"What?" I say. "I thought I had to."

"No," he says. "You could have stayed with me this year and finished out high school in Montague. I thought you wanted to go with your mother."

"I didn't realize I had a choice," I said. When Mom told me I was coming with her, I had thought that was what my dad wanted, too. I still would have left with my mother, but it's nice to know I had an option—that my dad wasn't so eager to get rid of me.

After dinner, my dad takes me back to the apartment and sees my mother. She's put on this deep red lipstick I haven't seen her wear in a while and a pretty lavender blouse with black pants. I feel a sad distance between them. They sit on opposite ends of the room and their conversation in front of me seems overly formal and less familiar than it did at Thanksgiving. When my dad leaves to go back to the hotel, he tells my mom that he'll meet her outside Berkeley Prep the next day for the big conference and that perhaps afterwards they can get a coffee so just the two of them can talk. I wonder if she thought he might stay over.

The next day, my mom leaves for the meeting at Berkeley Prep while I hang around the apartment, anxious to see what happens. There's too much free time to think about Connor and how much I miss him. I can't help it, but I reach for the phone and try calling him again, even though he hasn't taken any of the calls I've made since Saturday night. I'm surprised when he picks up.

"Yeah, what do you want? I'm walking into school," he says.

"I'm so happy you answered," I say. "Can I please see you in person? I'll tell you everything you want to know."

"What is there to talk about?" His voice sounds cold. "How you're a liar? How I was completely up front with you from day one and you messed with me? You seem one way, but you're really another. Talk about getting sideswiped."

"Connor, listen to me. That boy in the picture was just a dare, and it happened before we even got together. And everything else on the Wall was supposed to be protected."

"But the stuff that happened between us was private. I didn't think you were going to blab about it to those friends of yours."

"It was part of a secret—"

"I'm walking into school now," he cuts me off. "I can't talk."

"Connor, wait," I say.

"Yeah, what?" he says, annoyed. "There are teachers around. I'm not allowed to be on this thing."

"I didn't get to tell you . . ." I say.

"What?" he says. "Hurry. I'm hanging up."

"I'm falling for you, too. . . ." I say.

I wait and listen for his response, but there's no answer on the other end of the phone. Then I hear the sound of a man's voice. I assume Connor must be getting in trouble with a teacher, because when I look down at the screen on my phone, I see that the call's been ended.

Finally at around noon, my mom comes home. I'm happily surprised to see my father is still with her.

"So tell me what happened," I say as soon as they walk in the door.

They both fill me in on the meeting. It was attended by the principal, Mrs. Hanover, and the Revelers' parents. The principal wanted to have all the girls suspended, but the parents argued for a softer stance. Victoria's mother, as a member of the Parent Council, seemed to have an especially strong influence. They agreed on an in-school suspension for the rest of the semester. We were to report to school every day on time, but the four of us would be separated and assigned to sit in one of the academic department offices. This way we would be always in the presence of teachers who could monitor our behavior.

We were expected to focus on all our schoolwork with minimal social interaction, meaning no extracurriculars. Also, our parents were encouraged to institute an eight-o'clock curfew every night, even on the weekends. And if any of us ever created anything like the Wall again while at Berkeley Prep, we would get kicked out of the school permanently.

Principal Hudgins said she would hold a faculty meeting to clearly outline expectations and restrictions for students' behavior so something like this wouldn't happen again, and there would be revisions to next year's student handbook.

"And there's something else your father and I need to tell you. . . ." my mom begins. "We're sorry to tell you now, but we feel it's important to start setting a stronger precedent for honesty."

I take one look at them and know what's coming next. They have these serious expressions on their faces.

After they use the word *divorced,* I basically tune out the rest of what they have to say. Any other words that dribble out of their mouths don't really matter anymore.

CHAPTER nineteen

The trees that the butterflies spend the winter in also serve as a lumber source for local communities and big logging companies. Logging not only removes the trees, it opens up the forest canopy. The overhead holes expose the butterflies to the elements, increasing the chance that they won't be able to survive.

The next morning, I show up to Berkeley Prep and report in to Mrs. Hanover. She tells me that I'm assigned to sit in the history-department office during my in-school suspension. When I walk into the office, I notice Mr. Z busy grading papers at his desk. He looks at me, gives a small nod, and then turns back to his work.

Mrs. Hanover directs me to a space in the side of the room where there's an extra chair and a place for me to sit. Then she hands me a packet of assignments she collected from my teachers. I'm expected to stay here for the rest of the day doing my schoolwork. For lunch, I'm supposed to go to the lunchroom and bring my tray of food back up here to eat.

As soon as Mrs. Hanover leaves, I begin to go through the packet of work that I have ahead of me. There're questions on *The Wild Duck* for Modern Drama, worksheets for French, pages of math problems for pre-calculus, and an assignment to write a short paper in astronomy. I notice there's nothing for philosophy, but a note from Mr. Z. *Talk to me in person about your assignment.*

I turn around and go over to him. "I got your note," I said.

"Pull up a seat," he says, and puts down his pen.

I grab a chair and sit down across from him.

"I heard about what happened," he says. "What was the name of that thing again, where you wrote everyone's secrets? Mr. Broussard told me, but I forgot."

I look down, embarrassed. "The Wall," I say.

He nods his head. "For your last assignment this semester, I want you to take what you've learned from my class and apply it to that wall of yours. From what it sounds like, you created your own form of the hat experiment."

"How do you mean?" I ask.

"You need to figure that out for yourself," he says. "Now, get to work."

I go back to my seat and think for a while about what Mr. Z is asking me, and then I get it.

Victoria tried to lay down the truth on the Wall, but in many ways, it was like the baseball cap Mr. Z brought to class. He took the cap apart piece by piece and made us think about at what moment it was no longer a hat. It was the same thing with the truth on our Wall. When was something we wrote on it absolutely true, and when was it gossip? The line seemed too difficult to draw.

As I walk out of school that day, I bump into a group of Snobby Indies buying gum at a magazine and candy store around the corner. They all watch as I walk by, and Olivia comes over to me. "I'm still really pissed," she says to me. "But we heard you took it down. So thanks."

"It had to be done," I say.

"The weird thing is . . ." Olivia says to me, her voice quieter so her friends can't hear. "It's kinda nice knowing that there're other kids in our grade who are as messed up as me. It puts us all on an even playing field."

"Do you think everyone in our class is gonna hate me for the rest of the year?" I ask her.

"It depends," she says. "Some kids will. But I think over winter break, things will calm down. Something else will happen to get people all upset, and they'll start to forget about this."

At the end of that week, I call Connor again. He finally agrees to talk to me in person. We meet on Friday after school on the stoop outside E. E. Cummings's old apartment on Patchin Place. I spot him walking over to me along the cobblestone pathway. It's wonderful to see him again, but there's also a sadness to that familiarity. Maybe because it's not the same as it used to be.

We sit down on the stoop together. "I made a mistake," I say. "I'll never do it again. I just wish we could work this out."

"You should have thought of that sooner. I mean, you've acted like a psycho girlfriend."

"I apologize. I got wrapped up in this world that Victoria created, and I didn't see a way out."

"So in the meantime, you lie to me?"

"I'm so sorry that I hurt you, but please forgive me. I still want to be with you more than anything," I tell him.

"I don't know. . . ." Connor says, and looks away. "I don't think that's a good idea right now."

I look away. "Wow," I say softly. I guess I thought if I could just talk to him face-to-face, he'd forgive me.

"But I'm not saying I never will," Connor continues. "Maybe we could just hang out for a while. That way I can see if you're really crazy or if this was just a one-time deal." Then he lets out a smile. "I'm teasing you about the crazy part. I'm banking that you learned your lesson."

"I did," I say. "You will see. I'm so sorry."

"You're staying in town for winter break, right?" he asks.

"I think I'm going to visit my dad for a few days, but otherwise I'll be around."

"I'm going to Bermuda with my mom and her boyfriend. Maybe I'll call you when I get back," he says.

"That would only be the best thing ever," I said.

"Talk to you," he said.

"Sounds like a plan." I watch him walk away. This wasn't the way I wanted things to go. I hoped that we would end up in each other's arms, maybe even making out on a brownstone's steps in the middle of the day. The way he said he'll call me doesn't convince me a hundred percent. There's a chance he will, but no guarantee. One thing I'm sure of is that I'll never mess with someone's trust ever again.

It's funny, but I feel like I was taught that if you say,

"I'm sorry," it will make everything better. But I can see now that doesn't work in all cases. Sometimes it can clean the slate, soften the blow, speed up the healing, but there are a few occasions when the cut goes too deep. Then those two words will never quite take you back to where you were before.

When I leave Patchin Place, I walk along Bleecker Street and come across a used music store. I walk inside and talk to the college-looking kid who works there. "Do you have an album by the Persuaders called *Made to Be Loved*?" I ask.

I follow the kid as he walks down and looks through a stack of records. "Nope, don't got it," he says. "But we do have another album by them called *Thin Line Between Love and Hate*."

"All right," I say. "I'll take that one." I pay and head back out of the store. Then I take the subway uptown to Anne Marie's building. When the doorman calls up to her, I ask if I can talk to whoever answers. A young guy picks up, and I explain to him that I'm a friend of Anne Marie's from Berkeley and I want to check on her. He tells me he's Anne Marie's brother and that I should tell the doorman to let me come upstairs.

Anne Marie's brother is standing with the door open. He has huge lambchop sideburns and is every bit as cute as Anne Marie said.

"She's in the den watching TV," he tells me, and points me in the right direction.

When Anne Marie sees me, she gives a small smile. "I didn't think you would come by to visit," she says.

"I brought you something," I say, and hand her the record. "I hope you don't have it already."

She smiles and examines the song list. "Thanks. Nice find. It'll be a sweet addition to my collection."

"I'm glad you like it."

"Guess what?" she says, then pauses the TV show she's watching and turns to me. "I won. Mrs. Hanover called today and told me she's taking the Golden Wreath away from Victoria and giving it to me. She also said she hoped I would feel good enough to return to school in January, and I was welcome whenever I felt ready to come back."

"That's great news," I say. "You deserved it the whole time." I grab a pillow from the edge of the couch and put it on my lap.

"I haven't told my mom yet about winning," Anne Marie says. "I like keeping it to myself and not feeling like I have to report in to her all the time anymore." She looks down at her black Chinese slippers. "Grace told me about what she saw. . . ."

"Anne Marie," I say. "I just want you to know how sorry I am."

"I was just surprised 'cause I thought that we were buddies," she says.

"I know," I say. "We are. I royally messed up and I wish I could take back anything that I may have done to hurt you. But I know I can't. And I understand, of course, if you never want to talk to me again, but I just had to come tell you in person . . . that you are so smart and unique and you have such a big heart. When I heard about what happened . . ."

"Shh," Anne Marie says. "I don't want to talk about it, okay? I have my shrink for that kind of stuff now."

"I just want to say, if you ever need anything, I'm there

for you. And I get that it may take a while to build back your trust, but I hope you'll give me a chance. Just let me know if I can ever do anything to make things better."

"Just being here is nice. And maybe you can put that album on," Anne Marie says, and nods to her brother's DJ equipment set up on one end of the den. "I want to hear it."

I walk over, but I'm not sure how to turn the record player on. Anne Marie comes over and shows me how. The title track comes on and we listen to it together.

"Listen to that harmony," Anne Marie says. "See, the Persuaders knew how to mix their soul with a lot of rhythm and blues. This track was their first hit. It's all about the painful consequences of what happens to a man who takes his woman for granted."

I hang out with Anne Marie for a few hours, and she plays more music from her collection for me. She's really eager to share everything she knows about funk and soul. When it's time for me to leave, she asks me if I'll come back again this weekend to visit her.

"Count me in," I tell her.

CHAPTER TWENTY

Migrating butterflies have some sort of map genetically imprinted on their brains. They are born knowing everything they need to survive.

As I walk through Central Park toward home, I think about the Wall. I still feel like there's a struggle going on between the kinds of the things kids really feel and the way our parents and other adults want us to feel. I also haven't yet decided where I draw my own lines between what I want to keep private and what I feel is right to expose.

But as I think back on the last few months, I realize that the amazing thing about it is how we're not in this metamorphosis from childhood to adulthood alone. There are thousands of other girls out there right now going through what I am, migrating through these rites of passage in one massive flock. It's like there's something ingrained on our genetic code that shows us where to go, even though we've never traveled this way before. But if we keep flying, we'll eventually find our way home.

I would like to thank my publisher, Regina Hayes, and editor, Joy Peskin. In addition, the wonderful team at Viking, including Nico Medina for his brilliant copyediting and Linda McCarthy and Theresa Evangelista for their imaginative designs.

Many thanks to Brian Levy, Josie Freedman, and Stephanie Lehmann.

My four muses: Sasha Hecht, Maggie Weile, Caity Quinlan, and Kara Krushel.

Much appreciation to Phil Schappert and Scott Shalaway, and the other butterfly scientists and naturalists whose books inspire me and who fight for the conservation of these bright-winged creatures.

Also, Sabrina Lupero, Eve Glassman, Wendy Gross, Christine Whitledge, Annie Aackley, Susannah Gora, and the rest of the true confidantes whom I've grown up with.

Much gratitude to Steve Bello and Dave Thomas for their insight and encouragement; my big bro, David, for keeping it real and for taking me to those meteor showers in Malibu; and my mom for her creativity, inspiration, and love.